W9-DEM-222

WHERE SHE BELONGS

WHERE SHE BELONGS

CINDY PROCTER-KING

FIVE STAR
A part of Gale, Cengage Learning

GALE
CENGAGE Learning·

Detroit • New York • San Francisco • New Haven, Conn • Waterville, Maine • London

GALE
CENGAGE Learning®

Copyright © 2011 by Cindy Procter-King.
Five Star Publishing, a part of Gale, Cengage Learning.

LIBRARY OF CONGRESS CATALOGING-IN-PUBLICATION DATA

Procter-King, Cindy.
   Where she belongs / Cindy Procter-King. — 1st ed.
   p. cm.
   ISBN-13: 978-1-4328-2545-4 (hardcover)
   ISBN-10: 1-4328-2545-3 (hardcover)
   1. Mothers and daughters—Fiction. 2. Foresters—Fiction. 3. British Columbia—Fiction. I. Title.
PR9199.4.P775W47 2011
813'.6—dc23   2011033050

First Edition. First Printing: December 2011.
Published in 2011 in conjunction with Tekno Books.

In memory of Andy, brother of my heart. Taken too soon.
June 1, 1956–July 22, 1981

ACKNOWLEDGMENTS

As always, I have to give a shout-out to my husband, Steven King, for his understanding and support when we decided I should remain at home after the kids started school so I could write while raising our sons. Also, thanks, Steve, for kicking that mean-tempered black bear in the head when she treed you in the forests outside Clearwater, B.C. Not only did your quick thinking save me from enduring horrible memories of what she might have done to you while our oldest child was enjoying his first birthday party, but the experience provided inspiration for this story.

Where She Belongs is a "book of my heart." I drafted the novel several years ago, after we left Clearwater. While the setting is loosely based on my memories of that wonderful North Thompson Valley community, Destiny Falls has evolved into an undoubtedly fictional setting in my mind (for one thing, there isn't a lake in the middle of Destiny Falls!). The manuscript required a lot of work, so I set it aside. From time to time, I'd revise it and send it to critique partners for review. As a result, I have several people to thank for helping me hone my writing skill and develop this story. Most notably, I must thank Mary J. Forbes and Brenda K. Jernigan. I am indebted to you both. My appreciation also goes out to Verna Baak, Diane Dyrdal, Starla Criser, Karen Logue, Marie Murtagh, and Jamie Sobrato. If I've forgotten someone, I apologize.

Thanks to my dear childhood friend, Line Lauzon, who allowed me to pick her brains about her job as a shoe buyer in Montreal years ago. All errors and fictional liberties are mine.

Finally, thank you to my editor, Denise Dietz, for rescuing me from another potential lengthy submission wait and allowing my voice to shine through with her edits. I'm thrilled to join the Five Star/Cengage family.

CHAPTER ONE

Jess Morgan scanned the arrivals area of the small British Columbia airport. Her best friend was supposed to have met her at the luggage carousel thirty minutes ago. Granted, Jess hadn't visited in ages, but it wasn't like Molly Davis to be late.

Especially under these circumstances. Pete's heart attack. The funeral. Jess's mother left alone to deal with both.

A headache battered her temples as the exhaustion of the cross-country flight fell over her. Heels tapping, she wheeled her suitcase to a kiosk advertising North Thompson Valley attractions: whitewater rafting, helicopter skiing, and hiking and camping at majestic Destiny Falls, a few kilometers north of her hometown bearing the same name.

And a far cry from her life in Toronto.

Toto, I don't think we're in Kansas anymore. Destiny Falls hadn't felt like home in years.

Heart squeezing, she released the suitcase handle and set down her carry-on. She retrieved her cell phone from her purse. *Damn it. Dead battery.*

Slipping the cell into her coat pocket, she scanned the Kamloops airport for a pay phone. A flight announcement blared over the loudspeakers. Nearby, a young mother fussed with a baby in a stroller while two little boys with her kissed their father goodbye.

The picture of the cozy family stirred old longings inside Jess. Had she stayed in Destiny Falls—had fate not stolen the

9

option—she could have been that woman, in love and knee-deep in diapers. And not wanting it any other way.

Behind the young family, a phone stall beckoned. Shaking off bad memories, Jess grabbed her carry-on. A man in his early thirties jogged up, his dark blond hair buffeted by the chilly March breeze she'd felt coming off the plane.

"Jess?"

"Yes?" Well-worn jeans hugged his lean hips, and an ivory cotton shirt peeked from his unbuttoned jean jacket. Tall, broad-shouldered, with a square jaw and angular features, he looked familiar, but she couldn't place him. A crooked white scar bisected his right eyebrow, drawing her attention to his light blue eyes.

Wait a minute. "Adam?" She blinked. Amazing. She hadn't seen him in thirteen, no, nearly fourteen years, considering her rapidly approaching twenty-eighth birthday.

Memories flooded her mind from those few carefree summer weeks a lifetime ago. Adam had been visiting his aunt and uncle's farm in Destiny Falls. The object of her first older-guy crush, he'd ignored her.

How old had he been then? Seventeen. Which placed him at thirty-one now.

His scar held the same rugged appeal as when he'd been seventeen.

"Yeah, that's right. Adam Wright." His faded-denim gaze flicked over her. A faint buzzing spread through her—darn jet lag. "Molly sent me to get you."

"Oh? I was about to call her. Is she in the car?"

"No, I'm your ride."

Jess frowned. Adam had lived in Kamloops the summer they'd met, but she knew from Molly's emails that he'd moved to Destiny Falls several years ago. Why would he make the ninety-minute drive down the winding country highway when

10

last night she'd arranged her ride with Molly?

Her stomach pitched. "What's wrong?"

He pushed a hand into a front jeans pocket. "Molly stopped by your mother's place on her way down here, then decided she should stay in Destiny Falls and keep Nora company. So she asked if I'd mind coming. Sorry I'm late, but I left as soon as she called."

A reasonable explanation—except Jess's mother was very guarded. She held her grief close to her, sharing it with no one. That was how she'd dealt with Jess's father's death and with every other crisis in her life.

Lines of discomfort bracketed Adam's mouth. "Molly doesn't want you worrying about your mom. It'll be after ten when we get back, and she didn't think Nora should have to wait up for you without someone there to help her pass the time."

Jess nodded. Her mother usually went to bed at nine. And it would be like Molly to take stock of a situation and do what she deemed best—whether the recipient of her good intentions wanted her to or not.

"How is my mother? Did Molly say?"

"Pete's heart attack came without warning, Jess. It caught your mother by surprise. She talked about you at the funeral on Monday, said she'd left you a message."

Jess shifted on her new Italian leather pumps. A hint of censure shadowed Adam's gaze, mirroring her thoughts of the last twenty-four hours. She should have been here for her mother. Instead of dashing around the shoe shows in Europe, gathering ideas for her upcoming buying trip, she should have been in Destiny Falls, helping Mom get through Pete's funeral.

"I was overseas on business." Her need to explain herself rankled. She loved her mother, but they weren't Norman Rockwell material, and they never truly had been. Especially not since Jess's father died and Pete had entered the picture. "I only

11

returned to Toronto yesterday."

"Too bad she couldn't reach your cell or email."

"She didn't try." She didn't have the number or email address, so how could she? Her poor mother had been forced to leave a message on the answering machine in Jess's empty apartment.

"Yeah, well, it was a nice service. I've never seen that little church crammed so full. Everyone in town knew Pete."

"You went?" Jess picked up her carry-on. As far as she knew, Adam wasn't well acquainted with her mom. But of course everyone in Destiny Falls knew Pete. He was—*had been*—the manager of the sole supermarket in the area.

He nodded, reaching for her bag. His faint, woodsy scent drifted to her. "Let me get your luggage." Voice low, he slid the carry-on from her grasp.

Jess drew away swiftly, nerves humming. Her purse strap slid down her arm, and she dragged it back up. "Thanks." She wouldn't argue. She'd spent most of the last two days on planes. She just wanted to get there already.

He wheeled her suitcase toward the exit. "My dog's in the truck. Hope you don't mind. She was alone a lot today, so I didn't want to leave her. She rides in back and won't bother you."

"Um, that's okay." Was Adam married? Nearly everyone in Destiny Falls was.

She glanced at his hand. He didn't wear a ring, and Molly had never mentioned a wife or kids. But he looked like a family man, strong and capable, handsome, tall.

She rolled her eyes. *Get a grip, Jess.* What did it matter if the man had eight wives? After tonight, she wouldn't see him again. She hadn't visited Destiny Falls since her bitter argument with Pete four Christmases ago. She had just a few days off work, postponing several meetings to make it happen.

12

While she was here, her only concern was for Mom.

The headlights of Adam's big SUV illuminated the dirt driveway leading to the farmhouse Jess's grandfather had built. Her hand tensed on the armrest as she struggled to contain the mixed surge of anxiety and homecoming that always assaulted her at this point. The time away hadn't mellowed her conflicting emotions. And the long drive with Adam hadn't helped.

Initially, they'd exchanged idle small talk about the weather and changes in the valley. But his subtle disapproval of her—for what, missing Pete's funeral?—had worsened her tendency to withdraw when jet-lagged.

Eventually, he'd focused on driving while she'd stared out the passenger window, fervently wishing Molly had picked her up.

He parked next to Molly's red family sedan. "We're here."

"Thanks. I appreciate the ride."

He slid her a glance. "No problem."

Right. She unbuckled her seatbelt. As she retrieved her purse, he opened her door. Not wanting to insult him, she accepted his help climbing out of the truck.

"I'll get your suitcase." His deep voice sounded tight.

Conscious of his assessing gaze and the warm, rough texture of his large hand, she sidestepped him, mumbling another thank-you.

Turning, she faced the house she'd grown up in, where she'd once dreamed of Danny and babies and building a life in Destiny Falls. Her breath caught. Little had changed in four years. Fresh paint livened up the place, but it was still the same buttercup yellow with glossy white trim. A light shone at the side entrance, another on the front porch. A crescent moon glimmered above the forested mountains in a cloudless, star-studded sky.

The late-March breeze swirled her coat around her legs.

Adam stepped beside her, carrying the luggage. "Ready?"

No.

But she couldn't explain her ambivalent feelings to this man she barely knew. Instead, she asked, "Do you want to let out your dog?"

He shook his head. "Sheba's okay in the cargo hold for now. I'm not staying long, anyway."

Good. He made her nervous.

She headed to the side door, and he followed her in. She hung her coat on the row of pegs in the small mudroom.

"Mom?" She smoothed her knit dress, releasing static that had accumulated in the SUV. "Mom? Are you down here? Molly?"

No answer. "They must be upstairs," she murmured.

She entered the kitchen and set her purse on the antique pine trestle table. On the maple buffet banking the rear wall, sympathy cards and fading bouquets flanked a small bowl of potpourri. The scents of cinnamon and dried orange blossoms lifted into the air.

Jess stared at the cards, chest tightening. Like usual, she felt like an intruder in her childhood home—Pete's legacy. At Waverly Foods, he'd welcomed his customers with a ready smile. At home, he'd valued privacy. So much so that Jess had felt unwanted and, on her infrequent visits from university, increasingly out of place.

"Where do you want your luggage?" Adam asked.

"By the buffet is great, thanks." *Please leave.*

His shoes scuffed on the linoleum. Jess headed to the plaster archway that opened into the living room. Moments later, he joined her.

Hadn't he said he wouldn't stay long? What did he want, a tip?

She stepped into the living room. The huge stone fireplace

14

and navy chintz sofa swept into view, and her stomach bottomed out. *Dad.*

The last time she'd seen him, he'd been reading a newspaper in the overstuffed armchair Pete's swivel rocker had replaced long ago. The braided area rug had disappeared, too, although her mother's framed needlepoint designs still graced the walls and the hardwood floor gleamed.

Closing her eyes, Jess staunched the flow of sadness. If she surrendered to memories of her father, painful visions of Danny would follow.

Those she couldn't handle. Not now. She had to keep them at bay.

She called again from the bottom of the stairs. "Mom? Molly?"

Molly appeared around the upstairs corner, wearing jeans and a simple white blouse.

"Jess!" Red bob swinging, Molly raced down the steps. "How I wish it were under different circumstances, but, oh, Jess, it feels so good to see you again," she said as they hugged.

"It's good to see you, too, Moll. You cut your hair." Jess squeezed her best friend tightly. "I can't believe it. I'd forgotten how short you are."

"That's what you always say." Molly turned her face toward Adam. "We were the same height when we met in grade six, but something happened to Jess in high school."

"Something didn't happen to *you*, you mean," he replied with a smile.

Arrowing him a watch-it-buster glance, Molly touched Jess's arm. "How did things go at the airport, hon? Did Adam find you okay?"

She nodded. "Is Mom in bed?"

"Yes, although I haven't convinced her to try to get some sleep."

15

"That's all right. I can see her then."

"She'd like that. First, though, Jess, I should tell you . . ." Molly's gaze slipped to Adam. A hint of a frown firmed his mouth as unspoken communication passed between the cousins.

"Tell me what, Moll?"

"It's just that your mother . . ." Molly sighed. "She's taking Pete's death pretty hard, not at all like she usually . . . I don't know . . . conducts herself, I guess."

"What? Why didn't you say so last night?" What was going on?

"Jess, she'll be okay now that you're here."

Jess didn't wait around to hear any more. She raced up the stairs and took the hall to the right. Hand over her heart, she peeked into the master bedroom. Her mom sat up in the old double bed, plump pillows supporting her back against the iron headboard. Her ruffle-necked nightgown made her look small and fragile. Red splotched her cheeks, aging her beyond her fifty-nine years.

"Mom?" Jess gripped the cold glass doorknob. The closet door stood open, Pete's clothes in plain view. His glasses and wallet lay on the pine dresser, as if in wait for his return.

"Jessie?" Her mom's voice broke as she glanced up. "Oh, Jessie, at last, you're home!" Eyes brimming with tears, she held her arms open.

Jess raced to the bed and hugged her mother over the layers of pale yellow sheets and a wedding-band-patterned quilt. "It's okay. It'll be okay. I'm here, Mom. I'm here." The words were like a litany she didn't quite believe. Not once had she seen her mother like this after her father died.

Her mom sobbed against her shoulder. "Jessie, I don't know what to do! Peter was my world. I'm all alone now."

"You're not alone, Mom. I'm here for you." She sat on the bed and pushed the short, graying, brown curls off her mother's moist forehead.

"B-bless you. Molly has been wonderful. Everyone has been so kind. But it's not the same—it could never be—as having my Jessie-girl home again."

The pet name from childhood touched her. "I came as soon as I could." Obviously, not soon enough.

"I know, and I'm grateful. But it's been f-far too long." Red-rimmed hazel eyes searched Jess's face. "I know we've had our d-differences. It was difficult for you to accept Peter, and that always put a strain between us. But I want you to know how much I need you, Jessie. I want—"

"Oh, Mom. We'll have plenty of time to talk tomorrow, all right? Right now you need your rest."

Her mother nodded. Jess hugged her for several silent moments, stroking her soft curls, listening to her ragged breathing. She smelled of talcum powder and floral-scented soap . . . and childhood memories.

When the world had been safe and secure, free of heartache.

Everything had changed. *Everything.* Why hadn't she let her mother know how to reach her? Why had she allowed the troubles of the past to taint their relationship for so long?

Her eyes burned. Why had her mother done likewise? Dad's and Danny's deaths had been a hundred times more horrific than Pete's. Yet it had taken the loss of a man Jess hadn't even liked for her mother to open up.

To break down.

The bedroom door creaked behind them. Molly's quiet voice drifted in. "Excuse me, Jess? Mrs. Olson?"

Jess blinked back hot tears. "Come in, Moll." She pulled several tissues from the box on the nightstand and passed them to her mom.

"Thank you, Jessie. I must thank you, too, Molly. It's very sweet of you to take time away from your kids to be with me."

17

"I'm glad to help, Mrs. Olson. I put the kettle on to boil for a pot of herbal tea, if you'd like some."

Jess's mother nodded.

"Sounds good, Molly," Jess said brightly—feeling anything but. She kissed her mother's damp cheek and rose from the bed. "I'll bring up a tray."

"Thank you." Her mother's smile trembled.

"Stay, Jess," Molly said. "I'll do it."

"Thanks, but I'd like to." She needed to get out of here before she lost it—the last thing her mother needed. A few minutes alone in the kitchen would calm her. She just needed those few minutes.

Thank God Adam would be gone by now. She didn't care how she'd felt about him as a teenager, she couldn't handle his unspoken recriminations and very adult small-town judgments with her heart and head in such a state.

Crouched before the big stone fireplace, Adam pushed at the embers with a poker, listening for the whistle of the kettle like he'd promised Molly in case she got hung up with Jess and Nora before he left.

Jess Morgan. He shook his head. Man, had she changed. Pete had mentioned her from time to time when he and Adam had worked together with the Destiny Falls Young Achievers, and Molly was always eager to relate some cute teenage tale about the pair of them.

However, tonight, the edge he'd often heard in Pete's voice took precedence, raising questions Adam knew damn well weren't his business. Like what kind of woman didn't visit her mother in four years? Didn't know her flesh and blood well enough to realize that of course Pete's death would devastate Nora? Who didn't call before leaving the country, heavy work schedule or not?

18

That Jess might have grown into the self-absorbed type of woman Adam avoided dredged up a restlessness he'd thought long buried.

He'd *liked* his memories of Jess from that long-ago summer. Her innocence and trusting nature, her faith in all life had to offer. She'd been shy and beautiful, even at fourteen. Tall, leggy, tons of curly black hair, and eyes the color of melted toffee. If she'd been a year or two older—

But she hadn't been and so he'd kept his distance, thinking fondly of her when Molly recounted an especially funny story. Foolishly, he hadn't expected his memories of Jess to change.

For *her* to change.

But who didn't change as they grew up?

He placed a log on the fire, the seams of his jean jacket straining. At the clicking of heels, he glanced up to see Jess descending the stairs. Her long, dark curls veiled her face.

Fake-coughing, he stood. Her head snapped up, eyes wide and startled, filled with pain.

"Sorry." She wiped her cheeks. "I thought you'd left."

Gut knotting, he closed the fire screen. "I decided I'd tend the fire while Molly made the tea." He hooked the poker onto the old brass stand.

"She's upstairs," Jess said unnecessarily, clutching the post at the base of the steps.

He nodded and moved toward her. "How's your mom?"

"N-not good." Stepping off the stairs, she drew in a sharp, short breath.

Aw, hell. He couldn't stand to see a woman cry. Or try *not* to cry, in this case.

He placed a hand on her shoulder, grazing her hair. Her back bunched into knots beneath her light gray knit dress.

"I'm sorry," he murmured. "Is there anything I can do?"

Her eyes sparkled with checked tears, lashes clinging together

19

like starbursts. Damp and spiked. *Beautiful.*

"No, I—" A lone tear rolled down her face.

He rubbed the tension between her shoulder blades. "Your mom will make it through this, Jess. Molly told me she's a strong woman."

"No. I mean, yes. I mean—" Turning away, she hugged her arms. "Usually, my mother *is* a strong woman. But the way she's acting tonight . . . she looks like she's been crying for hours. It's not like her, and it worries me."

"She's grieving. It's a normal process."

"Maybe for some people. Not for my mom."

"Sure, it is," Adam tried again, gently. "Sorrow, denial, anger—they're all a part of grief." He knew too well. "Maybe you can't see it that way because you're mourning for Pete, too."

She shot him a strange look.

"Think of it this way. Your mom's husband died a week ago tonight—in the same bed she's lying in now—and her only child couldn't be here to attend the funeral with her. Now, I know this is a lot to absorb. I know she's having a rough night. But, given the circumstances, I'd say she's holding up fine."

Jess glanced away. "You don't understand. My mother isn't an emotional woman—not like this. She keeps her feelings under close wraps. That's how she deals with things. It's her way."

"So she's a private person. Her husband's death is a pretty good reason to act out of character."

"Not in my experience, it isn't."

The kettle whistled and sputtered from the kitchen.

"The tea." She took off. "I forgot about it."

So had he.

Adam trailed her into the large kitchen. She worked efficiently, as if on autopilot, grabbing the teabags Molly had left on the counter and dropping them into a china teapot. She

20

filled the teapot with boiling water, then crossed her arms with her back to him and spoke so quietly that the ticking of the wall clock reached his ears.

"My grandmother died when my mom was twelve. Cancer. By the time the doctors found the mass, her death was painful and very quick. My mother was forced to grow up overnight. She helped my aunt with the running of the house so my grandfather could keep working the farm. She never had time for grief, at least not in the way she's expressing it now."

Her voice thickened. "When Dad and—" She broke off. Inhaled. Started again. "When my father died, it was the same. I'll never forget that day. Hearing the news, feeling the shock, the terror. I felt like I was disintegrating, but Mom never cracked, not once. She never cried in front of me. I used to think she never cried for him at all."

Adam scraped his hand over his mouth. *Damn it.* He didn't know much about Jess's father. Only his name, Frank Morgan. Molly had never volunteered the information, and he'd never had reason to ask.

Until now.

"How old were you?"

"Eighteen. An adult, I suppose, but in many ways I felt as sheltered as a child." A slow breath seeped out of her. "I really don't want to talk about my father anymore, okay?"

"Okay." Adam leaned on the counter so he could see her face. He felt for her, although he couldn't claim to understand her. He'd never lost a parent, but he'd conquered his own childhood demons years ago. As a result, he didn't believe in hiding from trouble or running away. In his personal life, as in his forestry consulting business, he believed in holding out for the long haul. Putting down roots and watching them grow.

He intended to live out his days in the tiny sawmilling community that had always anchored him. Nothing—not the cal-

21

lous realities of the boom/bust logging industry, not the pain of the woman he'd once loved destroying their future with her recklessness—would dissuade him from strengthening his commitment to place. To home.

Adversity encouraged him to push harder to achieve his goals.

However, for Jess, he suspected that, like his father and his ex-fiancée, hardship prompted her to hide, and the unexpected sent her packing.

Still, she drew out something in him.

A dark curl tumbled over her cheek, but he didn't brush it away. If he touched her, he might feel compelled to offer her the comfort of his arms. Her rigid stance shouted that she wouldn't welcome the gesture.

"As for your mother's grief—"

"I can handle it now that I know. I just wish I'd known." Her gaze fixed on the rose-sprigged teapot.

"That I'd told you at the airport."

"Yes. If you knew how upset she was tonight."

"Well, I'm guilty there. I did know. But Molly felt your mom's anxiety had a lot to do with waiting for you to come home. She didn't want me to alarm you, Jess." He maintained a low, even tone. *Look at me. Let me know I'm doing some good here.*

She massaged her forehead as if ten bass drums boomed inside it. "I guess you're right," she said without conviction. "I'm not very good with surprises. Especially ones like this."

She glanced at him then, and he held her gaze. Hers spoke of secrets in shadows, luring, summoning, captivating him.

Was the shy but happy girl he once knew hiding in there somewhere?

A blush dusted her face, and she reached for a tray from the fridge top.

Molly swept into the room. "How's the tea coming?"

"Almost ready." Jess retrieved china cups and saucers from

birch cupboards, her movements swift and choppy. Self-conscious.

Molly studied her. "Are you okay? The way I went about this—"

"I'm fine." A curt note colored Jess's voice, and she paused. "Moll, I'm sorry. It's okay, and I'm okay. I'll be fine, really."

Molly glanced at him. *She's not fine,* resonated in her concerned expression.

He turned up a hand: *Whatever you need from me, Cuz.*

Gratitude smoothed his cousin's features. "Do you want me to stay longer?" she asked Jess. "I'll call the sitter and make the arrangements."

"A babysitter? Where's Tim?"

"Coaching basketball in Vancouver. The high school boys made it to the provincial championships." Molly lifted the receiver of a sky-blue wall phone.

"So you had to hire a babysitter? Why didn't you say so? I could have rented a car in Kamloops."

"Then need to keep it the whole time you're here? There still isn't a car rental place in town, Jess. Besides, I didn't mind."

Jess strode to the table and opened her purse. "I'm paying for the sitter. How much—"

"Jess, no." Molly hung up. "Please don't change the subject. I don't want to leave you in the lurch. You work like a dog on your trips. You must be wiped out."

"I'll go to sleep when Mom does."

"Yeah, in the rocking chair in her room. I know you can take care of your mom. What worries me is whether you can take care of you."

Molly's gaze remained unyielding, and Adam pushed off the counter. His cousin could be a mule at times, but Jess was right—Molly needed to return to her kids.

"Molly, you go. I can stay another hour or so."

23

Jess raised a hand. "It's not necessary."

"Actually, it sounds like the perfect solution." Molly smiled. "Thank you, Adam. You're a sweetheart."

No, a mind-reader. Molly and her husband were his friends *and* family. They spotted one another all the time. "Anything for you, short stuff."

"Don't I have a say in this?" Frustration edged Jess's voice.

"Please don't argue with me, hon." Molly retrieved her navy jacket from the back of a chair. "What can it hurt to have Adam around? You shouldn't have to cope alone."

"I live alone. I'm accustomed to coping."

"This is different, and you know it." Molly pulled on her jacket and withdrew keys from the pocket. "I'm calling Adam tomorrow," she said, her voice firm, "and I don't want to hear that you kicked him out." She crossed the kitchen and stretched to kiss his cheek. "Thank you," she whispered near his ear. "Make sure she goes to bed before you leave, maybe fix her something to eat, too."

"Yes, boss."

Face tight, Jess walked Molly to the mudroom door. Returning to the kitchen, she bee-lined to the counter and pressed a hand against the teapot.

"Warm," she muttered as if he'd personally cooled the contents. "Mom likes it scalding." She poured the tea into the sink, re-boiled the remaining hot water in the kettle, then topped off the teapot and covered it with a patchwork cozy.

"It's no problem for me to stick around, you know," Adam said to her back.

She picked up the tray and faced him, shoulders squaring. "Look, I know you mean well, but I'm perfectly capable of caring for my mother. And myself. Thank you for the offer, but there's really no need for you to stay."

If that were true, his cousin wouldn't have insisted. "How

24

about fear of Molly?"

"Funny, you don't look like a coward."

"I'm not. I'm not questioning your competence, either, but this is Destiny Falls—we help each other out. I've met your mother several times. I doubt she'd object to my being here."

Her eyes closed briefly. "That's not the point."

"Then what is?"

"That I can do this on my own."

"I'll keep out of the way unless you need something. Besides, I told Molly I'd stay."

"Do you always do what Molly wants?"

"Sometimes. Mostly, I just do what I want. It's less hassle that way."

"You don't give up, is that it?"

Adam laughed, scratching his jaw. Her don't-crowd-me act might work with her Toronto pals, but she didn't intimidate him. "Perseverance is my middle name. Face it, Jess, you're stuck with me. I'm not going anywhere."

CHAPTER TWO

The nightstand clock read ten past midnight before her mother finally fell asleep. Now Jess sat in the rocking chair by the bed, holding her mother's hand and watching the steady rise and fall of her chest beneath the wedding-band quilt. A peaceful expression graced her mom's features, and Jess sighed with relief.

Her mom really needed this rest. Her grief for Pete was overwhelming, beyond anything Jess had imagined. Yet, why should the change in how her mother coped with loss surprise her? After all, when in the nine years since Dad and Danny died had she honestly tried to understand what her mother thought or felt?

Her resentment of Peter Olson had always stood in the way of developing the close relationship several of her Toronto friends shared with their mothers. Pete's thinly disguised dislike of *her* had played a major part, too.

However, continuing to blame Pete for their lack of intimacy was an easy solution to a complicated issue. The problem dug much deeper.

How deep or why, specifically, Jess couldn't say. But it was time she found out.

Her mom mumbled in her sleep, turning on her side to face Jess. As soon as peaceful slumber claimed her again, Jess tucked her hand beneath the quilt and quietly pushed back the rocking chair. She kissed her mom's forehead, then lowered the bedside lamp. The tea tray could wait until morning.

Leaving the bedroom door ajar, she stepped into the hall and leaned against the daisy-flecked wallpaper. Toes pinching, she pulled off the pumps she'd forgotten until now. *Ugh.* The soles of her feet throbbed almost as much as her head. A hot shower before bed would feel wonderful. However, for all she knew, Adam Wright still skulked around downstairs.

Damn him.

He reminded her of Molly—persistent, tenacious, steadfast. All positive qualities she admired in her friend but found unsettling in Adam.

Especially when combined with his striking blue eyes and disarming smile.

Why couldn't he have left when she'd asked him to? But no, not Molly's cousin. Apparently, bullheadedness ran in both branches of the Wright family. Jess had wanted privacy, so of course he'd insisted on making toast. When she'd maintained she wasn't hungry, he'd said he meant the snack for her mom. Jess had felt like an uncaring fool.

Minutes later, once she was busy consoling Mom, a light rap had sounded on the bedroom door. She'd gone to thank Adam for his thoughtfulness only to discover the plate of warm, buttered toast resting on a blue gingham placemat on the floor, a blossom plucked from a sympathy bouquet poking from a water glass beside it.

And Adam nowhere in sight.

The kind gesture had moved her—and still did—as she replayed the scene in her mind.

But she didn't want to feel anything for Adam Wright. She just wanted him and the uneasiness he stirred within her gone.

The mudroom door had slammed moments ago. Had he finally taken the hint?

She picked up her shoes and padded into the bathroom for

some aspirin. Beside her, the shower beckoned. If not for Adam . . .

She tossed down her shoes. Enough! She wanted a shower— she'd take one. This was her childhood home, not his. She couldn't allow his presence to dictate her actions, like she'd always done with Pete.

She turned on the shower. Unless her mom had finally tossed it out, her ratty, pink chenille bathrobe still hung in her old bedroom. With luck, her matted, purple bunny slippers huddled in the closet.

One look at her in that get-up, and Adam Wright, if he hadn't left already, would head for the hills.

Twenty minutes later, Jess left her room with her hair wet from her shower and the bunny slippers slapping the floor. Her suitcase with her favorite PJs remained downstairs. She hadn't been about to risk bumping into Adam wearing nothing but her robe to get it. However, a rummage through the dresser had produced a granny nightgown, which she wore beneath the old robe. She'd scrubbed her face free of makeup and vanquished her headache with the aspirin. If not for the chance that Molly's cousin hung around, she'd be ready for bed.

She checked on her sleeping mother, then went downstairs. The living room was empty and the fire dead, but the lights, though dimmed, still glowed. A tantalizing scent teased her nostrils. Pancakes? Her stomach growled.

She entered the kitchen. Pancake mix dusted the orange countertop, several cupboards stood open, and a batter-clumped whisk lay beside a glass measuring cup. At the stove with his back to her, Adam blithely flipped pancakes. His jean jacket sprawled on the chair by the phone, one sleeve brushing the floor.

Not only was he here, he'd ransacked the place! "What are

you doing?"

He faced her. His gaze lowered to the bunny slippers, and his mouth twitched. "Molly said to feed you."

Molly said. "I thought you'd left." Jess tightened the bathrobe's frayed belt. "Didn't the door slam?"

"Yeah, sorry. I didn't expect it to swing shut so fast."

She didn't want him apologizing. It made her feel mean. "So you *were* leaving?"

"I didn't say that." Amusement flickered in his light blue eyes.

I sound like a witch. And probably looked ridiculous. She refused to squirm beneath his penetrating gaze, though. *She* belonged here—he didn't.

Yet Adam Wright looked more at home in her mother's kitchen than Jess had felt in years.

"I went to get my dog. That's why the door slammed," he said in a deep, mellow voice. "She's on the back porch. Hope that's okay. The truck drives her stir-crazy after awhile."

"Oh." Heat climbed her neck. First her mom, now the dog, even Jess—didn't he treat anyone like trash? It would be a lot easier to follow through on her plan of kicking him out if he did. "You shouldn't leave her on the porch. Mom leases the pasture to the neighbors. The horses wander up to the fence sometimes, even at night."

"Sheba doesn't chase horses. An irate mare nipped her in the rear when she was a puppy. She learned her lesson." His gaze drifted over Jess, cheeky and bold. "Nice housecoat."

The heat exploded, splashing her face and shooting sparks to her nerve-endings. So much for putting him off-guard. The man couldn't be swayed.

She focused on an invisible spot above his left shoulder. "It's cold out. You should bring her in."

"It's nearly April. Not cold for a German shepherd who sleeps

29

outdoors eight months of the year."

"It doesn't matter. She can come in." She forced herself to meet his gaze. With the ivory shirt setting off his wide shoulders and his hips encased in the low-riding jeans, he dominated the country kitchen. Hopefully, he would seem less imposing with his dog around, less likely to cause her to combust again. She couldn't kick him out now that he'd fixed the pancakes. She did have *some* manners.

"We'll put her in the mudroom," she said. "If she barks, there's less chance Mom will hear her."

"You'll eat with me, then?" Half-turning, he transferred the browned pancakes to a platter. He ladled three more dollops of batter onto the hot pan, and the thick mixture sizzled.

"I guess." Her grumbling stomach seconded the motion.

"You guess? That's your invite?"

Her face warmed. "I'm asking."

"Asking what?"

"For you to stay." She smiled stiffly.

"Stay and . . . ?"

"Eat."

"Stay and eat. Okay, great. I will. Thanks." He lowered the element beneath the gurgling coffeepot. "Like pulling teeth," he murmured.

A smile played around his mouth as he winked, and images of the seventeen-year-old guy who'd once teased her and Molly filled her mind.

Her tummy fluttered. For a second, she almost felt "thirteen going on fourteen" again. Adam had shot her that same killer wink when she'd caught him staring at her over the triple-patty Load 'Em Up Special he'd inhaled during her and Molly's double fourteenth birthday party at a long-defunct burger joint.

However, back then, coerced by his aunt to join the family outing, he'd winked at Jess to torment her—no different than

30

tormenting his cousin. Now, he probably got his jollies by keeping the rude city girl off-balance.

The trick was not to let him know how well it worked.

He strolled to the back door and let in his dog.

"Hi, girl," Jess said when Sheba nosed past her. The German shepherd's tail wagged, and her brown eyes glittered.

"She likes you."

Sheba's winking master sounded surprised. *Score one for Rude City Girl.* How gratifying to up-end him for once.

Jess tore a bit of warm pancake from the stack on the platter and fed the piece to the dog. Sheba gobbled the tidbit, then woofed softly. Jess rewarded her with another chunk of pancake.

"Of course she likes me." She wiped her hands on a tea towel, then flipped the remaining pancakes on the stove. "When I was a kid, I had a German shepherd who could have been her twin. She loved pancakes, too."

Adam gazed at her with a new light in his eyes. Respect or bafflement? *Hard to tell.*

"What did you call her?"

"Sheena."

He flashed a devastating grin. "Great minds."

Jess smiled back at him before she could stop herself. Something subtle had changed between them. Because they liked the same breed of dog?

Whatever, she'd take it over the unease stretching between them earlier.

She closed the cupboards while he settled Sheba in the mudroom with a bowl of fresh water and a promise for an entire pancake if she didn't bark again.

"By the way," Jess said while he was out of view. "Thanks again for getting me from the airport so Molly could stay here with Mom. She liked the toast. You were right, she *was* hungry. She loved the flower. I left the glass on her dresser."

See? She could do this. Humor the man to placate Molly, then send him on his way.

He emerged from the mudroom, wiping his hands on his butt. "It was no big deal."

"Sure it was." Jess stacked pancakes on the platter. "You said Mom wouldn't mind if you stayed, and you were right about that, too. She said you knew Pete from some group that mentors teenagers?"

He nodded. "Destiny Falls Young Achievers."

"Well, I'm sure you could have found a better way to spend your Friday night. I appreciate everything you've done. I really do. I'm sorry if I've come off a little, um, rude."

"You haven't been rude."

"I wasn't the height of graciousness when you offered to stay."

"When I wouldn't leave, you mean?"

"Something like that."

"Don't worry about it. I didn't get you from the airport to score points in the good guy department, Jess. I went because Molly asked me to and because I respect your mom. As for staying, that's turning out to my benefit, I think. It's not every day I have a chance to make pancakes at midnight. Now I get to share a nice meal with you and a couple of damn cute purple bunnies."

His smile, slow and incredibly sexy, warmed her from her soon-to-frizz curls down to her rabbit-eared toes. "You're okay, Adam Wright, you know that?"

"How about you taste my pancakes and then you can judge my okay-ability?"

She smiled back. Darn it, but it was difficult not to.

"Deal."

Adam riffled through the buffet drawer where Jess had said her mom stored tablecloths. Apparently, Nora was a stickler for protecting the original finish of the old table. Adam wouldn't know an antique from a well-used piece of furniture if they both clubbed him in the face, but he admired Jess's desire not to disrupt her mother's routines. After rolling out the *un*welcome mat with the disapproving vibes he'd given off earlier, he wanted to help make her feel as comfortable as possible.

He chose the first cloth beneath a pile of napkins, then moved Jess's purse onto a chair out of the way. He arranged the tablecloth and located a bottle of pancake syrup while she washed the messy counter.

"Plates and cups?" he asked as she rinsed the washcloth and folded it over the faucet.

"I'll bring them. You can get the butter, though. Thanks."

He retrieved the butter and cream from the fridge and joined her at the table. She stood motionless, staring at the tablecloth, the stacked plates sitting by her hand.

Uh-oh. "Jess?"

Her gaze lifted. "It's nothing," she murmured, glancing away. "Just nostalgia."

Bull. He put down the cream and butter dish. Her dark hair hung past her shoulders in tight spirals, starting to dry. When she'd showered, she'd removed her makeup, and shadows smudged the skin beneath her eyes. She looked impossibly young and vulnerable.

He rested a hand on her shoulder, and her fingers twitched on the table.

"This was my dad's favorite tablecloth," she whispered. "I didn't realize Mom still had it."

Way to go, Wright. Pick the wrong freaking tablecloth.

"Why wouldn't she?"

He watched Jess's shoulders rise then slowly lower. "Mom made this tablecloth when I was eight, because Dad used to bring her buttercups. I even embroidered a couple. We worked on it together, for him. One of the few things we did together." Her fingers glided over a loosely stitched buttercup. "See here? My masterpiece."

"You still miss him."

She nodded.

Adam's gut twisted. How awful it must feel to lose a loving parent. The difficult years with Pop had often felt like a loss. Their constant moving and Pop's drinking, his self-condemnation and sadness. Through the hard times, Adam had clung tightly to the good memories. With the help of his mother and his older brother, he'd hung on.

Maybe Jess, faced with the depth of her mother's grief, was only trying to hold on to the sweet, whispery havens of her youth, too.

"It must be rough, losing first your dad and then a stepfa—" *Damn it.* He'd nearly mentioned Pete again. The last time hadn't proven successful.

Her fingers fluttered on the tablecloth. "My feelings for Pete are complicated. I loved my dad very much. When Mom and Pete got married . . ." She moistened her lips. "My mom and I had a lot of problems. Pete and I never warmed to each another." She looked up. "I'm sorry, we'd better eat if you want to get home before morning." Off she went, collecting cutlery, coffee, and the pancake platter with exaggerated effort.

She'd just hung out her "Closed" sign. Adam recognized the indicators from earlier in the evening in the self-conscious way she moved around the kitchen, pink bathrobe flowing around the ugly nightgown that did a horrible job of disguising her curves.

Well, all right, then. She didn't need him butting in on her limited time with Nora, stirring up emotions best discussed with her mother, not him.

34

He poured the decaffeinated coffee and pulled out their chairs. While they ate, he made polite conversation, asking about her job as a buyer for Arlington Shoes. It was a name he recognized from a Kamloops mall as a pricey national chain—classy and sophisticated like Jess, when she wasn't swathed in faded pink cotton.

Even now, wearing the tattered robe, she radiated an elegance that fascinated even as it reminded him they lived in two different worlds.

Jess lived in the world Crysta had left him for.

But he wouldn't think about his ex-fiancée and what he discovered he'd lost when he'd tracked her down.

Especially not what he had lost.

"What does a shoe buyer do, anyway?" he asked between forkfuls of syrup-drenched pancake. "Go shopping with a vengeance?"

Jess smiled, and he gave himself a mental pat on the back for managing to encourage her to unwind.

"Attend trade shows, meet sales reps, decide which styles to buy or arrange to manufacture for our stores." She glanced at him over her coffee cup. "There's a lot of travel involved."

"I'll bet." To destinations nowhere near as ordinary as rural B.C. "Such as?"

"Europe, South America, Asia."

"Sounds glamorous compared to trekking through the bush."

Her gaze wavered. "You're a logger?"

"Nope." He downed more pancakes. "Consulting forester."

"You have your own company?"

"Don't sound so shocked."

"I'm not. Not that you own a consulting firm, just that it's located in Destiny Falls."

Why did city dwellers always assume that hicks from the sticks were business no-minds?

35

"Why do you say that?"

She sipped her coffee. "The small population, for one. Wouldn't a regional center like Kamloops make a better base for your company than a tiny place like Destiny Falls?"

"Not necessarily. In fact, if we're talking small contracts, the more local the firm, the better." Warming to his subject, he swabbed pancakes in syrup. "The Vancouver firms that hunt the big contracts—that's where my competition lies. Right now I'm bidding on a contract that'll bring in several months of work. Not only for me and the guys I usually hire, but also as summer jobs for our university kids. To win it, I need to convince the timber-company bigwigs that I can provide the same bang for their buck."

Jess nodded, although her thoughtful gaze held doubts.

"It's not only a matter of coming in cheaper." Adam drank his coffee. "I have a good reputation with small contracts, but can I be trusted with a big one? I need to prove I'm reliable, dependable, rock-solid. My success with current jobs is paramount. There's no margin for error."

"I know where you're coming from there. Mistakes in merchandising can be disastrous." She set down her cup and lifted a forkful of pancake. "It sounds like winning this contract means a lot to you," she said before closing her full lips around the fork's tines.

He tore his gaze away from the tempting sight.

"It does. The Vancouver firm I'm probably competing against rarely hires locals. The town gets a boost from the cash their guys spend while they're here, but then they leave again." Like Jess would. Like Crysta did—taking his future with her. "What good does that do a struggling community like Destiny Falls?"

"I see your point."

"The purpose of the program Pete and I ran for Destiny Falls Young Achievers is to help kids with bright futures realize they don't have to leave the area for work. After they earn their degrees, they can return to make their homes here. Assist in building the local economy instead of taking their money and expertise elsewhere."

"Expanding your business will help them realize that?"

"That's the plan. I won't sacrifice my lifestyle to do this, Jess, but I don't think I'll have to. I'll continue doing fieldwork and bidding on small jobs when it suits me, and I'll tackle the administrative load from my home office. The point behind winning *this* contract is simply to get started. To get the kids believing they can achieve success in their hometown, too."

She sliced her pancakes. "It sounds like when you commit to something, you give it your all."

"I wouldn't have it any other way. I told you perseverance was my middle name."

She blushed, a delightful rosy glow. "You make hard work sound easy."

"No. Worthwhile."

Her gaze swept to the ceiling. Was she thinking of her mother? *Good.* He liked that. And what it suggested about her.

She cared. Perhaps more than she wanted to admit.

Who knew, maybe she'd realize she owed it to Nora to put in more than a cursory appearance. Maybe she'd hang around town a while and try to sort through whatever had gone wrong between them.

Or maybe he was pushing his own set of values on her, hoping to see something that wasn't there.

Either way, it didn't really matter. He'd promised to repair his aunt and uncle's rotting fence this weekend. Next week looked jam-packed: meetings, fieldwork, a trip up the valley come Tuesday or Wednesday. By the time he returned to Destiny Falls, Jess Morgan could well be gone.

As would the chance to get to know her better.

The idea bothered him much more than it should.

CHAPTER THREE

What must Jessie think of me?

Nora Olson sat beside her grown daughter in Peter's cherished classic luxury coupe. The morning sun streaming through the open garage door mocked her. She was an anxious mess.

She glanced at Jessie, who struggled to start the car's rebuilt engine. In the four days since her daughter had come home, they'd shared several talks. However, each time Jessie broached difficult issues, Nora balked. She didn't mean to. Her heartache for the mistakes of Jessie's childhood haunted her, and her anguish over losing Peter remained too raw. Yet, witnessing Jessie's confusion over her visible grief for Peter ate at her.

Her daughter deserved an explanation. But how could she tell Jessie that Peter was the true love of her life, that his steady influence had always nourished her while her tumultuous feelings for Jessie's father had left her drained? Jessie had adored Frank so, and Frank, who'd loved big and boisterous and grand, had doted on their only child.

Nora couldn't destroy Jessie's memories by exposing another side of Frank—and further revealing her own flaws.

Her daughter might think her weak, and she couldn't bear that. Jessie was all she had now, and Nora was too big a coward to risk their fragile bond.

Shredding her tissue, she watched Jessie turn the key again. The engine clicked, nothing else. Not even a whir or a whine.

39

"It's no use. The battery's dead." Jessie pulled out the key and looked at her. "When did you last drive the car?"

"Not since before—" She couldn't even say the words. "Not for some time. Peter used it mainly for work, you see, and what with our friends helping me out . . ."

Jessie's golden-brown eyes softened. Her lashes were long and dark, like Frank's had been. "It's okay, Mom. I knew your lawyer appointment was today. I should have checked the car before now."

Jessie had never understood Peter's love for the classic automobile, or why Nora hadn't insisted on a more reliable source of transportation. The answer was simple. She hadn't required her own car, because she and Peter had done everything together.

"But Peter tinkered with this car all the time. Why would it act up now that he's—" Her breath hitched. "Darn it, I remember now. Peter parked in the driveway the day he—that Friday, and I didn't move the car into the garage until the next night. Did I forget to turn off the headlights?" Since her husband's passing, sometimes she truly thought she was losing her mind.

Jessie checked the headlight knob. "Looks like that was it, all right." She pushed the knob back in. "Why did you move the car?"

"For Monday, for the . . . after the service, so the guests would have room to park." Tears blurred her vision, and she gripped the remnants of her tissue. She refused to dissolve into another useless bout of weeping. The lawyer expected her. They had to go.

"Oh, Mom." Jessie unbuckled her seatbelt and slid across the bench seat. "I wish I'd been here to handle things for you. I know I keep saying that, but it's true."

Nora dabbed her nose with the tissue. "To have you here

with me now, Jessie, means the world. And for you to phone your boss yesterday and arrange to stay longer than we thought you could is far more than I'd hoped for. I'm imposing on your career, I know I am, and it means so much, you staying here."

"You're my mother," Jessie said softly, caressing her shoulder. "I want to be here with you, for you."

Even though I wasn't there for you?

She didn't deserve her daughter's understanding.

However, with Peter gone, Jessie seemed eager to improve their relationship. Hope leapt in Nora's chest that some good might arise from her husband's death. Finally, a chance to rectify past wrongs, when her daughter paced cold hospital halls while the Galloway boy struggled to survive, when only Molly could reach her.

An awful time, the logging accident and the heartache that followed. One they desperately needed to address.

"But what about your job?" she asked. Jessie had spoken to her boss for an hour yesterday and again briefly today. Each time, Nora had noted tiny lines of stress marring her daughter's face. However, when she'd asked, Jessie had assured her that everything was fine. "Isn't six weeks too long to be away?"

"Mom, we've been through this. Please don't worry about my job. It's well within my rights to take this leave of absence, and Gareth knows it. Besides, it's not like I'm falling off the face of the earth. My assistant will call or email with questions. Molly says wireless is spotty around town, but if I have problems I can use her broadband connection with my laptop."

Nora nodded half-heartedly. Wireless? Broadband? She didn't even own a computer. She was a dinosaur.

And, heaven help her, as much as she wanted to, she couldn't force Jessie to reveal details of the life her daughter would rather keep hidden. She'd surrendered a mother's license to pry years ago.

"Should we go back to the house?" The cheerfulness in Jessie's voice rang false. "You can freshen up, and I'll make tea."

"But the lawyer—I don't want to miss her."

"I'll call. We can reschedule."

"Jessie, she only comes to town on Tuesdays, and I need to put the business of Peter's will behind me."

Her daughter glanced at her watch. "No time for tea, then." She withdrew her cell phone from her purse.

"Who are you calling?"

"Directory assistance. Is that taxi service still operating?"

"Yes, but he just has the one car."

"Don't worry. We might be a little late, but we'll get there. I promise, Mom, I won't let you down."

"Any other changes?"

"Nope. Same as last year." Adam smiled at the middle-aged clerk at the counter. "Thanks, Nancy," he said when she hit the computer key to print his auto insurance forms.

She trundled toward the shared office printer several feet away. While waiting, he scanned a pamphlet about wood stoves and chimney fires. Behind him, one of the rented office doors clicked open. He glanced over his shoulder. *Jess.*

Her black curls tumbled over her light-colored blouse. She carried a sweater over one arm and gripped a paper in her other hand. Tan pants, low shoes, and an expensive-looking purse completed the picture. She looked so at odds with the farming prints and forest fire prevention posters decorating the country office, it wasn't funny, but that didn't stop a satisfying warmth from stealing through him.

He hadn't expected to see her again. When he'd left Friday night, he'd said to call if she needed anything, but she hadn't. He'd refused to intrude on her limited time with her mom by visiting the farmhouse uninvited.

"Hi," he said as she neared the counter. The insurance office was a public place. He could intrude all he wanted here.

Her gaze flew to him. "Oh, hi. Sorry, I was preoccupied. Do you have business here?"

"Insurance for the SUV. Mine expires tomorrow." He tossed the fire safety pamphlet onto a magazine-strewn side table. "How about you?"

She looked back at the bank of rented offices. "The lawyer. Mom's in with her now. I'm not sure why, but she doesn't seem to want me to stay."

"No?" He hoped things hadn't soured between them. Family was important, especially during rough times. And Jess's mother was going through a doozy. "What did she say?"

"Just that she'd be okay on her own. Which, normally, I could accept. But lately she hasn't been herself, as I've mentioned. Now today . . ."

"Pete's will?" he guessed, and she nodded.

"I thought we'd planned our day over breakfast. First the lawyer, then the grocery shopping. We were even going to drop in at The Clothes Horse to see Molly. Of course, that was before the car conked out."

"That old Monte?"

"Yes. The battery, I think. The car's not the problem, though. At breakfast Mom said she wanted me with her when she saw the lawyer, but now she's sending me to Waverly Foods alone." Jess chewed her lipstick, worry darkening her gaze.

"Maybe she's not ready to visit the store, Jess. Lawyers, life insurance—that's just paper. But Pete managed Waverly Foods for over twenty years. The place is bound to remind her of him."

"I didn't think of that."

"Makes sense, though."

Another nod. "She's right that we can take the groceries back

43

with us in the taxi, and we are running low on essentials." She glanced at the lawyer's office again, her voice softening.

Adam touched her wrist. His hand grazed the cuff of her blouse, and his fingers brushed smooth skin. "Forget the taxi. I can help you out."

"Aren't you working?" She switched her grocery list to her other hand, and his fingers fell away.

"I'm between meetings with the Forest Service. Might as well put the time to good use." *For the sake of Pete's widow.* "I'll take you and Nora home when you're ready. Later, once I've finished my town work, I'll drop by and jumpstart the car. Save you the bother of calling a garage."

"It's no bother."

"I insist."

The worry in her gaze receded. "Thanks, Adam. That would be nice."

Nice. Yeah, that was him. A regular Boy Scout.

"Let's get those groceries. Give your mother one less thing to worry about."

After another glance to the lawyer's office, she murmured her agreement.

"Give me a second." He returned to the counter and paid for his insurance. Finished, he opened the door and followed Jess out to the sidewalk bordering the small shopping center. Tiny patches of melting snow dotted the banks of the parking lot in testament to the long winter, but the air was brisk and the sky clear, proclaiming spring's arrival. The sun shone brightly on the heavily forested mountains surrounding the community.

He stopped at his dusty vehicle. "It's a beautiful day." *Beautiful woman, too.* "Let's leave the SUV parked here and walk. We can bring the groceries back with a cart." He chucked the insurance papers through the open window. They landed on the driver's seat.

44

A smile tipped Jess's mouth. "Aren't you worried someone will steal that?"

"In this town? Half the time we don't even lock our doors. So, nope."

Her smile grew. "You don't have to come with me, Adam. You can finish your business, and I'll meet you back here."

"No way. Banking bores me." Not true. He enjoyed monitoring his finances. Good thing, or he wouldn't make much of a businessman. However, Jess needed a diversion from worrying about her mother. Her concern for Nora impressed the hell out of him, but all that anxiety would give her ulcers.

"All right. I'd better wear my sweater if we're walking. It's cooler than I expected." She set her purse on the hood of his truck. "You didn't bring Sheba along." She gestured toward the cargo hold.

"She's better off at home when I've got a town day. Here, let me help you."

Moving behind her, he took the sweater and held it while she slipped on first one sleeve, then the other. The backs of her arms brushed his jean jacket in a movement that, at another time and with another woman, might be considered intimate. Traces of her flowery shampoo drifted to his nostrils. His chest squeezed, and he hauled in a breath as arousal sped through him. A vision of Jess pulled snug back against him, his hips burning into her shapely rear, flashed through his mind.

Clearing his throat, he stepped away. She retrieved her purse, the spring-time color in her cheeks alerting him that their nearness had affected her, as well.

Whether positively or negatively, he hadn't a clue.

"I'll have to buy a spring jacket, I guess. My work coat would look out of place here." She glanced at a jeans-clad young woman struggling to settle a toddler into his car seat three parking spaces away. "I see the uniform of the day is still denim, huh?"

Not sure if she expected an answer, he guided her toward Waverly Foods. "You're sticking around, then?"

She nodded. "I called my boss and explained the situation. He wasn't happy I'll be gone so long, seeing as I just returned from Europe. But he approved a six-week leave of absence, provided I'm back by the middle of May."

Six weeks. Five weeks longer than Molly had mentioned. The extra time would be good for Jess and Nora, and chances were he and Jess would continue bumping into one another. Counting outlying farms and ranches, Destiny Falls boasted a population of less than fifteen hundred.

"Why mid-May?"

"I've been building contacts for a buying trip to Asia at the end of May. Even with Gareth—that's my boss—and my assistant keeping me up to date through email and phone calls, I'll need office time to prepare."

He nodded. "Your mother must love the idea of having you in town for the next six weeks." So did he, although he shouldn't. He had nothing to gain from pursuing his attraction to Jess.

"She really needs me right now, Adam." They passed the bank and drugstore. Jess strode to the row of grocery carts outside Waverly Foods. "More than she ever has before."

He pulled out a cart for her, and the clanking of metal frames pierced the air. "You could always move back home for good. I bet your mom would love that."

She frowned. "I'm not moving home. My job—"

"Sorry." He lifted a hand. "I don't know where that comment came from." Wishful thinking? A woman as beautiful and interesting as Jess Morgan didn't waltz into town every day. But how would a merchandising executive get her thrills in a tiny community like Destiny Falls? Twiddling her shoelaces? Compared to her globetrotting career, the limited job opportunities would probably leave her feeling as suffocated as they'd left Crysta. "I believe in equal rights as much as the next guy." He didn't want to come across like some small-town Neanderthal who thought women belonged pregnant and barefoot in the kitchen.

"Oh, yeah?" She smiled. "How much does the next guy believe in them?"

He laughed. "I'd better take my foot out of my mouth before I'm forced to swallow it." At this rate, he might as well hire a taxidermist to stitch the damn thing into place.

"Good idea." She turned and sailed in through the automatic door, leaving him to push the shopping cart behind her.

He had a great view.

Jess attacked her mother's grocery shopping list with the same determination she usually reserved for making risky buying decisions. Adam's comment outside the store had unnerved her and unleashed a torrent of guilt. The only way she'd been able to deal with her reaction was by uttering a shallow joke—which only proved how shallow *she* was and how miserably out of touch with what her mother might need or want.

In the days since she'd learned about Pete's death, she'd never once considered moving back to Destiny Falls. Neither had she entertained the notion that her mother might *want* her to. Her life, though stressful and hectic, provided a certain structure she'd come to rely on since Dad and Danny died. The prospect of losing that psychological safety net terrified her.

In Toronto, she felt distanced from her memories. However, in Destiny Falls, they confronted her wherever she went. After the accident, Danny's family left town, but the places where she and Danny had hung out, and some of their mutual friends,

47

remained here. The dreams she and Danny had shared. Their young love. *Her first lover.*

The joy and passion they'd gifted to each other.

He would have been my husband.

She couldn't handle living with the reminders every day.

Grateful Adam had abandoned the subject as quickly as he'd brought it up, she allowed him to direct her around the supermarket. He located items as she read them off her list, introducing her to the butcher and the bakery clerk, as well as several customers who either knew her mother or had known Pete. Everyone offered their condolences. By the time they reached the checkouts, Jess had become thoroughly re-acquainted with the know-thy-neighbor philosophy of Destiny Falls.

"Good morning," the cashier, a buxom blonde woman about her mother's age, greeted cheerfully. The woman's gaze flitted from Jess to Adam as they placed the groceries on the conveyor. "Nice day, eh?"

Jess smiled and nodded. The cart empty, she fetched her wallet from her purse while Adam began bagging groceries at the end of the checkout. The cashier peered at her.

"Excuse me, sweetie, don't I know you?"

Jess read the woman's nametag: THELMA. The name tweaked, but nothing substantial popped to mind. "I'm Jess Morgan, Nora Olson's daughter. I'm visiting for a few weeks. I haven't been back in a while, but I was born here."

Recognition lit Thelma's gaze. "Oooh." She offered her sympathies on Pete, then asked about Jess's mother, who, it turned out, was a friend. "I thought you looked familiar, sweetie. You take after your father, you know." Thelma continued scanning grocery items. "Yes, I knew him, too. Of course, that was long ago, and he didn't have family here, did he?"

Jess shook her head, skin prickling. "They're in

48

Saskatchewan." Unlike most Destiny Falls residents, Frank Morgan hadn't been born of local pioneer stock. When he'd first moved to town, people treated him like an outsider. Now Jess was an outsider here, too.

More to the point, she felt like one.

Thelma's friendly gaze narrowed again. "Yes, you look a lot like your father did, tall and dark. Although you have that lovely natural curl I've always remembered. That's your mother's blessing."

Jess tried a smile. *Another topic of conversation, please?*

Thelma tapped a finger to pursed lips. "It's been ages since you moved away." Her eyes brightened. "Say, didn't you know the Galloway boy? What was his name? Davy?"

"Danny." Jess sucked in a breath. *Wrong topic.* She didn't want to talk about Danny Galloway in the middle of a supermarket checkout line, of all places. She didn't want to talk about him at all. His memory was too precious.

Hers. No one else's.

She unsnapped her wallet and withdrew her debit card. To her relief, Thelma picked up on her reluctance to discuss Danny and didn't ask about him again. Gaze understanding, she waved a hand.

"You can put away that card, sweetie. Your mother runs a monthly tab. All you gotta do is sign." She tallied the amount on a carbon copy pad and passed the pad to Jess. "She'll keep getting the staff discount this way."

Jess glanced up. "Thank you. That's very kind." Her word sufficing as credit—there was an advantage to small-town living she'd completely forgotten. "I'd like to pay for all her groceries while I'm here, plus any outstanding balance from March."

"You bet." Thelma scribbled a note on the pad. Then she took over bagging groceries while Adam placed them in the cart. "Will you be around the Victoria Day long weekend?" she

49

asked Jess. In honor of the former queen's birthday, the national holiday occurred on the third or fourth Monday in May. "You wouldn't want to miss the Lumberjack Festival. They wind up with a slo-pitch tournament, and sometimes it can get pretty interesting, eh, Adam?"

Jess lifted her eyebrows. *The Lumberjack Festival. Wow.* "You still hold that?"

Thelma grinned. "Your dad was a master. Always winning the axe-throwing and obstacle pole bucking competitions. And wasn't he Best All-Around Logger a year or two?"

"Three." In a row. Once upon a time, the trophy had proudly graced their fireplace mantel.

But those days were long gone.

"I won't be here then, actually." Returning her wallet to her purse, she asked Adam, "Do you participate in the logger sports?"

He shook his head. "I leave that to the guys with the chain-saws. Thelma's just trying to embarrass me."

"Am not," Thelma teased.

"Are, too," he kidded back. Glancing at Jess, he placed another bag in the cart. "Destiny Falls Young Achievers sponsors the festival's slo-pitch tournament. Last year Pete decided we should hold a silent charity auction at the dinner-dance afterward."

Thelma chuckled, hands on her ample hips. "And what happens? Adam here puts up two days forestry work training as a prize. What was the training, now? Timber cruising?"

"Traversing. Compass and line work."

"Compass, that was it. Well, my Wendy, how shocked was *she* to learn she'd won the prize? Her sister put down her name as a lark and then had to buck up for DFYA. Kylie insisted Wendy take the training, but Wendy wasn't too happy about it, was she, Adam?" Thelma flashed a toothy grin. "My Wendy's not cut out for bush work. Was probably way more trouble to Adam than she was worth."

"Now, Thelma." Adam's voice held a friendly warning.

"Well, it's true. In fact, Wendy has so little talent for bush work that she finally convinced Adam to let her off the hook. Cooked him a wonderful meal to thank him for it, too. And, you know, this boy hasn't called her since? Wendy was willing to offer another meal or two, but Adam?" Thelma clucked her tongue. "You work too hard, sweetie. It's admirable, but it ain't no way to make babies. Don't you think your mom and dad would love it if you gave them a little grandchild someday?"

Adam's ears reddened. "I'll keep that in mind, Thelma. Thank you, as always, for the entertaining chat."

"Bye, now." Thelma waved before greeting her next customer.

Or victim, depending on one's perspective. Jess's mouth curved.

Adam shot her a glance. "You're not smiling, are you?"

"Never." She held back her laughter until they left the store. Then it spilled out, releasing the tension she'd bottled all morning. Oh, it felt so good to laugh again.

Adam pushed the shopping cart beside her, the wheels scrunching the stones that were scattered in the parking lot. "You think Thelma's pretty funny, huh?"

"I'll admit, you took it well." Jess crossed her arms against the brisk breeze.

"She means no harm. Wendy's the youngest of four daughters. Thelma wants her to get married, and she becomes carried away in the encouragement department sometimes."

"Thelma wants *you* to marry Wendy?" Jess wouldn't doubt it. With his thick shock of dark blond hair, that sexy scar cutting across one eyebrow, and the muscular build evident beneath his denim jacket, Adam Wright exuded a masculine, hometown charm.

Definite son-in-law material, anyway.

51

"Thelma wants *anyone* to marry Wendy," he said with a grin.

They reached the SUV. He opened the cargo door and began transferring grocery bags. "But Wendy's only twenty-one. That's ten years between us—not my thing. And she's certainly not ready to settle down, no matter what Thelma thinks." He glanced at her. "Can I ask you something now?"

"Sure."

"Who's Danny?"

Chapter Four

As soon as he asked the question, Adam wished he could retract it. A moment ago, Jess had been laughing. Now her gaze lowered, face sobering.

"Someone." A halting tone shadowed her voice.

No kidding. "And not my business, I take it." Molly had never mentioned a Danny Galloway. Why not? "Forget it. I shouldn't have asked." He'd give anything to see Jess smile again. That soft, slow smile that lit her entire face.

"It's okay." She glanced up. "I'm the one who should apologize, Adam. You've done so much for my mother and me. But, Danny . . . it's . . ."

"Personal. I get it."

She nodded, sadness dulling her gaze. Because of her mother? This Danny? One thing was certain. Adam wouldn't ask. For several agonizing months after he'd found Crysta living in a grungy Vancouver apartment and she'd coldly relayed what had happened, burying pain had been his trademark. He knew how it felt to want to keep hurt hidden.

He placed the last grocery bag in the truck. Jess toed a cluster of pebbles. "I should go back inside and wait for Mom."

"I'll return the cart. I won't be long."

"Thank you. We'll be here."

She disappeared into the insurance office, the bell above the door tinkling. He'd leave her alone for now, give her some space. He'd rather stay, but he'd go.

53

But, hell, the urge to discover what made her tick drove through him.

He wanted his mind free of her. Needed his fill of her.

He wanted to know her secrets

Pete's old car rumbled behind Jess, and she turned from tidying the workbench in her mother's detached garage. She couldn't imagine touching Peter Olson's things when he was alive. However, now her cleaning spree represented one less task to leave to her grieving mother. Besides, she'd needed to muster her composure while Adam drove the car for thirty minutes to retain the charge. Her response when he'd asked about Danny this morning embarrassed her. Losing the love of her life at eighteen had been devastating, but nine years had passed. There was no excuse for her rudeness.

Adam parked the forest-green car beside his burgundy SUV. As he climbed out, she handed him his wrapped jumper cables in exchange for the keys.

"How's the battery?" she asked.

"Good now, I think." He walked around the big hood of the car and stowed the cables in his truck. "Hopefully, your mom won't leave the headlights on again. Old batteries drain easily. If it happens, let me know. I'll put it on my charger overnight."

"With a car this old, shouldn't Pete have had a charger?" They'd located Pete's dusty jumper cables, but Adam had elected to use his own, newer set.

"Maybe he loaned it to a friend who forgot to return it. Or he planned to buy a new battery, so didn't feel like he needed one. Pete wouldn't intentionally leave your mother stranded, Jess."

Point taken. Pete hadn't intended to die.

Nodding, she slipped the keys into her pants pocket. "Anything else? The car sounded rough when you left."

Adam shut the SUV's door and faced her over the car. The bare bulb hanging from the rafters burned brightly in the late afternoon light, burnishing his dark blond hair. For a moment, her heart raced with the attraction that had caused her dozens of sleepless teenage nights.

"It's difficult to tell with these classic cars. Pete probably knew all her quirks. I know he planned to finish restoring her. He repaired the body rust when he had her repainted, and the upholstery's in fantastic shape. The same can't be said for the transmission. I think your mother's in for some trouble there."

Wonderful. "How can you tell it's the transmission?"

"The ride should feel smooth when an automatic shifts gears, but the tranny clunks, sometimes grinds—not good signs."

"It's that bad?"

"It's a gradual thing, Jess. Part of old age. The engine sounds good, but the tranny's a separate issue. It could last another few years or tank out tomorrow." He scratched his jaw. "Do you think your mom would consider buying a new car?"

"Gosh, I don't know. Pete loved this old gas guzzler. He had it in storage for ages, then sold their import and started driving it again." Jess ran a hand over the long hood of the car. The lingering engine heat suffused her palm. "To ask Mom to part with it now is like asking her to part with a piece of *him.*"

Adam strode toward her. "A friend of mine's a good mechanic. He'll look at it for you."

"I'll talk to Mom about it in a couple of days."

"Don't put it off. You don't want her having transmission trouble after you leave."

"Yes, but there's no point rushing her into something she isn't up to handling yet. Isn't that what you said to me about the grocery shopping this morning?"

"I'm sure you'll know best when to discuss it with your mom." His hand settled on the hood a scant inch from hers.

Her fingers twitched. She would not move them and risk making him feel like he carried a contagious disease. "I'd hate to see her stuck without reliable transportation, especially come winter."

The hot car hood cooked her hand. Specific lower regions of her body warmed up, too—for reasons that had zippy to do with engine heat.

God, what a time to redevelop a teenage crush.

"I *will* talk to her, Adam."

"I know. I didn't mean to imply otherwise." He brushed grime off her sweater sleeve. His gaze lifted to meet hers. "You're all dirty." His thumb grazed her cheek, and her skin tingled. This was crazy!

"How did things go with the lawyer?" he asked. "Nora was quiet after the meeting."

Don't step back, she ordered herself. *Don't relay how much his touch affects you.* "She needed time alone, um, to pull herself together. She's doing better now, though. A friend dropped by to see her this afternoon. That helped."

Adam's faded-denim gaze pinned her in place. "The meeting went well?"

She shrugged. "Pete left her in a good position financially. The house and land were paid off before she married him, and he had life insurance. If she wanted to buy a new car, she could. I'd be willing to help her out, too, of course."

"Of course." He seemed to lean toward her slightly. Or she toward him? Awareness of him licked at her nerve-endings like a constant, low-burning flame.

"Would you like to stay for dinner? Mom wanted me to ask." A lie. The question had popped out. "Molly brought over a casserole while you were gone. It's heating in the oven. She and Mom are showing the horses to the kids," she stupidly tacked on. Her rambling betrayed her nerves, which was silly. She'd had relationships with other men since Danny. She could deal with this unwelcome attraction to Adam.

"Do you want me to stay?" he asked softly.

"Um . . ."

"I'm trying to be honest here, Jess. You're in town for six weeks—that's a fair while. I could keep my distance. However, the more I think about it, the more I realize I don't want to. I'd like to see you while you're here."

"You mean as in dating?"

"If that's what you want to call it. Although there aren't many places in Destiny Falls I could take you on a formal date."

Then what did he have in mind? A hook-up? "Well, I don't sleep around."

He laughed. "That's gratifying to hear, because I wouldn't dream of sharing you." The scent of his aftershave floated to her, a heady mixture of moss and musk. "I was thinking more along the lines of getting to know each other better, one on one. However, if you'd like, we could always discuss our sleeping habits later."

Her face burned. Now he knew the thought of having sex with him had crossed her mind. She wanted to crawl beneath the car and hide.

"Is there someone in Toronto?" he asked.

Say yes. "No, but—"

"Think about it for a few days. I'll catch you on the weekend."

"You're not staying for dinner?" Her *mother* would be crushed.

"Can't. Remember that big contract I mentioned Friday? I'm initiating some silviculture surveys up past Valemount tomorrow. They're of the same nature, though smaller and less intensive. It's another opportunity to show what MountainTop can do, so I'm leaving tonight."

"Silviculture?"

"Textbook definition—the growing and tending of trees. We're doing mainly survival assessments of blocks planted three years ago."

"How long does starting the contract take?"

"Two or three days. Why, miss me already?"

She smiled. "No."

"Hm, I'd better not touch that one. I doubt the old ego could take it." He pressed a chaste kiss to her cheek. As he drew back, his gaze moved over her face. No longer teasing, but serious, seductive, searching.

Instinctively, her lips parted. Adam must have read an answer in the tiny movement, because in the next instant his mouth covered hers. A soft gasp rose in her throat and merged with his low moan of approval.

The horses' whinnies drifted to her ears. Then Molly's voice, calling instructions to her children. Not as distant as the horses, but growing louder. Near the garage's open side door—

Jess broke the kiss, stepping back.

A few seconds later, Molly breezed in. "You two finished?"

"Not by a long shot," Adam murmured, his gaze trained on Jess.

A sensual shiver scooted up her spine. She looked at Molly. "Hi. Where's Mom?"

"Making lemonade with the kids. How's the car?"

"Battery's charged," Adam replied, glancing at his watch. "I have to go." He smiled at Jess. "Take care, and remember what I said about the transmission." He walked around the car and climbed into his truck, then opened the window and revved the engine.

"Are you leaving for Valemount right away?" Jess asked.

"As soon as I get Sheba."

She rubbed her neck beneath her hair. "Thanks for helping with the car."

"No problem." His gaze rested on her, then shifted to Molly.

58

"Catch you later, Cuz."

"Bye." To Molly's credit, she remained quiet until the SUV spewed a trail of dust down the driveway. Then she grinned at Jess. "Well?"

"What?"

"Come on, Jess, I saw how Adam was looking at you." Molly's voice lilted. "My cousin li-ikes you."

"He barely knows me."

"True, but if I know him—"

"Sorry to burst your bubble, Moll, but I'm not getting involved with your cousin." Even if the warmth of his kiss heated her lips like summer.

"Relax, I was kidding." Molly looped an arm around Jess's waist, and they strolled to the door. "Are you coming to dinner with Tim and me on Friday?"

"I don't know. I haven't talked to Mom about it yet."

"I mentioned it to her. I hope you don't mind. She thinks it's a good idea."

"She does?" Friday would mark two weeks since Pete's heart attack. Death milestones were excruciating.

Molly nodded. "Thelma Matthews called. She wants to visit your mom, and Friday's the only night she can. Besides, you're never in town for Tim's and my anniversary. You were my maid of honor. You have to come."

"But shouldn't a wedding anniversary be a private celebration?" Jess flipped off the light and followed Molly outside.

"We will be alone, after dinner. Tim's parents are taking the kids overnight. We want you there, as one of our guests. An evening without rug rats—it'll be fun."

Jess smiled. "You're persistent."

"Family trait."

"Okay, I'll talk to Mom. If it's all right with her and if Thelma's here, I'll come."

"Great. That'll make four, counting Adam. He and Tim are best friends." Molly lifted a hand to shade her eyes from the sun. "Is that okay? We asked him before, you know . . ."

Pete died. "Um, sure. Whatever you want, Moll." *No big deal.*

She was attending for Molly and Tim. Nothing to do with Adam.

Jess dreamt about Adam that night. Wednesday and Thursday nights, too. Wild dreams. Hot dreams. Fantastically erotic.

Waking Friday, her skin damp between her breasts, she attributed the dreams to an advanced case of stress-deprivation. In Toronto, work swamped her to the point that she rarely dreamed about anything but budgets and sales analyses and endless samples of women's shoes. She hadn't had a proper vacation in years, and the effects were taking their toll. Tension headaches and dissatisfaction were commonplace. However, her concern for her mother aside, these last few restful days in Destiny Falls had helped her realize life didn't have to feel so taxing. Surely she could succeed at her job without sacrificing her health and relationships.

Her first priority in achieving her objective lay naturally with her mom. When not at her laptop, the sheer pleasure of making up for lost mother-daughter time filled her days.

However, her nights belonged to Adam. Rather, her idea of him. The fantasy. After her torrid dreams, seeing him at the restaurant tonight was bound to feel anti-climactic.

Deciding to shower after breakfast, she tamed her curls with a hair pick and donned her old bathrobe. Downstairs, a framed portrait of Pete on the fireplace mantel caught her eye—his manager's picture from Waverly Foods. Marie Shaverton from the bakery department had visited yesterday. Had she delivered the portrait to Mom?

Padding to the mantel, Jess gazed at the glossy picture. Pete's thinning, gray-blond hair fluffed across his scalp, and a glint of light refracted off his silver-rimmed glasses. From behind the lenses, his eyes smiled a welcome. As did his mouth.

A sincere smile of greeting for his customers. A gentle glance for the wife he'd cherished. But not once had he bestowed that look of compassion and understanding upon Jess.

Can't you see what you're doing to her? His voice, clipped and harsh, punched through layers of memory. *Why bother coming home anymore, when all you do is throw up walls around her? Your mother doesn't need more grief in her life, girlie!*

Jess tugged in a breath. "You were right, Pete," she whispered to the portrait. "Mom didn't need more hurt in her life. Well, neither did I."

Nor had she deserved the cold shoulder he'd continually shown her in subtle ways: a snide remark in a pleasant tone when her mom was out of earshot, moving her coat if she mistakenly hung it on his peg. Four Christmases ago, when they'd fought so bitterly, had been the fifth without her dad and Danny. Jess had announced her transfer from Vancouver to Toronto, her new job beginning mid-January. Mom had taken the news poorly. They'd argued, and Pete had stepped in, as usual—Mom's protector. His animosity had chased Jess away days earlier than her time between jobs granted.

Worse, both she and her mom had allowed it to happen.

Never again.

It's my turn, Pete. You can't hurt me anymore.

"Jessie?"

She glanced over her shoulder. Her mother stood in the kitchen archway, dressed in cords and a floral top, egg whisk in hand.

"Hi, Mom. Pete looks good here." Jess's resentment wilted. It was time to move on.

"Thank you, sweetie. I think so, too." Her mom smiled. "I'm

about to scramble eggs. Would you like to make the toast?"

Adam skipped onto Nora Olson's front porch, energy and excitement sweeping through him. Talk about a severe bout of spring fever. His attraction to Jess had hit him like a sledgehammer. Now, three days after kissing her, he still saw stars. Working out of town hadn't diminished his need to learn what drove her, like he'd half-hoped it would.

A woman hadn't crept under his skin like this in ages. Winning the Jamison Forest Products contract consumed most of his time, so lately his social life blew. Oddly, he hadn't really missed it. However, while he loved his work, bunking with two other guys in a cramped rental cabin while initiating the silviculture surveys couldn't compare to the thought of spending an evening in the company of Jess Morgan.

She was one beautiful woman. And intelligent, and caring.

Loosening his tie, he peeked through the sheer curtains draping the living room window. Nora crossed to the kitchen, while Jess, sitting on the swivel rocker, hunched over a laptop. Probably working. Despite her sudden leave of absence, evidently she'd already made arrangements to remain informed. Good for her. Unlike Crysta, Jess was fully capable of dividing her attention between career and family. Her devotion to her mother proved that.

He knocked on the door. Jess's head lifted, but she didn't glance his way. She wore her hair swept up from her temples and caught in a pretty clasp atop her head. Her black curls cascaded over her shoulders, and he recognized her light gray dress from meeting her at the airport.

He liked that dress. The soft fabric hugged her curves just so. His fingers itched to follow.

She called to her mom in the kitchen, then snapped shut the computer and placed it on the coffee table. Getting up, she started to the door. He straightened and adjusted his tie again.

His blood pumped. Adrenaline rush.

"You should steer clear of her, bud."

Big problem there, Wright.

He didn't think he could.

Glancing at her watch, Jess opened the door. "Right on time, Thel—" *Not Thelma.* "Adam!" Wearing a beige sports jacket, dressy trousers, and hunter-green tie. Her pulse jumped. "Why are you here?"

He grinned. "Is that any way to greet your date?" He leaned against the doorjamb, crowding her, obviously enjoying her flustered expression.

"Date?" Molly hadn't said boo about Adam acting as her date. In fact, when she and Molly confirmed their dinner plans this morning, Molly had said he might return from Valemount later than anticipated. "Weren't we meeting at the Wander-Inn? That's where I'm meeting Tim and Molly."

Even minus his customary jeans, he exuded casual confidence as he lifted one shoulder in a sexy shrug. "I made good time on the road, so thought I'd pick you up. Use one vehicle instead of two. Save the car for your mom, in case she needs it."

"Well, um, thanks for thinking of me, but I can't leave yet. Thelma's coming over to play crib with Mom. I'd like to stay until she arrives."

Her mom's soft footfalls sounded on the hardwood floor. Jess made room for her in the doorway, and the cool evening air wrapped around them. "It's Adam, Mom, not Thelma like we thought when we heard the knock."

Her mom nodded. "I'd figured something of the sort when I didn't hear Thelma's voice straight off." She shook his hand. "Hello, Adam."

"Hi. I hear you're playing crib with Thelma Matthews tonight."

"Yes, when Peter was alive, we used to play with Thelma and Vince all the time."

"I play a mean game of crib myself. Maybe I could interest you and Jess in a little tournament sometime?"

"That would be nice. Wouldn't it, Jessie?" Her mother beamed.

"Um, sure." Jess cleared her throat. "Adam came to see if I needed a ride, but I explained it wouldn't be necessary."

"Oh, Jessie, don't worry on my account. I know I haven't been myself lately, but I'm starting to feel better. Thelma will be along shortly. Look, there's her car now."

Jess glanced around Adam. A car turned in off Old Village Road, its headlights gleaming in the twilight. The sedan stopped next to Adam's SUV, and Thelma climbed out, waving.

Jess looked at him. His blue gaze challenged: *Any other roadblocks?*

He had her. And, damn it, he knew it. Her mother would consider her ill-mannered if she refused the ride now.

"Just a minute." She retrieved her coat and purse from the brass tree near the door. She pulled on the coat while the others exchanged hellos. Adam rocked on his heels, ever nonchalant.

Ever distracting.

"Don't you two make a charming couple," Thelma said once Jess stepped onto the porch. "Dress pants and a sports coat, Adam? That's not like you." She commented to Jess in earnest tones, "The man rarely sheds his jeans, honey. Make the most of it while you can."

Adam laughed. "Thelma, do you have any idea what you said?"

Thelma's face reddened. "I did not." She smacked his arm. "Mr. Wright, you're awful."

64

Jess squirmed while her mother chuckled softly.

"We're double-dating with Tim and Molly Davis," Adam said. His mischievous gaze dared Jess to correct him. So she did.

"We're meeting Tim and Molly for dinner, he means." She and Adam were not dating, and she didn't appreciate him teasing her in front of Mom and Thelma.

She waited until the door closed behind the two women. "Adam Wright," she reprimanded like a mother might a naughty child.

"Yes?" All innocence. All adult, impertinent male.

She tried to remain irritated, but his jaunty expression got the better of her. Tonight belonged to Tim and Molly. She owed it to her friends to make the evening work, even if doing so meant letting Adam's behavior slide. "Forget it."

His eyebrows perked. "You're coming with me, then?"

"Do I have a choice?"

"Only if you want to embarrass me in front of Thelma."

"She's inside."

"Yeah, but I think I saw her peeking through the curtains."

Jess smirked. "Oh, sure."

He pushed his hands into his trouser pockets. "Well, you can't say I don't try."

"No, that's the one thing about you I could never say." And it just might lead to her undoing.

65

CHAPTER FIVE

Adam didn't believe in waiting for what he wanted. As Pete's recent passing testified, life was too short not to grab it and give it a good shake. However, recalling Jess's tenuous relationship with her stepfather, he refrained from mentioning his renewed philosophy over dinner. Instead, assisted by an excellent meal, fine wine, and the friendly ribbing he always enjoyed with Tim and Molly, he concentrated on encouraging Jess to relax. By the time their group finished eating, a festive atmosphere enveloped the small table in the candlelit dining room now empty of other patrons. Music played in the background, and a fire crackled on the hearth, creating a cozy mood.

Ellen, a ruddy-faced woman in her fifties who ran the rustic inn with her husband, whisked away their dinner plates with a promise to return with dessert. Adam topped off the wineglasses and announced, "Time for another toast."

"Here, here!" Jess lifted her glass alongside his.

Adam motioned his glass toward Tim and Molly. "You two married young," he said, then paused. "Well, you were young, anyway, Molly."

Tim snorted. "Enough with the age jokes already. I'm barely a year older than you are, Wright."

"Yeah, but you play left field like you're ninety."

"You wish! The Educators are gonna clean up this year. Your Mountaineers don't stand a chance."

"Time out, *boys*," Molly said with an amused glance toward

66

Jess. "I realize slo-pitch starts next week, but I don't think Jess and I can tolerate another round of your macho need to out-brag each other. You can act out your childhood fantasies on the softball field if you'd like, but the subject is hereby banned from this dining room."

"Yes, dear. Sorry, dear." Tim slouched his lanky frame in his chair, and Molly giggled.

"Much better." She turned to Jess. "Have to keep him in line, you know." She nodded to Adam. "Come on, cousin. Toast us."

"Okay, all kidding aside, you two have one of the best things I've ever seen going in a couple. You made a commitment to each other seven years ago, and you've stuck it out even through the rough times like when Tim lost his job to the school board funding fiasco."

"Thank God that's behind us," Molly commented, her gaze tender as she glanced at Tim. "I know you weren't happy working in the sawmill, honey, but you did it anyway, so we wouldn't have to move. Now you're back teaching Phys. Ed. again. Everything turned out for the best."

Tim clasped her hand on the tablecloth, his brown eyes gleaming.

"Exactly," Adam said to Tim. "You applied to other school districts and received decent offers. You could have taken the easy route and left town, like so many other of our friends have done. Instead, you chose to stay right here, where Molly has her roots and where your kids feel at home. That kind of love and commitment is rare these days. You have a wonderful home and family. Congratulations on your seventh anniversary, Tim and Molly. Here's to many more."

"Thanks, Adam," Molly said. "That means a lot to me."

"Me, too, pal," Tim added.

"Congratulations, Tim and Moll," Jess chimed in, and wineglasses clinked all around.

Within moments, Ellen brought the coffee and desserts. Sparklers fizzled atop the strawberry cheesecake slices she placed in front of Molly and Tim. She congratulated the couple, then poured the coffee and left for the desk in the lobby visible through the dining room's open French doors.

Molly pushed her camera toward Adam and snuggled beneath Tim's arm. "Be a dear, Adam. Another shot of Tim and me?"

"What? I've taken three already." He picked up the camera, anyway, and snapped the picture while the sparklers danced. "Happy?" He passed the digital back to her.

"Not yet. Now I want one of you and Jess." Molly lifted the camera. "I know you couldn't help missing the wedding, Adam, because of your stupid appendix bursting, but I'd like at least one shot of Tim's AWOL best man with my maid of honor, even if it's seven years late."

She didn't have to ask twice. Adam scooted his chair close to Jess's and looped an arm around her slender shoulders. The kitten-soft fabric of her dress cushioned his fingers, and her spine tensed slightly.

Pleased with his ability to get a rise out of her, he squeezed her arm while Molly snapped the picture.

Conversation continued in a steady flow while they ate dessert. A string of quiet ballads played in the background, intensifying the intimate atmosphere. When the poignant strains of a popular love song drifted over the sound system, Tim smiled at his wife and she smiled back. Without saying a word, he led her to the center of the tiny dining room. Molly tucked her head against his chest, and they moved to the slow, romantic beat.

Adam glanced at Jess. She relaxed in her chair, hands folded on her lap, a faraway expression on her face as she watched Tim and Molly waltz.

"Penny for your thoughts?" he asked, but she didn't budge.

Her gaze grew hazy. Had she even heard him?

What are you thinking, Jess? That Tim and Molly have it all?

Or, like Crysta, did she believe marriage was a one-way ticket to Nowheresville?

His gut clenched. He didn't want to think about Crysta Jenkins—his love for her had died with her betrayal. However, on a night like this, the memories re-surfaced. Two years ago, he and Crysta had attended another of Tim and Molly's famous anniversary dinners. They'd announced their engagement, Crysta three months pregnant with his baby. The unborn child he'd thought she'd wanted as much as he had.

He'd been wrong.

Let it go. Be here. Now.

He focused on Jess. As if she sensed the weight of his thoughts, her head turned. Her gaze slowly lowered, then drifted back up.

Locked with his.

His chest tightened, and thoughts of Crysta vanished. *Here. Now. Action. Reach out. Do it.*

Who was he to question instinct? Living in the past was a definite route to the doldrums. He couldn't look at Jess without wanting her, and he couldn't survive the next five weeks without learning if she wanted him, too.

He drained his coffee and pushed back his chair. "Want to dance?" He offered his hand.

Her gaze flicked to the meager floor space. "There's not enough room."

"We'll make room. Humor me."

Biting her lower lip, she rose. He accompanied her to the makeshift dance floor as the romantic song wound down. No matter, they'd take the next one.

He pushed back a table and moved two chairs. Ellen stared with undisguised interest from the inn desk.

Molly and Tim strolled over hand-in-hand. With a nod toward Ellen, Tim asked, "Wreaking havoc again, Wright?"

"Look who's talking." Adam stepped in beside Jess.

"Don't pin it on us, pal. We're heading home to wreak some havoc of our own."

Light pink dusted Molly's cheeks. "The kids are staying at my parents' tonight."

Adam laughed. "No explanations necessary, Cuz. Anniversary sex. Sounds good."

"Oh, yeah," Tim said.

Molly ignored them. "What time are you coming to the store tomorrow, Jess?"

Jess's eyes were bright, her skin flushed. Because of the sex talk? Adam hoped so.

Avoiding his gaze, she replied, "Around eleven, after I drop Mom off at the hairdresser's. Is that a good time?"

"Sounds perfect. Is she joining us for lunch afterward?"

"If you don't mind."

"Of course not. I'll see you both then."

Adam paid the bill as Tim and Molly left—his treat, in honor of the celebration. Then, hands in trouser pockets, he returned to Jess. "You're visiting the store?"

She nodded. "I'm in dire need of some jeans if I want to at least look like I fit in around here. I packed in such a rush, I didn't bring a single pair."

An image of her curvy behind in tight jeans flitted through his mind. He approved.

"Still want to dance?"

Her gaze flickered. A slow, sultry country ballad with a heavy, steady backbeat wove around them. Interpreting her silence as a tentative yes, he clasped her hand and swung her around so she couldn't see Ellen spying on them.

He placed his hand on her back, and a small tremor rippled

70

through her. Nerves? Anticipation? Lust? He couldn't tell which, but he could definitely feel it. Beneath his palm, on her back. Beneath her silky-soft dress.

Lowering his head, he whispered, "Pretend it's just you and me. One dance. That's all I ask."

He half-expected a quick rejection. Instead, to his intense pleasure, she closed her eyes and swayed with him to the beat. She didn't speak. Neither did he. Heat flooded him, and he pulled her close.

She didn't resist.

Adam stifled a groan as the music flowed over them. Sweet heaven, if she moved this well with him on the dance floor, how would she respond to his touch in bed?

He hardened, and her eyes flew open. Surprise and passion mingled in her gaze.

"Sorry," he murmured. But he really wasn't.

Velvet eyes. "It's okay."

Taking his time, enjoying the seductive tension, he brushed her lips with a light kiss. Her fingers tightened on the back of his neck. He pressed his lips to hers and tasted the strawberry-laced recesses of her mouth.

His gut contracted. Blood surged to thrum in his veins. He lost himself in her heat, her scent, the sensual dance her tongue shared with his.

The clattering of cups snapped him to his senses. He broke the kiss, his breath releasing in a soft hiss. Ellen stood less than four feet away, gathering the coffee things from their table. Arching a disapproving eyebrow, she trundled out of the dining room.

Slowing their tempo to a near standstill, Adam glanced at Jess. "Looks like the Mom in this Mom-and-Pop operation is trying to tell us something." He grazed her lower lip with his thumb.

She smiled. Softly, warmly. Uncertain. "We should go."

"Home?" He kept her hand clasped in his. Home was the last place he wanted her to go.

"I'm not sure."

Understanding dawned within him. She wanted to be with him tonight—perhaps as much as he wanted to be with her. But she'd already told him she didn't sleep around. He liked that. As a matter of fact, he liked it a hell of a lot. For reasons he suspected it wasn't wise to examine at this point, if ever.

"I know somewhere. It's not much, but it's private." Tipping up her chin, he gazed into her almond-shaped eyes. "Trust me, Jess. We'll take this as slow as you need."

Jess studied Adam in the shadowy interior of his SUV. He drove toward her mother's house. Had he changed his mind about taking her somewhere private? Did she want him to? She couldn't recall the last time she'd acted so impulsively with a man. What was it about Adam Wright that inspired her to let down her guard?

He slid a glance her way. "Curious?"

"You could say that." Although questioning her sanity was more accurate.

"Well, your curiosity's about to be satisfied." He steered the truck onto a narrow dirt road leading into a pasture. Parking in the middle of the field, he switched off the engine. "We're here."

"Where?" Jess rolled down her window to the fresh, pure fragrance of grand old fir trees. They towered around the field's perimeter in silhouette against the moonlit sky. A huge wooden screen, dingy with neglect, stood at the far end of the field. "The old drive-in! I'd forgotten it was here!"

"Don't say that." Adam's mellow voice reached out to her. "Old man Worthington might have been crazy trying to make another go of this place after the video stores put it out of business, but some of my best summer memories revolve around the Starlite."

Hers, too. The drive-in had gone bankrupt a second time before she and Danny started dating, but she'd spent several starry evenings here the summer she'd turned fourteen.

The summer she'd met Adam.

He nudged her thigh. "Remember how my brother and cousins and I got saddled with watching you and Molly when her parents went to that concert in Kamloops? We tried to ditch you to catch a Clint Eastwood marathon, but Molly threatened to squeal on us unless we took you both along."

Gazing out the window, Jess nodded. "You remember that?" As far as she knew, he'd barely realized she existed then.

"Definitely."

She faced him. He leaned with one jacket-clad arm propped on the steering wheel. A lock of dark blond hair fell over his forehead, reminding her of the handsome teenager she'd worshipped in secret that summer.

"I don't know why Molly threatened to tell. Both of us were babysitting at that age. We could have stayed on the farm alone."

"Yeah, but my Aunt Sheila had put her foot down, and she can be a mean one to cross. So my tough-guy cousins caved."

Jess laughed. "Luke said he'd pay for the boys, but not for me and Molly—"

"So we buried you girls in a ton of blankets in the back of Luke's van and smuggled you into the drive-in. Later, we learned that six could have got in for the same price as four that night, because of a carload special—"

"Which Molly had known about all along! What pests we were."

"Not to me. Granted, I could have done without Molly at that age, but you"—he brushed the tip of her nose with a finger, and a delicious ripple whispered through her—"were another

73

matter. I'd met you at my uncle's corral before, but that night at the drive-in was the first time I really saw you."

"Uh-huh." She refused to take him seriously, or the effect his touch had on her. "That's why you panted after the grade-twelve girls in the next car all night."

He shrugged. "I was seventeen. The other guys would have razzed me all summer if they'd known I had the hots for a girl entering grade nine. To a guy of seventeen, a fourteen-year-old girl is practically a baby."

"Unless said fourteen-year-old is as well-endowed as her grade-twelve counterparts."

"Yes, unless that." His arm slid off the steering wheel. "Plus, my aunt would have killed me if she'd had any inkling how I felt about you. I'm talking wringing my neck, busting my kneecaps, and sending-me-home-incapable-of-fathering-kids killed me. And then my mom would have gotten in on the act. She had rules. My brother and I could date girls our own ages, one or two years younger at most."

Jess laughed. His mother sounded like her dad.

"I liked you then, but you were far too young to even consider doing anything about it. Luckily, a few years have passed."

Jess arched her eyebrows. He sounded awfully self-confident. "Is that why you brought me here? To do something about it?"

He shook his head. "This isn't some master seduction scene, unless you want it to be. Even then, with you leaving in a month, I'm not sure we should pursue it." He caressed a strand of her hair between two fingers. The gentle, pulling action tickled her scalp. "I packed some blankets in the cargo hold, some coffee and Kahlua. I thought we could sit back there with the door open, share a drink, and look at the stars. Anything else is your call."

Jess drew in a breath, deciding then and there that she could trust this man completely when it came to saying no to sex. He

74

didn't seem to have a dishonorable bone in his body. "I love hot coffee drinks."

"All right, then. Let's go."

She let herself out and met him at the rear of the truck. Her skin prickled in the cool night air as he raised the cargo door and spread out a blanket on the rough carpeting. He helped her climb in, then sat beside her, unfolded another blanket, and wrapped it around her shoulders like a shawl.

"I guarantee the premises to be free of dog hair," he said once her legs dangled over the bumper and she'd unbuttoned her coat for comfort. He passed her two mugs from a bag. Then he pulled out a thermos and a small bottle of Kahlua. "I vacuumed before picking you up, and the blankets are clean."

He thinks of everything. "Impressive."

"Why, thank you."

She held out the mugs while he mixed their drinks. Accepting a mug, he raised it.

"To Tim and Molly's seventh anniversary, to you and I getting to know each other again, and to this romantic, abandoned drive-in its owner refuses to sell."

They tapped mugs. Jess sipped her coffee. "How did you and Molly become such good friends? Seeing as you ignored her when we were all teenagers, I mean."

Adam's arm bumped hers through the blanket. The small scar on his eyebrow bobbed. "Maturity. Mine, not Molly's. We all grow up eventually. When I did, thankfully Molly forgave me for tormenting her when we were kids." He drank from his mug. "Living with her parents when I first came to work here helped."

"You lived with the McLeans? I didn't know that."

He nodded. "A few weeks during the summer when I was twenty-three. There were no vacancies at the apartments, so I stayed with my aunt and uncle. Molly and I spent a lot of time together. We've been close ever since."

Jess smiled at his mention of "the apartments." She hadn't heard that phrase in ages. "When did Tim move here?" She sipped her drink. The rich flavors of coffee and Kahlua lingered on her tongue . . . much like Adam's nearness lingered on her senses.

"The end of August that same year. Two vacancies had opened at the apartments, so I moved in, and that's when Tim and Molly met. He was the other new tenant and quickly became my friend."

Jess giggled, and Adam looked at her.

"Sorry," she murmured. "It's the way that building still gets called 'the apartments.' Like it's 'the town hall' or 'the recreation center.' Except Destiny Falls doesn't have a town hall or a rec center."

"Well, it is the only apartment building in town. Calling it the Park Avenue Gardens sounds a bit pretentious, don't you think?"

A tiny muscle flexed in his jaw. Had she insulted him? "You really like living here, don't you?"

"Of course, I do. It's my hometown."

"You mean you think of it as your hometown." She'd thought he hailed from Kamloops.

"No, I mean it *is* my hometown." He downed his drink. "I was born in Destiny Falls. My family didn't start bouncing around the province until I turned six."

Something else she hadn't known. "You moved a lot?"

"Yep."

She finished her coffee, passed him the mug, and watched as he deposited it with his in the bag. "Why did your parents move so much?"

"Pop's job." He shifted closer to her on the blanket. "I wasn't happy about it. At the time, neither was my brother. In the end, we made do. Kevin and his family live in Merritt now, Mom

76

and Pop in Louis Creek."

"No one's in Kamloops?"

He shook his head. "And no one's here except me, Molly, and her folks."

"So you wanted to live where you were raised."

"Yeah. There's no place like it. I've moved around enough to know. You were lucky, living in one place as a kid. I don't know, it anchors you."

"I agree." The sense of belonging she'd taken for granted before Dad and Danny died had felt rooted in the community. Despite its limitations, Destiny Falls was a wonderful place to grow up. "No kid wants to leave their friends or change schools." An image of Adam as a little boy—all big blue eyes and tousled blond hair—popped into her mind.

"Exactly." His tone softened. "Kevin didn't mind the moving as much as I did. I know it sounds cliché, but when I moved back here at twenty-three, I felt like I was coming home." He gazed at her. Cupping her hand, he held it in her lap. "Looks like we have something in common, after all."

I don't know about that. Jess closed her eyes briefly against the pleasurable friction of his thumb on her palm. Unlike Adam, she neither lived in Destiny Falls currently, nor did she desire to.

In a way, she was just passing through. Anything that might happen between them would be just as fleeting and transitory.

But, oh, at the moment, how she wanted it to happen.

She tilted her face toward him, parting her lips, knowing she shouldn't kiss him again and risk leading him on. However, a secret place inside her prodded her to let caution scatter like the stars in the ink-black sky.

She had to taste him—like she had on the dance floor.

She had to taste him one more time.

CHAPTER SIX

Adam smiled as if he could read her mind. His free hand lifted to her chin, his big fingers splaying along her jaw. Then the smile slowly faded from his lips and his mouth descended.

His lips caressed hers, coaxing a response. Moaning, Jess shut her eyes again. His tongue slid along her lower lip, then dipped, warm and moist, into her mouth.

Coffee. Syrupy Kahlua. Adam.

Desire spiraled, dizzying her. Angling her head, she welcomed his kiss, and he gathered her into his arms with a groan.

A bittersweet yearning tunneled through her. His hands roved over her back and shoulders before they settled on the unbuttoned front of her coat. He pushed aside the fabric and spanned her waist with his hands, his touch both protective and assertive: *Mine. I want. You.*

A sensual shudder gripped her. She arched her back. His hands glided up her dress to cup her breasts. Too soon. Not soon enough. Her nipples tightened. She arched again, and the blanket fell, collapsing in a bulky heap behind them.

The crisp night air swept over her, raising tingling goose bumps along her skin. Adam mumbled something indecipherable against her mouth, then scattered kisses down her throat. Pausing at the hollow of her collarbone, he sucked her sensitized skin until her breath came in short gasps. Mind-numbing. Seeking. *I want.* From him. From her, too.

She pulled back. She hadn't known a simple kiss could take

her so far so fast. "Adam." She placed her hands on his chest, and he lifted his head. His blue gaze, so near, swirled through her. "I think I'd better call in my option."

"Call in your what?" His gaze fogged.

"Before things get out of hand." He'd said anything beyond a drink was her call. She'd believed him.

He released a breath. "All right. Under one condition."

"Oh, so now there's a condition?"

"Just this." His mouth claimed hers in one last, probing kiss. He smoothed her coat lapels over her breasts and latched the button at her waist, as if secreting away a present meant for another day. "This is a surprise for me, too, you know. When I brought you here, I didn't intend to paw you like a horny teenager." He touched a finger to her lower lip. "When you want to continue where we left off, please let me know."

A desperate aching filled her. She wanted to continue now. She wanted to pull him down on the blankets with her and make love beneath the sparkling dome of stars. But they'd already gone too far. Considering she'd stayed in Destiny Falls for reasons that had nothing to do with him, they'd already gone *way* too far.

"Adam, I don't think . . ." She tugged in a breath. "Wanting something and acting on it are two different things."

"Mm-hm." He toyed with her coat. "The way I see it, we're bound to wind up together sooner or later, while you're here. I happen to be rooting for the sooner—now. I was fooling myself before."

" 'Together' as in 'sleeping together' or 'together' as in 'a couple'?"

"Either works for me."

His handsome features settled into a casual mask she didn't believe for a second. That long-ago summer aside, she'd only known him a week, but she understood him well enough to realize she had no business even fantasizing about sleeping with him. He didn't do anything halfway, and she needed to devote all her attention to her mother in the short time she was home.

"But that's the problem." She sat up straighter, accidentally jostling him. He repositioned himself next to her, planting an arm on a raised knee. "I can't allow myself to become involved with you in either way."

"Why not?"

"My mother." Her chest knotted. "She really needs me right now, Adam. I won't be here that long, but while I am, I can't afford to split my focus between her needs and yours."

"Split your focus? That sounds impersonal."

"I'm sorry. But you strike me as a guy who expects a certain degree of attention in a relationship."

"If by that you mean spending a reasonable amount of time together, I agree."

"Well, I can't do it."

"Jess, I admire your concern for your mother, but you're telling me you can't be there for Nora and still take some time out for yourself, too?"

"That's exactly what I'm saying." Although it didn't sound as rational coming from him. Jumping onto the soft earth, she glanced at her watch. "It's getting late. Thelma has probably left by now, and Mom might be waiting up for me. I need to go."

"Oh, no, you don't." Pushing out of the cargo hold, he grasped her arm. "What's going on here, Jess? You're using your mother as some sort of excuse. I'm not sure why, but you are."

"That's ridiculous. Let me go." His grip slackened. She shook her arm free. "I think you'd better take me home now."

"What are you afraid of? I'm not the big bad wolf. I'm just a guy who wants to be with you."

She shook her head. "I don't want to talk about this. My mother is who is important to me right now. She's who I should be with. Not you. Not this." She tramped to the passenger door. Yanking it open, she grabbed her purse. "I'm asking you to drive me home. If you won't, I'll walk. Either way, I'm going."

The mudroom door slammed. Nora glanced up from the sweater she was crocheting for Thelma's forthcoming grandchild. The door had been making a racket for weeks. Peter had planned to fix it, but now it fell to her to assume the tasks he'd performed with love and caring.

Her heart wrenched. *Darling Peter.* She missed him so.

Thank God she had Jessie to lean on for a few weeks. How she wished they could erase the bad years and start over. Yet, sometimes working through the past was the only way to move forward. This was one of those times.

She set her crocheting on the coffee table. Smoothing her slacks, she rose from the sofa and entered the kitchen. "Jessie?"

"Hi, Mom." Strain resonated in her daughter's voice. Jessie hung her coat and purse on the mudroom pegs. "I noticed Thelma's car isn't here."

"She left thirty minutes ago." Nora suppressed a frown. Color splotched Jessie's cheeks, and forced gaiety widened her eyes— problem signs she recognized from Jessie's childhood. Whenever Jessie had felt troubled, she'd put on a brave face for Nora and confide in Frank. Unfortunately, Nora had encouraged the practice. Her guilt over her inability to provide Frank with the big family he'd always wanted had proven a harsh master.

Twit.

She approached her daughter. "Is something wrong?"

"No. I had a great time."

"It's . . . well, you look upset." Lord, she was terrible at this. "Did something happen?"

"Of course not." Jessie brushed back her dark curls. "Besides, we need to focus on you." She slipped her arm through Nora's, and they strolled into the living room. "How was your night? Did you beat Thelma at crib?"

"We each won two games, then had coffee."

"No best of five?"

"Thelma wanted to talk. Our chat was nice. It helped me."

"I'm glad, Mom. It's important for your friends to support you right now."

She nodded. "But it feels even more wonderful to have your support, Jessie. You don't know what your being home means to me."

"It means a lot to me, too, Mom." Warmth softened her daughter's voice. They stopped in front of the dying fire. "Have you thought about the car repairs I mentioned at breakfast?"

Nora blinked. How had her concern for her daughter evolved into a discussion about Peter's car?

Suddenly, a vision of her husband lying cold and still in the casket swamped her mind. A chill crawled over her. *Peter.*

"Yes," she managed. "I trust Adam. Peter respected him, and he—Peter loved that car. If it needs a new transmission to run well, that's what I'd like to do."

"I'll call the garage tomorrow."

Nora patted her daughter's hand. "Now you, sweetie. We always talk about me. I'd like to talk about you." For too long, she'd allowed Peter's resentment of Frank's only child to come between her and her daughter. She should have risen to Jessie's defense more often, especially during the first years of her hasty second marriage.

Stupidly, she'd hoped that Jessie's difficulties with Peter would resolve over time. What an idiot she'd been. Her passive nature was a poor excuse.

"Jessie?" she said when her daughter didn't reply.

"Mom, I told you, I'm not upset. Just tired."

There must be more. Nora's maternal instincts weren't that

rusty. However, if she persisted, she could push Jessie further away. "You're sure? If there's something you need to talk about . . ."

"There isn't. I'm exhausted. Are you coming to bed?"

"Not yet." Her mother's heart counseled patience. Jessie needed space. The least she could do was provide it. "The fire's not out, and I'd like to finish my crocheting."

They exchanged goodnight kisses, and Jessie climbed the stairs. As she reached the top, she turned. "Please don't worry about me, Mom. Everything's fine."

Nora didn't believe her.

Adam sank into the recliner in front of the blaring TV and popped open an ice-cold beer. Stewing over his idiotic behavior with Jess, he reached over the armrest and scratched Sheba's ears, then drank several slugs of the chilly brew.

He plunked down the can on the end table and stared at the hand-hewn log walls of the great room in his large, comfortable home. A house built for children he'd yet to conceive, for a wife he'd never known. Although, once, he'd nearly held both within his grasp.

Don't think of that now.

How could he not? At times like this, the emptiness of the big house taunted him. Crysta had confessed her pregnancy and, *wham,* he'd bought a ring, dug out blueprints, started dreaming. They'd live in the cabin on the five-acre property until he finished their home, he'd said. He hadn't asked, he'd told her, describing his vision in detail. Part him: the logs, their rough edges, the huge beams. Part her: the airy, open spaces and contemporary, high ceilings. A perfect blending of him and Crysta.

Except she hadn't wanted any part of his dreams. Or him, as it had turned out.

83

Only a masochist would continue building a house that had chased away his fiancée. However, working with the logs had kept Adam sane when anguish brandished its sword. He'd loved Crysta and their unborn baby. Boy or girl?

I'll never know.

His jaw stiffened. He grabbed the beer and took another swallow.

Come this October, their child would have turned two, not much younger than Molly's Kaitlin. Had the baby been a girl, the pair might have become playmates.

Swearing, Adam plunked down the beer again. Logically, he realized Crysta would have left town no matter what he'd said or did. She hadn't wanted a life here. She'd wanted to break free, let loose, party. But Destiny Falls wasn't much of a party town, and Adam had been dumb enough to believe the surprise pregnancy would soothe her urge to roam.

However, she might not have developed such contempt for the baby growing inside her if she hadn't felt cornered. If he hadn't made her feel that way.

Now, to a lesser degree but enough to irk him, he'd committed the same crime with Jess—a woman he'd known one week!

"Some guys never learn, huh, Sheba?" The dog's ears pricked. He scratched her head. "Some guys need to write it a hundred times on the whiteboard, and even then we don't learn."

Damn it, he should have accepted it when she broke off their kiss at the drive-in. Instead, he'd subtly pressured her until he'd scared her away. When he'd dropped her off at her mother's house, she wouldn't even let him walk her to the door. He'd considered overriding her protest, but one glance at her stiff-backed demeanor had convinced him to let the matter die. Unlike his attraction to her, which continued to burn strong and bright.

Fed up with the blasting roar of the TV, he thumbed the

remote. "I have to make it right, Sheeb." Or face the distinct possibility that Jess would avoid him over the next five weeks—an uncomfortable situation for everyone. Him, Nora, Molly. And Jess.

He had to make it right.

"This is it, Jess—The Clothes Horse!" Molly twirled between the racks of jeans and tops jamming the tiny, turquoise-and-yellow shop. "What do you think?"

"It looks great, Moll," Jess said with false enthusiasm. She'd promised this time to Molly, and her friend deserved her full attention, but she couldn't stop thinking about her mistakes with Adam last night.

Whatever had possessed her to go to the drive-in with him? To agree to go anywhere they might be alone? Their slow-dance at the restaurant had advertised his intentions like a billboard. He'd wanted her, and, damn it, she'd felt the same. However, he'd been prepared to indulge their attraction, and she hadn't. With her boss squawking about how her extended leave worsened his workload, enough complications filled her life without Adam pulling her in yet another direction.

Pushing thoughts of him from her mind, she examined the belts and accessories near the cash register. "Nice selection." She glanced at Molly. "I like the layout of the store, the colors and atmosphere."

"My boss has a good eye."

"So do you." She mustered a smile. "To think this building once housed a Laundromat and arcade."

Molly leaned on the counter. "They changed locations a few years ago. The building owner took the opportunity to split two units into three—the hairdresser's, the gift shop, and the boutique." She propped her chin on a raised hand. "Not bad for Destiny Falls, eh? Remember how we used to dream about

85

opening a place like this together? We wanted to call it MJ's."

Jess nodded. "We were ahead of our time. I can't imagine a store like this succeeding in Destiny Falls eight or nine years ago." She sorted through the jeans rack.

"Times change, Jess, even in this teensy ol' burg. My boss says she wouldn't consider selling if not for her health issues. Too bad she can't afford a full-time manager."

"But that's where you come in." Jess checked the size on a pair of jeans and draped them over her arm to try on. "How does Tim feel about your idea to buy the place?"

"He's all for it. I loved staying home when the kids were babies, but Sean starts kindergarten in September and Kaitlin wants to attend preschool. It's time to do something for myself, you know? The financing's a little sticky. After living on one income for years, we have squat in savings." She shrugged. "I haven't really looked into it yet."

"You should. If your boss is serious about selling, the timing's perfect."

Leaving the counter, Molly riffled through the next rack. "I don't want to pressure her. Barb knows I'm interested. When the time is right for her, we'll talk." She chose a pair of black jeans and handed them to Jess. "That makes four pairs. Are you ready to brave the dressing rooms?"

"I still need tops and a spring jacket. I wouldn't mind trying on some belts, too."

Molly laughed. "Boy, am I gonna make a killing off you today."

"It's not like I don't own a pair of jeans, Molly. I just forgot to pack them."

"They're probably all designer labels, too. Welcome back to the real world, hon."

Jess tossed her friend a mock-haughty look before heading to the dressing room. Leaving three pairs of jeans on the hook outside the door, she entered the mirror-less space—the first thing she would change if she owned the store. Who wanted to check out the presence or absence of a muffin-top in view of other customers?

She shucked off her shoes and pants, then pulled on the first pair of jeans.

"Wasn't last night fun?" Molly asked from the other side of the door. "I haven't laughed that much in ages. How long did you and Adam stay at the restaurant after Tim and I left?"

"A few minutes. The waitress didn't approve of the dancing, so we had one waltz then went." *One waltz.* It sounded so innocent. It had felt anything but.

"He took you straight home?"

"Not really." Opening the door, Jess stepped out to the wall mirror. "We drove to the old drive-in and talked." She studied the fit of the blue jeans in the mirror.

"That make-out haven?"

"It was empty."

"Except for you two!"

"Nothing happened, Moll."

"Did I ask?" Molly's reflection grinned at her. "Come on, Jess, would it really be so horrible if something had happened?"

"Yes." Satisfied with the fit of the jeans, Jess faced her friend. "I like your cousin, Moll. That's the problem. I could get to like him too much."

"Go, Jess!"

"No, no, no! I refuse to start something with Adam I know I'll have to finish in a few weeks."

"Who says you'd have to finish?"

"Molly! If Gareth gets his promotion, I'm a shoo-in for his job."

"*Shoe*-in. Good one."

"I'm serious, Moll. He's all over me about a junior buyer

quitting while I was in Europe."

"How is that your fault?"

"It's not. But he was counting on me to hire and train a replacement before I leave for Asia. Now I can't."

"Because you had the audacity to visit your grieving mother? What an ass."

Jess's lips twitched. "If I want to replace him, I need his recommendation. I can't afford to alienate the dickhead."

Molly crossed her arms. "How would dating my cousin alienate your dickhead boss?"

"Adam's a distraction I don't need." A sexy, bullheaded distraction.

Molly's voice softened. "Jess, it's been years since Danny."

"This isn't about Danny." Oh, crap, is it?

"Uh-huh."

Sighing, Jess ran her hands over the crisp new denim covering her thighs. "Okay, maybe in a way it's a bit about Danny. Think about it, Molly. You married Tim, and I would have married Danny. Two best friends raising their kids together while co-owning a store like this one."

"You still miss him."

"He's a part of me. The way he died—"

"I know."

"Then support my choices, Moll."

"I do. But you're not the only person to survive heartache. Adam's had his share."

Don't ask. "What do you mean?" Too late.

"Remember Crysta Jenkins?" Molly fiddled with a display of sunglasses. "Tall, blue eyes, blonde hair? She was three years behind us in high school. They dated a couple of years ago. Adam fell in love with her."

Jess's pulse blipped. "What happened?" God help her, she really wanted to know.

88

"It's his story to tell. However, I can say they got engaged at warp speed, and she left him ten days later."

"That's awful." *Poor Adam.*

"And when I say 'left him,' I mean she left him, and she left Destiny Falls. At first he didn't realize she'd skipped town, and her mother wouldn't tell him. He spent weeks looking for her."

"Why wouldn't her mother tell him?"

The shop door tinkled and two teenage girls entered. They arrowed for the jeans rack.

Molly glanced back. "Oh, those girls said they'd return today. They might need my help."

"Way to evade my question, Moll."

Molly passed her a pair of black jeans. "His story, remember? Those low-riders look great on you. Now try these."

Jess held up the skinny jeans. "I don't know. They sure look tight."

"You've got the figure for them. Try them on." Molly grinned. "Spoilsport."

"All right, all right!"

As Molly headed for the teenagers, Jess re-entered the dressing room. Fingers clumsy, she unzipped the blue jeans. Damn it, why should Molly's story about Adam bother her? So he'd been engaged once. The man was thirty-one years old. She couldn't expect him not to have a romantic history.

She peeled off the jeans and hung them on her "to buy" hook. Then she wriggled into the stretchy black pair. Molly's footsteps approached on the wood floor outside the door. Jess flexed her knees, the give of Lycra easing her movements. "I don't know about these skinny jeans, Molly. They feel great, but, wow, they're tight." The footsteps stopped. "Molly?"

A husky male voice said, "Not last I checked. But I'll offer my opinion on those jeans. That is, if you're brave enough to come out."

89

Jess's stomach back-flipped. "Adam?" Wasn't it enough that he'd invaded her peace of mind—must he also disrupt her shopping?

She whipped open the door. "Do you always show up where you're not expected?"

His gaze roamed over her from head to toe, and the corner of his mouth tipped up. Images of the amazing kisses they'd shared flooded her mind.

"Only when it's to my advantage. Nice jeans."

Liquid heat rushed through her. With her blouse haphazardly tucked in and her feet devoid of shoes, she felt half-dressed, somehow exposed, as if he'd interrupted her in her bedroom instead of in a public store where he had every right to be.

He looked so good in jeans, a black T-shirt, and that battered denim jacket. Big. Strong. Sexy. And, as usual, too damn close.

"I didn't realize The Clothes Horse carried jeans for men," she said tightly.

"I dropped off an old ball glove I promised Sean. Now that I'm here, though . . ." He glanced at his watch. "It's nearly noon. Do you have plans for lunch?"

"You know I do. With Mom and Molly, once the owner of the shop arrives."

"Great. I'll join you."

Oh, no, he wouldn't. Her emotions had run the gamut this week. She shouldn't be anywhere near Adam Wright and his clear blue mesmerizing gaze.

"It's women only, Adam."

"How about after lunch?"

"I'm spending the day with my mom."

"Just an hour, Jess. We need to talk."

"We talked last night."

"So that's it?"

"Looks like."

"Man, you're stubborn. We talked about your mother then, Jess. Now I'd like to talk about us."

"Well, I'm afraid that's impossible." She poked her chin in the air—and immediately felt about ten years old.

He chuckled. "Oh, yeah? Why?"

"Because there isn't an 'us.' " She peered around him. Molly and the teenagers were enjoying an animated conversation about belly-button rings and hadn't heard them. A faded baseball glove rested on the cash counter, corroborating Adam's story.

"But there could be." His low whisper urged her to look at him again. "After last night, you can't deny it." He clapped a hand to his chest. "I swear, those jeans should be outlawed."

She huffed out a breath. "You don't get it, do you?" she whispered. "I won't become involved with you, at least not like last night. Do I need to hit you over the head with a brick to make you realize that?"

"Probably."

She blinked. *Do. Not. Smile.* "You've been a friend to me this last week, and I appreciate everything you've done. But I'm not prepared to take our relationship any further."

"At least you can use the R word to describe what's happening between us."

"I'd rather use the F word."

"You're telling me to take off?" A pained expression pinched his face.

Now she did smile. "No. I mean friendship, with a capital F. I'm sorry, but that's all I can offer right now."

Hooking his thumbs in his belt loops, he nodded. "I saw the car out front. Have you talked to your mom about the transmission?"

Jess peered at him. "You're accepting my offer of friendship?"

"Yes." His blue eyes twinkled. "Don't tell me now you're disappointed?"

91

Oh, God, was she?

Don't go there.

"Um, I booked an appointment with your mechanic friend for Monday. He said the transmission will take a week, maybe more, depending on the availability of parts and if any other work is required."

"What will you use for transportation?"

"The taxi. The garage doesn't have a courtesy car, and Tim and Molly both need their cars for work."

"Take my SUV. I don't need it."

"I can't do that."

"I'll use my bush pickup. In fact, to make it easier, I'll meet you at the garage. You can keep the SUV as long as you need. What time is your appointment?"

"Quarter to four. You're sure?"

"Of course, *friend.*"

Another smile tugged her lips, and she rolled her eyes. Before she could toss out a comeback, Molly approached them, lugging a stack of jeans.

"You're freaking out my customers, big guy," she admonished her cousin. "They won't use the dressing rooms while you're here."

"Why not?"

"You intimidate them. You're older, but not that old, if you get my drift. They might start drooling."

He snorted. "I'm leaving in a minute."

"Thanks." Molly piled the jeans on the corner bench in the second dressing room. Turning, she said, "Those skinny jeans look fantastic, Jess. Are you buying them?"

"I haven't decided."

"Well, get the lead out. I'm lining up some tops for you to look at."

Adam remained silent until Molly strolled out of earshot.

They concluded the arrangements for his SUV, and Jess spun around to enter the dressing room. He smacked her butt, and she jumped, skin burning.

"I agree with Molly, buddy. You should buy these."

CHAPTER SEVEN

Adam waited by his SUV for Jess to return from the garage restroom. He'd never encountered a jumpier woman. While they'd discussed the car's issues with Ty, she'd either fiddled with her purse strap or developed a fascination with unsnapping and re-clasping her watch, but only when he'd glanced at or addressed her, never when Ty had. Maybe she wasn't as committed to their new "friendship" as she claimed.

He could only hope.

Seconds later, she appeared around the building, unzipping the short jacket she'd mentioned buying from Molly. Blue jeans hugged her hips, and a light purple top peeked from the dark gray jacket.

"Thank you for talking to the mechanic with me," she said as she reached him. "I know zilch about old cars. I might have steered Ty in the wrong direction without your help, pun not intended."

"You'd have done great on your own. But thanks for the thank you, anyway." He dangled the SUV keys at her. "The bush pickup's still at my place, and I need to feed Sheba before I go out again. Would you like to drive us back, or should I?"

Wariness entered her gaze. "Um, I should tell you—"

"Your license has been suspended?"

"No. It's your truck."

"Ah." He lifted his eyebrows. "Sounds like a case of BTP—Big Truck Paranoia." She chuckled, and he grinned. He loved

94

to tease her. "Don't sweat it, Jess, the truck's not a semi. She sits higher off the ground than your mother's car, but she handles like a dream." He passed her the keys, and she flipped them over in her hand.

"It's not the size. I know you'll laugh when I say this, but I can't drive a standard. I should have told you Saturday, but it slipped my mind."

"You mean to say you grew up in Destiny Falls, damn near the birthplace of the four-by-four, without learning to drive a stick?"

"I drove my dad's truck a few times. But that was over nine years ago."

"What about in Toronto?"

"I lease an automatic sedan. It's easier to maneuver in downtown traffic."

"Don't worry, the standard will come back to you. It's like riding a bike . . . or making love." He winked. "However, in the interests of preserving your sanity and mine, you could circle around the garage a few times. The property's big enough. Once you're comfortable with the clutch, I'll navigate you to my place. You turn right at Destiny Falls Crossroad, then take another right onto Red Rock Road. It's a few roads before the waterfall."

"Okay, okay, one step at a time. I have to master the clutch first."

"Then tarry no longer. Your carriage awaits." With a gentlemanly sweep of his hand, he opened the driver's door.

"Some carriage. But I appreciate the loan of it, anyway." As she climbed behind the steering wheel, she glanced at his dog in the cargo hold. "Poor Sheba. She won't like losing her warm, comfy spot back there."

"Are you kidding?" Adam strode to the passenger side and slid onto the seat. "Sheeb loves riding around in my bush pickup. She'd take it over this beast any day."

Jess drew in a breath. "I guess there's no postponing the inevitable, then." She turned the key in the ignition. *Thunk.* The truck lurched forward.

Adam winced. "You forgot the clutch."

"Sorry."

"That's okay. Just step on it before you start. Remember to release it slowly, but not too slow. You don't want to ride it when you're shifting gears."

"Clear as mud."

Spine stiffening, she stepped on the clutch and cranked the engine. A healthy roar filled the cab. The clutch depressed, and she experimented with the gearshift until she located reverse. Turning her head, she eased her foot off the clutch and backed up.

"Great! You're on your way."

She zapped him a smile that smacked him in the chest. Man, she was beautiful when she smiled.

Stepping on the clutch again, she shifted into first and steered around the garage. Adam talked her through the clutch and stick shift, careful not to flinch when she ground the gears a second time. Sheba whined in the cargo hold.

"Damn it," Jess said. "Sorry."

"You'll get the hang of it."

"Yeah, but when? My mother expects me back before midnight."

"My slo-pitch practice starts at six-thirty."

She glanced at the dashboard clock. "It's four-twenty. I'd better graduate to highway driving. Good thing the Crossroad isn't far."

"I'll let you know when to turn. Relax."

"Easy for you to say." But she slackened her death-grip on the steering wheel and took two more loops around the garage, engaging and releasing the clutch in better synchronization with the gearshift. She released a breath. Pride wreathed her face as she pulled onto the highway and accelerated to a few kilometers below the posted speed limit.

Adam clapped and whistled. She shot him a humor-filled glance.

"Another milestone!" he declared when she turned onto Destiny Falls Crossroad without riding the clutch.

"Oh, shut up," she tossed back lightly. "Can't you see I'm driving?"

"Yes, Mother." He slouched against the armrest like an insolent teenager. Pretending to watch the scenery, he monitored her progress from the corner of one eye. She returned her attention to the road, which curved and wound at a steady incline. The spruce and fir trees lining the shoulders increased in size and density as the houses facing the Crossroad gave way to treed acreage and forested mountains. The road narrowed, and soon thick brush obscured the signs.

"Shouldn't we have reached Red Rock Road by now?" she asked.

"We passed it five minutes ago."

"What? Why didn't you say something?"

"You told me to shut up."

"Oh, for—" She glared at him as if he were frustration incarnate. He wiggled his eyebrows like Bugs Bunny outfoxing Elmer Fudd. "Adam Wright! You tricked me on purpose!"

He showed his teeth. "Guilty."

"I don't believe this! I can't turn around now without taking us into the ditch. What should I do?"

"You tell me, Jess. You're in the driver's seat."

"Cute, Wright." Twin spots of color flared on her cheeks, giving her a just-been-kissed-and-not-too-thrilled-about-it look. "As if I'm not nervous enough learning to drive this behemoth, you have to play word games."

He shrugged. "You're tense. I'm helping you loosen up."

"I'll loosen a can of kick-butt on you if you're not careful."

"Come on, Jess, you're doing fine. The turn-off for the waterfall is up ahead. We'll drive around the campsites, check out the local wonder of nature. Have you visited the falls since you came home?"

"Mom's car hasn't exactly been reliable, remember?"

"So, I found a way around that. I thought you'd appreciate it."

"You're hopeless, you know that? The only reason you didn't breathe a word is because you knew you'd never get me in the middle of nowhere with you like this without resorting to another of your dirty tricks."

"Dirty tricks? *Moi?*" He crossed his heart over his shirt pocket. "My intentions are as honorable as my gender allows."

"Well, at least you score points for honesty." Reducing speed, she downshifted smoothly into third gear. "Where's this turn-off, anyway? My memory's rusty."

"That long, huh?" He pointed out a sign. "Take a left. Quick!"

Shifting jerkily into second, she swung the truck onto a narrow road. It bounced over a pothole, engine wailing like a wounded animal. "Sorry."

"Did I complain?"

"No. Thank you." She chose the fork to the right, following the loop of empty campsites nestled amid tall evergreens. Tourists rarely descended on the area until May. He and Jess would have the falls to themselves.

Good. He didn't feeling like sharing the scenery. Or the woman.

At his suggestion, she parked parallel to the viewing deck. As if stretched to the limits of her endurance, she crumpled against her seat and sighed. "We made it."

He laughed at her woebegone expression. "Who'd have

thought it? Jessica Morgan—busy merchandising executive and world traveler—humbled by a standard SUV."

"Humiliated is more like it. And please don't call me Jessica."

"Why not? It's a beautiful name."

"Maybe, but it's not mine."

"What's Jess short for, then?"

"Plain Jessie, with an 'i-e.' Mom named me for her father, Jesse Banks. She always said she didn't see the point in calling me Jessica when she never planned to use the name."

"So your birth certificate reads?"

"Jessie Noreen. Corny, huh?"

"I think it's great. Although unusual around here, a girl being named for her grandfather."

"Thank God his name wasn't Marvin." Her voice brimmed with warmth.

Adam liked her wit. Too bad she didn't display it more often. "I was named for my mom's father, too—Tom McLean. My middle name is Thomas."

"Really? I thought it was Perseverance."

"Very funny." He lowered his gaze to her lips. What he'd give to silence her smart mouth with a slow, deep kiss. Unfortunately, the last he knew, mature, adult "friends" didn't hook up in parked vehicles like a couple of sex-starved teenagers. "Now do you want to see the falls or what?"

If she'd replied "or what," he would have gone ahead and kissed her—damn the friendship. It was a farce, anyway. He knew it, and so did she. She just didn't want to admit it.

She didn't allow him the satisfaction of playing into his hand. Hopping out of the truck with a blithe, "That's why we're here," she raced ahead to the viewing deck, leaving him sitting there with heat licking his veins and a tight ache in his chest.

Jess zipped her new jacket against the breeze that had picked up

99

since they'd left the garage, then risked a glance back at the SUV. Adam remained in the passenger seat, gaining her a few moments of peace. All too soon, his door opened. Out he climbed, jean jacket in hand. He donned the coat over his blue flannel work shirt and strode to the cargo hold to retrieve his dog.

As he lifted the door, his broad back stretched faded denim, and her heart clambered in her chest. Sheba bounced out of the cargo hold with a cheerful-sounding bark.

Quickening her pace, Jess turned toward the viewing deck. Their friendship was a joke! Adam proved that every time he came near her. The connection between them felt super-charged, a crackling, humming energy that infused her with excitement as much as it did dread.

I don't need this.

Or did she?

She sucked in a breath. She was on vacation of sorts. Maybe a short-term thing with Adam was exactly what she did need.

He didn't want forever. And he drew her like a magnet.

How much longer could she withstand the pull?

Adam accompanied Sheba on her bathroom break near a remote section of the chain-link fence bordering the wedge-shaped canyon. He hadn't lured Jess to the waterfall for a repeat of the drive-in scenario, and he didn't want her worrying that he had. As much as it went against his nature not to go after what he wanted, he had to give her space or whatever was blos-soming between them would die.

You're crazy to want her, Wright. Never mind the number one stopper—her temporary visit. In three weeks, he needed to submit his bid for the Jamison Forest Products contract. Preparations, slo-pitch, and coordinating the Destiny Falls Young Achievers program without Pete's assistance would keep him hopping. He didn't have time for a relationship, short-lived or otherwise.

Cutting through the brush, he allowed Sheba to scamper ahead of him to the viewing deck. The dog barked at Jess's heels, eliciting her cautious laughter. Her gaze swung to meet his . . . still wary and guarded, yet lit with a soft expression that enthused him and gave him hope.

He joined woman and dog on the deck. Planting his hands on the rough cedar railing, he drank in the view. To their left, the majestic waterfall cascaded over a sheer cliff face, plummeting to the remnants of the ice-stocking that formed at its base each winter. Sparse stands of Lodgepole pine suffering from the ravages of a province-wide beetle infestation rimmed the canyon walls, as did clumps of Western red cedar and Western hemlock. To their right, the valley widened into a breathtaking vista of dense virgin forest.

The waterfall roared in his ears. He leaned in close to Jess. "Glad we came?"

She nodded, her dark curls fluttering in the moisture-scented breeze. "I forgot how peaceful it is."

"Especially before tourist season starts." He dragged in a lungful of clean canyon air. "I never get tired of coming here."

She looked at him. "Do you come often?"

"When I need to think. It's great stress relief."

"Sure beats rush hour."

He chuckled. Sheba nosed his thigh, and he scratched her head. Jess's gaze lingered on him.

"What?" he asked.

"Oh." She waved a hand. "I was remembering how Molly and I used to call this place 'Hick Falls,' in honor of our little one-horse town."

Adam laughed. "Her brothers called it 'Hickey Falls.' "

"And took advantage of that name often, no doubt."

"Did you?"

Color fanned her cheeks. "I guess every teenage couple comes here at some point. But I was shy in high school, and my father was the protective type. I rarely dated."

"I don't believe that. Even at fourteen, you were a knockout. Your dad must have wielded a pretty hefty chainsaw to scare off the boys."

"All but one," she murmured. An unmistakable sadness shadowed her tone.

Brushing off his hands, Adam ordered Sheba to lie down. The dog curled up behind them on the deck. "If you don't mind me asking, Jess, how did your father die?"

She gazed out at the waterfall. A pair of violet-blue swallows darted through the air, swooping and diving against the backdrop of the canyon in a graceful ballet. She watched the birds for several moments before returning her gaze to his.

"Widowmaker," she whispered.

Adam's blood froze. He'd heard his share of loggers' tales about loose limbs or large chunks of debris hurtling from a tree as it was being felled.

"He was killed cutting trees in the bush?" Icy fingers gripped him.

The thundering falls shrouded her voice as she nodded. "And so was my boyfriend. Danny."

Shit! "Damn it, Jess. I'm sorry."

Her eyes flickered shut, as if she couldn't hear him. "Dad should have checked the tree . . . he forgot to check the tree. He was training Danny. He should have been more careful." She bit her bottom lip. "That's the thing. No one really knows what happened. Danny couldn't remember. If Dad checked, it made no difference. A huge branch flung down on Danny. And then the . . . the falling tree struck Dad. It broke his neck. He was killed instantly."

Nausea swelled in Adam's gut. He covered her hand with his on the railing. She looked at him, eyes shining with unshed tears.

"Jess," he murmured. "You don't have to say any more."

Jess gazed at the big, strong forester standing beside her. "It's all right. I . . . I want to." She heard her voice break, felt his hand tighten over hers, offering warmth and security. "It feels good to tell you," she admitted. That, more than anything, surprised her. Caused something cold and dark and bleak to twist loose inside her. "Danny was more than my boyfriend. We began dating when I was sixteen. We planned to get engaged."

"What happened? Was he—?"

"Killed, too?" She shook her head. "He died, but not right away, like Dad did. Danny had surgery . . . but it didn't help. At best, he would have faced the rest of his life in a wheelchair." The old sorrow resurfaced, grabbing her by the throat. Yet she wanted—*needed*—to continue. "Those two weeks following the accident were horrible, attending Dad's funeral and surviving the aftermath while Danny knew he might be dying. I visited him in the Kamloops hospital every day."

She blinked back stinging tears. In that sterile hospital room, she'd pledged to love Danny Galloway forever. But her love— *their* love—hadn't been enough. She'd lost him, anyway. And the grief that had assaulted her when her father died spiraled out of control.

"My mom . . ." The words scraped from her throat and she swallowed. Adam squeezed her hand while the falls rushed endlessly before them. "Dad's death shocked us both. Then when Danny died . . . Adam, it was torture. But instead of reaching out to each other, Mom and I each suffered alone. It wasn't by choice. I didn't realize that her 'acceptance' of the accident"— she crooked two fingers into quotation marks—"was an act put

103

on for me. She wanted to be strong for me, but I couldn't see that. I wanted to be there for her, too, but I didn't know how. Not when she was being so damn stoic, so damn strong."

"Jess . . ."

"Please. I need to say this." She glanced at him. "I turned away from her."

"What do you mean?"

"Turned away, ran away. I hadn't planned to start university in Kamloops that September. I applied, but then Danny and I decided to wait a year so we could prove our independence and make some money." For her engagement ring and for their first apartment. A vision of Danny's earnest face at eighteen filled her mind: his scruffy dark hair and warm-cocoa eyes. "I was already working at Waverly Foods. After the accident, though, I couldn't handle living here, in this town—"

"The memories were too much for you." Adam's deep voice sounded gruff.

"Yes." *Thank you for understanding.* "A few weeks before high school graduation, we announced our decision to postpone our educations. Our parents were supportive. Dad asked Danny if he wanted to work in the bush that year. He wanted to be a forester, like you, so it seemed like a good idea, and the money was fantastic. He was supposed to stay on the landing—a bucker. His job was to de-limb the logs in preparation for loading. But fallers make the big money, and the foreman agreed that Danny was a natural."

"He took faller training?"

Her lungs ached. "My father was certified. He always resented having to jump through that hoop. He'd been logging and training fallers for decades, and suddenly the government required him to take a course from someone years younger without as much experience. He considered it red tape B.S." She inhaled sharply. "Danny would have taken the course. He couldn't fell

104

trees without it. But Dad thought giving him a head-start couldn't hurt. He began to pre-train him . . . but I blamed Mom. She let me believe she was behind the idea."

"She didn't want you angry with your father when he'd just died. You had enough to deal with already."

Jess nodded. "I left within the month. Accepted the university offer without consulting her and moved in with my Aunt Marion in Kamloops. Mom carried on, keeping tabs on me through my aunt, her sister. Neither of them told me. Then Mom ran into Pete in Waverly Foods one day, and they grew close again from there." She exhaled roughly. "I should have come home on the weekends more often, but I couldn't. Pete was there for her, though. He supported her when I couldn't."

"But who was there for you, Jess?"

"Molly."

"Not your mother, though. Not in the way you needed."

Numbness swathed her. She shook her head. "No, not my mom."

"Yet you blamed yourself for the problems you and she shared. Do you still blame yourself?" He cupped her face with one hand. His thumb brushed a hot, escaping tear.

Her throat tightened. "I don't see how I can't," she whispered. "When I think about those days now, it hurts, Adam. It hurts so damn much."

He swore, and the earthy word sounded oddly like an endearment. He pressed his lips to her cheek, her chin, and then wrapped her in his arms.

She released an anguished sigh against his chest. His unbuttoned jacket had flapped open, and his flannel work shirt cushioned her face. His heartbeat resounded in her ear, drowning out the noise of the falls. He stroked her hair, and she lifted her head.

His gaze met hers . . . and then he kissed her.

Once. Lightly.

Don't kiss him back. It was too soon, and painful memories packed her brain. But, damn it, his kiss felt too right to question. Lacing her fingers behind his neck, she urged down his head.

Their lips met softly, the moment tender. Gradually, the kiss deepened.

As before, as always with Adam, a compelling need swept through her. *It's right. It's wrong. Not now. Right now.*

She opened her mouth beneath his and relinquished herself to the pleasure of his kiss.

He moaned. His hand glided down her neck until his thumb rested in the hollow of her throat. Her pulse beat wildly. The heat of his palm flowed into her as his rough fingertips caressed her skin.

With a groan, he tore his mouth away. His breath raked from his chest. "Damn it, Jess, I didn't mean for that to happen."

She wanted him back. His lips, his arms. "I know."

He pushed her hair off her face. Tingles skated along her neck. "I hope you don't think I was trying to take advantage of the situation—of you," he murmured.

"I don't." She bore as much responsibility for the kiss as he did. Lying to herself wouldn't change that. "But . . . the kiss . . . us . . ."

"So now there's an us?" He smiled.

"There could be." The same words he'd uttered at The Clothes Horse Saturday. How ironic.

"There could be," he repeated, voice husky. "That's the best non-answer I've had all day. I'll take it."

106

CHAPTER EIGHT

Two days later, Jess had mastered the stick shift in Adam's SUV but hadn't come closer to deciding how far she wanted to pursue their attraction. In telling him about the past, she'd invited him into her life in a way she hadn't done with another man since Danny. She hadn't even mentioned Danny to her Toronto ex-boyfriends. The woodlands tragedy would have sounded as foreign to those career-obsessed city boys as paying for their lattes with rubles.

Wednesday morning, she drove to Molly's to email her assistant several large files, then ran errands. On her return, a faded blue pickup sat in her mother's driveway. Sheba napped in the sunshine that streamed over the truck bed.

Heart pounding, Jess parked the SUV in the garage. She hadn't heard from Sheba's handsome master since dropping him off at his big log house on Monday. She'd assumed he intended to give her a few days. Now, warmth spread through her. She really wanted to see him.

Entering the house through the mudroom, she set the groceries and her laptop case on the kitchen counter. Radio music drifted from the living room, and the orange-spice scent of her mother's favorite herbal tea laced the air.

She crossed to the archway. Adam and her mom played crib at the cherry-wood coffee table. Adam perched on the sofa, rubbing his jaw in concentration, while her mom pegged out points from the swivel rocker to his left.

In the moment before they noticed her, something inside Jess softened. Wearing jeans, a chambray shirt, and gray work socks on boot-less feet, he looked incredibly right sitting there. As if he belonged.

The man felt more comfortable in his skin than anyone she'd ever met. She wanted to find her place in this world more than anything. Could he show her how?

As if in answer, his head lifted and his clear blue gaze zeroed in on her. His sexy half-smile evoked every detail of their kiss at the waterfall, and her pulse fluttered.

"Hi." Her voice sounded wispy and insubstantial. Face heating, she cleared her throat.

"Hi, yourself." He got up. "Your mom said you went grocery shopping. Need help with the bags?"

"No, thanks. I already brought them in." Motioning for him to sit again, she strolled to the swivel rocker and kissed her mom's cheek. "Who's winning?"

"Can't you tell?"

"I am!" Mom's peg skipped past the skunk line. "I invited Adam to stay for lunch to thank him for lending us his SUV," she commented as if he visited every day. "Did you buy the salad things?"

Jess nodded. "And some macaroni and cheese. But I can fix you a sandwich, Adam, if you don't like packaged macaroni."

He patted his stomach. "I'm starving. A sandwich and mac?"

"And salad?"

"Looking at you makes me hungry."

"A salad, a sandwich, and macaroni, it is," Jess said. As she turned toward the kitchen, her shoe nudged an object sticking out from under the coffee table. Bending, she retrieved a photo album and flipped the first few pages of the suddenly familiar volume.

Her stomach sunk. "Oh, Mom, no, my baby pictures! Please

tell me you didn't show these to Adam."

"Why shouldn't I?"

"My favorite's the one of her bathing you in the kitchen sink," Adam said as he shuffled cards.

The nudie collection. Excellent.

"Jessie, you're my only child. Lord knows your father and I wanted more, but it didn't work out that way. I'm proud to show off your baby pictures to anyone willing to see them."

Eyes twinkling, Adam dealt the cards. "Maybe someday Jess will give you hordes of grandkids, and you can show off their pictures instead of hers."

"That would be nice." Her mother's tone was wistful.

Jess itched to kick his shin—hard. "Don't plan on it any time soon, Mom. My job's very busy, remember?"

"Yes, but if you met Mr. Right—"

"Somebody mention my name?" Adam's index finger bobbed.

Her mother's laugh competed with the country melody on the radio. "Adam, you're delightful. Isn't he, Jessie?"

"He's an absolute scream." Jess leveled the delight in question a stern look, then carried the album to the bookshelf flanking the fireplace. "I'll make lunch while you two finish your game." Shelving the album, she headed to the kitchen.

"Oh," her mom said. "Before I forget, your office called. They want you to call back before five o'clock their time."

"That was fast." Jess looked at her watch. Twelve-fifteen in B.C. meant three-fifteen Toronto time. "I'll do that first, then. My assistant must have a question about the files I sent."

Nora Olson was literally creaming him at crib. "Fifteen-two, fifteen-four, pair is six, pair is eight." Her little white peg bounced along the board.

"All right, I give, I give already." Faking bad sportsmanship,

Adam threw down his cards. His peg stood a good twenty points back.

"You can't give," Jess's mother informed him. "I've won."

"Okay, I concede defeat, then."

Her gaze flicked to the kitchen. "I see Jessie's finished her phone call." She rose. "I'd like to freshen up before lunch. Would you let her know?"

"Sure thing."

"Be back soon." She went upstairs.

Adam tucked the cards into their box and stored the pegs in the compartment on the underside of the crib board. Nora's spirits had improved greatly in the twelve days since Pete's heart attack. Although her sadness re-emerged now and then—in the sorrow-etched lines at her eyes and mouth, in her sudden, searching, lost-soul glances—she appeared much more at peace, and rested, and capable of moving on.

Jess's visit had done her mother a hell of a lot of good.

When Adam finished tidying their game, he strolled into the kitchen. His thick work socks muffled his steps as a hearty country song played on the living room radio. Jess placed a water-filled pot on the stove, a contemplative expression on her face.

He should cough or say something to announce his presence, but he really just wanted to stand there watching her. Her new blue jeans molded her curvy behind, and her leaf-green T-shirt and dark brown belt looked worlds away from the high heels and sophisticated dress she'd worn to the Wander-Inn Saturday night. Yet, Jess Morgan still exuded class. She probably exuded class nude.

Axe the fantasy, Wright. Before it affected him lower down.

She started unpacking groceries. He sidled up to the counter and dug into the second bag, earning himself a wide-eyed glance and a satisfying jump.

"Earth to Jess. Did I startle you?"

"As if you don't know. I was thinking."

"About what?"

"Oh . . . work." She withdrew vegetables from her bag and sat them on the counter.

"Problems?"

"Not really. My manager can be a jerk sometimes."

"Now you know why I work for myself."

"So you can be a jerk to your employees?"

He laughed. "You're quick."

"You're rubbing off on me."

He liked the sound of that. "You're not mad at me, then?" He pulled macaroni boxes out of his bag.

"Why would I be?"

"Because of what I said about giving your mother grandkids."

Her mouth pursed. "You did walk a fine line for a minute there. Make sure it doesn't happen again."

"Mmm. Bossy. Could have its perks."

She blushed. He passed her two soup cans. His skin burned as their fingers grazed. She stashed the cans in the cupboard. Then she flicked her hands in a shooing gesture near his chest.

He didn't move.

"Adam, please sit down. You're my guest." She hustled between the bags and cupboards, her swift movements a telltale indication that she felt the electricity buzzing between them as keenly as he did. "Where's Mom?"

"Upstairs for a minute." Or twenty, if he was lucky. He craved this alone time with Jess. She wielded her mother's transition to widowhood like a protective shield, but he'd bet Nora would love it if she developed new interests and relationships while she was in town. "In case you're wondering why I'm here, it's not to sit on my duff while you wait on me. If you won't let me help

111

put away groceries, I can start the salad."

"If you insist . . ." Her eyebrows lifted. "I hate chopping."

She handed him a knife and salad bowl. While he diced carrots and celery, she poured the pasta into the boiling water on the stove and stirred it with a wooden spoon.

"Why did you drop by in the middle of a work day?" she finally asked.

To see you. "Can't you guess?"

A soft smile touched her lips, and her gaze danced away.

"However, if you need a reason, I have a couple," he said. "Like wondering how you're making out with the SUV."

"Perfect." Her gaze remained glued to the macaroni pot.

"Then there's the Young Achievers group. The first meeting since Pete died is next week. The kids want to host a tribute. Would you and your mom like to come?"

Still stirring. "Definitely."

"How about dinner at my place Saturday?"

Her head snapped up. "Your place?"

"Don't look so terrified."

"I don't."

"You do."

"Well, I'm not."

"Uh-huh." He squeezed a plump tomato, then washed it and sliced it into wedges. "It's only dinner, Jess. I'm not asking you to marry me."

"No? That's a relief."

"Haw, haw."

Her head tipped. "You do know how to whip up a mean batch of pancakes."

"You're staying over?"

Mission accomplished: she laughed. "No."

He clapped a hand to his chest. "Jess, you wound me. But I was thinking something more low key, no pressure, like throwing steaks on the barbecue."

"Steak." Her nose scrunched. "A man's meal."

He shrugged. "I'm a man."

Heat flashed in her toffee-brown eyes. She retrieved a colander from a cupboard, then strolled to the fridge and produced a head of lettuce.

"Tell you what," she said in a non-Jess-like burst of spontaneity that threatened to knock off his work socks. "Make it grilled chicken, and you're on."

At seven the following morning, Jess strolled into the kitchen. The back porch door stood open, cool air streaming in. Coffee perked on the stove and a tiny vase of crocuses cheered the table.

Tightening her bathrobe sash, she went outside. Her mother sat in a cedar deck chair and stared at the horses grazing in the pasture. A blanket draped her shoulders and slippers peeked out from beneath her nightgown. With feather-like strokes of her fingertips, she caressed the weathered sheepskin jacket on her lap.

Crap. "Mom? Are you okay?"

Her head swung slowly, like someone in a trance. Eyes glistening with grief, she murmured, "I couldn't sleep." Her voice reflected a misplaced note of apology.

"Oh, Mom." Jess's heart ached. Yesterday, her mom had chatted happily with Adam over lunch. Then she'd joined Jess on a walk along the bank of one of two rivers that wended through town. However, tomorrow was Friday—three weeks since Pete had died. And this Sunday would bring Easter, Mom's first holiday without him.

Those were killers.

The agony of Jess's first holiday without her father and Danny had torn her apart. Danny's family hadn't moved yet, and his mother had invited Jess and her mom to Thanksgiving dinner during Jess's visit home from university. Mrs. Galloway had believed that sharing the mid-October Canadian holiday would comfort them all. However, Jess and her mom had already drifted apart, and the contrast between the isolated manner in which they'd dealt with their grief compared to the Galloways' supportive banding together had made everything worse.

By then, Mom had turned to Pete. She'd offered to talk, but Jess had refused. She hadn't trusted that what they might share wouldn't get back to the man whose very existence had infuriated her. It was like her parents' marriage had held no meaning, like her mom had bided time with Jess's father until she could be with Pete again.

Now, Jess knew better. Old emotions were powerful and complicated, and burying sorrow didn't solve anything. Her mother's grief for Pete would intensify unless they talked about it.

Sitting in the second chair, she tucked her bare feet beneath her robe and clasped her mom's hand on the armrest. "Is that Pete's coat?" she asked quietly.

Her mom nodded. "I only came out to pick the flowers. After I put them in water, something urged me to go outside again, almost like Peter was calling me. I went around the corner, and that's when I found this coat . . . hanging on the outside hook."

"It looks like an outdoorsman's coat." Like her dad might have worn. Not Peter Olson, bespectacled supermarket manager.

"Peter wore it on our walks. We walked several times a week, even in winter. He must have left it out here before he died." Her mom's gaze shifted to the pasture. The breeze ruffled her short, graying curls. "Peter and I had our routines. Every morning before he went to work we'd have coffee, watch the horses. It was his idea to lease out the fields and barn, you know."

Jess squeezed her mom's hand. "It was a good idea."

"Peter was a good man. I know you haven't always believed that, Jessie, but it's true. Yet, he could be difficult at times. I realize he was often rude to you."

Her chest pinched. "Because I reminded him of Dad," she whispered.

"Yes. That didn't excuse his behavior—or mine. I should have stood up for you, honey. I knew you were hurting."

"Mom, please don't do this to yourself. None of us were blameless."

Her mom shook her head. "Peter and I were to blame. You were so young."

"I was old enough to decide I wanted to marry Danny. Old enough to realize that suddenly leaving home would hurt you. I didn't have to act out around Pete, but I—" She swallowed. "He took you away from me."

A tear trickled down her mother's cheek. "Because I allowed him to."

"That's water under the bridge now, isn't it? I want it to be. Because, despite how upset I was with you back then, despite all my old hurt and anger, I do know that Pete was a good man. I know that you loved him and he loved you."

Torment drenched her mother's sigh. "And I know my love for Peter has always bothered you, Jessie. There are many different kinds of love, though. My love for your father was strong, so strong sometimes that it wore me out. Frank gave a lot, but he demanded a lot, too."

"I think I can see that now. I remember Dad as larger than life, full of exuberance and vitality. I imagine it was difficult keeping up with him."

"Yes. Peter was much more my equal. My love for Peter is . . . *was* . . . softer than the love I felt for your father. Peter was my husband, but he was also my friend . . . what I needed most."

"It wasn't that way with Dad?" Jess asked through a tight throat.

"Don't misunderstand me, Jessie." Her mother glanced at her, hazel eyes imploring. "Frank was a powerhouse, and I loved him deeply. Even when it was to my detriment—and yours—I put him first. Just like I did with Peter. You know your father and I wanted more children. But not because we didn't love you. I hope you realize that."

Jess blinked back tears. "Dad wanted a big family. I heard him say so countless times." In the pasture, the horses nickered, and the morning sun polished the dry grass gold. Soon, new spring growth would replace winter's remnants.

"Yes." One tiny, quiet word. "But I couldn't give him more children. We were married ten years before I became pregnant with you."

Jess shook her head. "How do you know it was you? Was your fertility tested?"

"No. Neither of us were tested, which makes my crime worse. Frank would have considered testing an insult, so I didn't push it. With my erratic cycle, it was easy to assume—"

"That it was your problem? Mom, it doesn't matter whose body was responsible. It was yours and Dad's inability to have more children, not yours alone."

"In hindsight, I understand that. But when you were little, I let my guilt come between us, between me and my sweet daughter."

"You did?" Jess asked hoarsely.

"I'm ashamed to admit it, but yes. Your father loved you so much . . ." Her mom's hand slipped out from hers, and the cedar armrest grazed Jess's palm. Then her mom's hand settled *on* hers. Smooth, gentle, the touch of love. "Frank didn't ask me to fade into the background. Because of my guilt, I pulled away from you. I thought he would be happier that way, so then you'd be happier, too." A sob broke free from her. "But I messed up everything. I sacrificed your love. Can you forgive me?"

"Mom, there's nothing to forgive. I love you."

Her mother smiled, but it quivered. "Your father burst into my life and stole my breath away. I wanted to give him everything, and I did, including you. When he died, and then Danny . . . Jessie, you were so lost and alone, and I was such a failure."

"Mom, you were never a failure."

"Yes, I was, and I need to accept that. I wasn't there for you. My sweet daughter, I'm so sorry."

"It's okay." She couldn't deny the absolution her mother obviously needed. She lifted their joined hands and kissed her mom's. "I mean it, Mom. I love you."

Happiness glimmered through her mom's tears. "And I love you."

Jess smiled. "I didn't come out here to dredge up the past. I want to talk about Pete, but not if it hurts you. Only to help you."

"Yet, how I feel about Peter is tied up with the past, Jessie. That's why I need to discuss it. Looking back, I realize I shouldn't have shut down when your father died. I hid my grief from you. How wrong I was to do so. Lord, how I wish we could have shared our pain."

A strange sense of peace fell over Jess. "This is the most honest conversation we've had in years."

"It gives one hope, doesn't it?"

Nodding, she laced their fingers together. "We can share our feelings now, Mom. About Dad. About Pete. He was a good man. I've known that for a long time. In a way, his death has brought me back to you. He's given us another chance. I'll forever be grateful to him for that."

"Another chance," her mom repeated softly. "You never fail

to surprise me, Jessie. What a wonderful way to think of Peter's passing. He's given us another chance."

"Hurry!"

"I am!" Jess squealed as fat raindrops pelted her scalp and chilled her shoulders through the magenta tunic sweater she wore over her new black jeans. Juggling the filled wineglasses and cutlery, she ducked through the open sliding glass door leading from Adam's sundeck into his spacious log home. She deposited her load on the dining table, then extracted the uncorked wine bottle from his arm, freeing him to set down their dinner plates. "Did we forget anything?"

"The pepper grinder." He slid shut the door. "I'll get it later, unless you need it now." He raked a hand through his rain-flecked hair, looking rumpled and relaxed and thoroughly male.

"I'm okay." She arranged the place settings and sat down. "I can't believe how fast the rain came up."

"At least we had the good sense to come in." He lowered his big frame onto the chair to her right. His leg grazed hers beneath the oak table, and he flashed a smile that made her whole body hum.

She took a calming sip of wine. She'd almost backed out of dinner tonight. After her talk with her mother on the back porch two days ago, she'd felt selfish stealing time for herself just when they were growing close. However, her mom had insisted that she follow through with her plans, and now she was glad she had. She'd missed Adam's sense of humor and generous nature. Add in his undeniable sex appeal and hometown charm, and she was amazed half the eligible women in Destiny Falls hadn't fallen in love with him.

Love?

Pulse tripping, she plunked down her wineglass. Love wasn't on her agenda. If she wanted to continue seeing Adam, she had

118

to make that clear.

To whom?

Oh, shut up, she chastised her nagging inner voice. She refused to let a lengthy self-examination ruin the evening. For once, she wanted to let go and enjoy herself, to push caution aside and pretend tomorrow wouldn't come.

"Did you finish your mapping yesterday?" she asked. An innocuous topic of conversation.

He nodded around a mouthful of grilled chicken. "Took all morning," he said once he'd swallowed. "I spent the afternoon in the bush. How about you?" He sipped his wine. "Is Arlington Shoes surviving without you?"

"Remarkably, yes. By the way, that wasn't my assistant who called Wednesday. It was my boss. Gareth."

"The jerk."

She laughed. "He spouts the company line about my leave of absence—it falls within my benefits package, how good it is for Mom, yada, yada. But then he drones on and on about the extra work it creates for him. My assistant is very capable, yet he wanted to rehash the spreadsheets I'd emailed her."

"Was there a mistake in them?"

"No. If there had been, Sarah would have contacted me."

"Maybe she's overwhelmed."

Jess shook her head. "She covers for me all the time when I'm traveling. She's used to it, and she's good at her job. Without her, I'd probably work seventy hours a week. As it is, I average fifty."

Adam whistled. "That's nuts."

She cut into her chicken, "Don't tell me you work short hours?" With several of his contracts originating throughout the valley, how could he?

"I didn't say that. The difference is that MountainTop is my company. I call the shots, and I have a life outside of work."

119

She swatted his arm. "I have a life."

"Oh, yeah? When?"

"When I'm not traveling." *Not really.*

"You ever sleep?"

"Okay, I don't have much of a life," she conceded. "I don't mind. I like keeping busy."

"Still, it must be nice to have a break." His husky voice rolled over her.

"It is." She pushed the rice around on her plate. His gaze lingered on her, and that odd little hum started up again. "I'm not used to so much free time, though."

He wagged his fork. "See? I was right."

She smiled. "Since coming home, sometimes I wake up thinking I need to meet a supplier or plan a promotion two days behind schedule. Then I remember I'm in Destiny Falls with absolutely nothing pressing to do."

"Except relax. Never underestimate the importance of relaxation."

So true. "And getting to know my mother again. If anything good has come out of Pete's heart attack, it's that."

He nodded. "How is she?"

"Coping." Since their breakthrough Thursday morning, talking to Mom about Pete was proving less and less difficult. "I took her to the waterfall today. I even avoided the pothole."

"Ah, yes, the offensive pothole. Did you grind the gears this time?"

"No, I did not grind your precious gears. That reminds me, though, I spoke to Ty yesterday. You were right about the car, although I hate to admit it right now."

"Okay, I take back the wisecrack about your driving. What did he say?"

"It's the transmission, all right. He ordered parts, but the car won't be ready until late next week. Is that a problem?"

"Should it be?"

"Don't you want your SUV back?"

"Not as long as you're in town. I'll make do with the pickup." He speared a chunk of grilled red pepper. "Keep the SUV. That way you and your mom will each have a vehicle once the car's fixed. It also gives me an excuse to check up on you, make sure you're not grinding my gears."

Jess fidgeted with her napkin. With one sentence, the thrust of their conversation had changed. Whatever she said to Adam now would either keep their relationship moving forward or bring it to an abrupt halt.

I'm not ready.

Her heart pounded.

But I want this.

"You don't need an excuse to see me," she murmured.

He looked at her, pleasurable expectation lighting his gaze. "I don't?"

"No." She shook her head. "You don't."

After dinner, they washed the dishes, Adam rinsing and Jess drying to the classic rock station he'd tuned in on the stereo. Once he'd stored the last plate in the cupboards, he fed Sheba in the carport, then hauled wood into the great room and built a fire while his beautiful guest hid in the kitchen, concocting dessert from her bag of "secret ingredients."

He kicked off his shoes and stoked the blaze in the rock fireplace separating the two rooms. "That dessert ready yet? This fire will only last three or four hours."

Her tinkling laugh sailed to him. "Almost." Five seconds passed. "Ready!" She stepped around the fireplace carrying two massive chocolate fudge sundaes, each topped with whipped cream and a maraschino cherry. "Ta-da!"

He chuckled. "You expect me to eat that monster?"

"It's to make up for asking you for grilled chicken when I know you had your heart set on red meat." She passed him a spoon and goblet. "You don't have to eat all of it."

"I'll give it the old college try." He sat cross-legged on the carpet.

Jess knelt beside him, plucking the cherry from her sundae and popping it into her mouth. Chewing slowly, she closed her eyes. Her sooty lashes fluttered against her pale skin. "Mmm."

Adam's heart rate skyrocketed. Did she have any idea how erotic she looked—or sounded? And how different from the stressed out woman he'd met two weeks ago. He'd thought her gorgeous then, but now her curly hair had grown wilder, her makeup was more subdued, and the tight black jeans she'd bought from Molly's store emphasized her curves in a manner he greatly appreciated.

He was even more attracted to this Jess.

Her eyes opened, and their gazes linked. She dipped her spoon into her ice cream. "You haven't tried your sundae."

"I've been too busy watching you."

"I love maraschino cherries. I used to sneak into the fridge and eat a whole jar at once. It drove Mom batty."

"I can imagine." He held her gaze, and she drew in a breath, legs squirming on the carpet.

Finally, she broke eye contact. Swallowing her ice cream, she glanced around the great room. "This house is amazing. Did you design it yourself?"

Nodding at her transparent change of subject, he dug into his sundae.

"You have good taste." She licked chocolate sauce from her spoon, pink tongue swirling.

Arousal shot through him. Shifting on the carpet, he lifted a knee. "Thanks. I helped with the construction and contracted out the trades."

"It's a big house for one man."

"One man and his dog." He winked. "My office is in the basement, and three bedrooms are upstairs." He'd intended the smallest bedroom as a nursery. Thinking the project would thrill his new fiancée, he'd shown Crysta the blueprints. She'd dismissed her sour expression as morning sickness. Joke on him.

"Three bedrooms is excellent resale value." Jess ate more ice cream.

"They'll come in handy when I have a family. Do you want kids?"

A wry smile touched her lips. "With my long hours, if I had a baby, I'd need a live-in nanny *and* a cooperative husband."

"You don't sound optimistic about the cooperative husband."

"Well, what do I know? Other than Danny, I've never come close to getting married."

"I have. Once. From my point of view. She—Crysta—had other plans."

Jess's gaze lowered. "Molly told me a bit about her."

"Like what?"

"Just that you were engaged and that Crysta left. Are you upset Molly said something?"

He shook his head. An old Rolling Stones song pounded on the stereo, and the heavy beat resounded in the great room. "At one time, it might have bothered me. But not now." He scooped whipped cream into his mouth. It slid, cool and slippery, down his throat. "I met Crysta a few years ago. We dated a couple of months." Then their protection failed, and they discovered she was pregnant. "If you think I'm pushy now, you should have seen me then." He rested his spoon in his goblet. "Short version, I pressured her, and she wasn't ready. Our breakup was ugly."

"Were you badly hurt?"

"Yep. But I'm over it." He wouldn't repeat his mistakes with Crysta with another woman—especially someone like Jess, only in town a few weeks. "Like I said, that was a couple of years ago. I mellowed once I hit thirty."

Jess's lips curved. "Not completely, I hope."

"No. Never completely."

"I don't mind. I like your persistence and determination. It makes me crazy sometimes, but I still like it." She swallowed a spoonful of fudge and ice cream. The dark sauce smudged her lower lip.

"And I like"—he drifted his gaze down her face—"how your mouth looks with chocolate sauce smeared at the corner."

"Where?" Her tongue darted out, missing the fudge.

Heat pulsed through him. "Not there."

"Here?"

"No."

Her tongue emerged again, and he pulled in a breath. *That does it.*

Bridging the gap between them, he kissed one side of her mouth. "There." He kissed her again, full on the lips. "And there."

Her gaze dipped, her breathing growing shallow. Slowly, she licked her lips, her tongue gliding over the spot his mouth had just touched. She glanced up. "Is there any more?"

"Oh, yeah." Lifting his spoon, he skimmed chocolate fudge onto the tip and held it to her mouth. Her gaze met his as her berry-red lips slicked over the fudge. "Don't swallow," he commanded.

She complied.

He lowered his mouth to hers, longing for a taste. Of chocolate. Of Jess. He parted her lips with a gentle pressure.

Greedy for more, he kissed her deeply. Coaxing. Then demanding.

A moan rose in her throat. Pulling away, he placed their spoons and goblets on the hearth. On his knees, he cupped her face. Desire shimmered in her eyes and her lips trembled. He hauled her into his arms.

Mouths fused, they toppled onto the carpet and rolled toward the heat of the fire. Lying on his side, Adam ran a hand up her soft sweater, over her breasts, then back down to her waist, her hips. Her breath released on another ragged moan.

Placing both hands on her firm bottom, he fitted her pelvis against his jeans. Need flashed through him, hot, urgent, and undeniably focused on this sexy, giving woman. *Jess, Jess, Jess.*

He kissed her lips, her chin, and throat. Her little, rocking movements scorched him with the knowledge that she was every bit as aroused as he was.

"Did you buy these jeans to drive me nuts?"

She shook her head. "It's an added, um, bonus. Molly wouldn't let me out of the store until I bought them. Part of our deal that I spend two hundred dollars during her, um, shift."

"Good for Molly. And this top . . ." He slipped a hand beneath her long sweater and toyed with the button of her jeans. "Did my cousin convince you to buy it, too?"

Her hands caressed his back. "I had it with me. I usually wear it over a skirt for a loose, layering effect."

He chuckled. "I have news for you, honey. This sweater doesn't layer over these jeans. It clings like a second skin." He popped open the button and inched down her zipper. "Now, this is more like what I'd call loose."

Her hips wriggled. "They *were* feeling snug."

He slipped a hand inside the back waistband of her jeans. His fingers skipped over the silky T-shaped ridge of her thong onto two smooth, bare mounds of flesh. His arousal hardened to granite.

Groaning, he kissed her deeply. Her breasts crushed against

125

his chest. "If you need me to stop, you'd better say so now because you're about to send me over the edge."

CHAPTER NINE

"I don't want you to stop," Jess murmured between his kisses. She needed him—oh, so much—but she had to establish some boundaries before they went any further. "Adam, I need you to understand . . . what we've talked about before." His warm lips nibbled her neck. Her skin tingled. "Ooh . . . you realize that this . . . us . . . you understand we're short term?"

"Because you're leaving in a month?" he asked, mouth sliding to her ear.

"Yes." His lips tugged her earlobe, and she wriggled against the tickling sensation. "I want to be with you . . . I feel things for you . . . sometimes it's so strong."

He kissed her eyelids. Gentle, tender, feather-light. "I feel it, too, honey. I want it, too."

"But it can only be . . . we can only have—"

"A summer romance?"

"I won't be here in the summer."

"Okay, then, just the spring."

"Just the spring," she echoed, fumbling with his shirt buttons. Shirt open, she covered his muscular chest with kisses and teased one flat nipple with a finger.

His breath raked in. "Easy, honey. I want this to last."

He peeled off his shirt, then removed her sweater and lowered her to the plush carpet as Aretha Franklin's powerful voice sang "Natural Woman" over the stereo. The firelight bathed his face in an amber glow as he kissed her again. She returned him kiss

127

for kiss. Desire burned in her veins. Embers sparked in her soul.

He planted hot kisses down her throat, caressed her bra. Unhooking the clasp with deft fingers, he tossed aside the lacy lingerie.

His large hands molded her breasts, thumbs flicking over her stiff nipples. She moaned, and his head lowered. His mouth skipped down her tummy to her belly button. His tongue darted in and out, in and out.

She grew moist and slick. "Adam."

"Yes?"

His voice vibrated against her stomach, and she smiled. She felt like she was glowing from the inside out. Warm, soft, melting.

And wilder than she'd thought possible.

She threaded her fingers in his hair. "Please don't stop."

"Sweetheart, this is just the beginning." Moving down, he lifted her legs one at a time and slipped off her shoes. Urging up her hips, he stripped off her jeans and socks, leaving her nude except for her black lace thong. His fingers slid beneath the scrap of fabric. He found her center and rubbed.

She rocked her hips as sensation spiraled. "Ooh, not fair. I want to touch you, too."

Sitting up, she helped him shed his jeans. He whipped off his socks and boxers. Even his appendectomy scar looked sexy as he stood before her, fully erect. She'd never seen another man so glorious. She'd never yearned for any man the way she yearned for Adam.

She coaxed him down to the carpet and wrapped her hand around his erection. A low groan issued from him.

His excitement fueled her. Skin against skin. Mouths joined, tongues darting. She couldn't get enough of him.

"Now," she whispered. "I can't wait much longer."

"You're not the only one." He kissed her. "We're forgetting

something, though." He grabbed his jeans and withdrew a condom packet from a front pocket. "Call me optimistic. I've been carrying this around for days."

A sweet, poignant emotion bloomed inside her. Not because he'd anticipated making love with her, but because he'd thought to protect her.

Together, they slid the sheath into place.

She removed her thong, then sank with him to the carpet. The DJ's voice announced the next song on the radio, but she couldn't decipher the words, couldn't concentrate on anything but her passionate need to make love with Adam.

He lifted his hips and entered her slowly. Inch by sleek, hot inch. Filling her. Driving her mad.

As if intent on torturing her, he stilled. Desire coiling, she tightened her inner muscles and thrust against him.

A wicked smile tipping his mouth, he began to move. Slowly again at first, then faster. Deeper.

He lowered his head to her breasts and tasted one nipple, then the other. Lips tugging, tongue swirling. Bringing her to the brink of release at the speed of light.

Jess tried to hold back, tried to contain the vortex swirling inside her. Then he rubbed her between her legs again, and she climaxed in a rush. "Adam!"

He pumped rapidly. Seconds later, his body throbbed, his breathing harsh with his own release.

He rested his head on her shoulder. "Jess, that was amazing. Honey, we're perfect together."

She held him tightly, a dozen emotions swelling within her. Meshing, conflicting. Making her sigh with contentment. Shaking her to her core.

For Adam had done much more than make love with her.

He'd touched her heart.

★ ★ ★ ★ ★

Adam woke after midnight to find himself alone in bed. Light from the loft hallway streamed through the open door. Noises of Jess moving around downstairs punctuated the stillness.

He sat up. He must have fallen asleep after they'd made love a second time. No wonder—the second time had been as intense as the first, and the first had nearly knocked him out, until Jess had suggested coming upstairs.

Shrugging into his robe, he left the room and glanced over the narrow log railing. Jess was pulling on her jeans in the semi-darkness of the great room, her dark curls tumbling over her bare shoulders. Her bra encased her breasts and socks clad her feet, but her sweater and shoes still lay scattered on the carpet alongside his discarded clothes.

"Hi," he said.

Her head lifted. "Hi."

"Leaving so soon?" "Dinner" had lasted longer than expected.

"I have to get home." She retrieved her sweater and tugged it on. "Mom will worry if I stay out all night."

"Call her." He descended the split-log steps.

She shook her head. "It's too late, and she has traditional values. If I stay, she'll know we slept together on our first date. I'm a bit surprised by that myself."

"It wasn't a date. It was dinner."

She laughed. "It was a date, and you know it."

"We could count Tim and Molly's anniversary as our first date," he said as he stepped off the bottom stair. "Lunch on Thursday was the second date. So tonight was our third."

Her lips twitched. "Typical male justification."

"Just so you know I'm not kicking you out." Reaching her, he picked up her trendy shoes. Erotic memories flooded his mind—Jess on her back on the carpet, her shoes cast aside and her hips raised as he peeled off her jeans.

130

Desire swelled. *Down, boy. It's not the time.*

"There'll be other nights," he half-whispered. Passing her the shoes, he kissed her.

"Thanks—I mean for my shoes."

"Not for the offer of other nights?"

"That, too. I'd planned to leave you a note." Morning-after jitters shaded her tone.

"A clean get-away. I've spoiled it now, haven't I?"

"I didn't want to wake you."

"I wouldn't have cared." Grazing her chin with one hand, he kissed her. "But I'm here now, so you don't have to write that note."

He kissed her again, harder, craving her lush mouth. Her hand clasped his wrist, and her lips parted. She held him there, deepening the kiss, dissolving his sudden notion that she was running out on him.

She broke away, gaze soft, and he brushed her lower lip with his thumb. "You'd better put on those shoes before I drag you back upstairs and have my way with you for a third time tonight."

Her small smile churned up the madness inside him. "Still frisky, are you?"

"I have a feeling 'frisky' will describe my general state of existence over the next several weeks."

"Poor boy."

"I'll work it out of my system by the time you leave town." His chest tightened. Her leaving was inevitable. That didn't mean he had to like it. "I'll need your help, though." He kissed her fingertips.

"What kind of help?" she asked lightly. "Part time? Full time? Day shift? Night?"

"Mostly nights. Although I'm sure we can fit in a day here and there."

131

"And the benefits?"

"You can set your own hours. Come and go as you please. As for the pay—"

"I'll take it in kisses."

"I was hoping you'd say that." He held her close, mouths joining. Her body heat seeped into him, and the lingering scent of their lovemaking swirled in his brain. As she leaned into him, her shoes wedged against his hip.

"I keep forgetting the purpose of those is to get you out of here," he murmured against her mouth.

"I'll put them on." She slipped on the shoes, gaze sweeping to the fireplace. The flames had diminished to embers, and chunks of fudge swam in melted ice cream in the goblets on the hearth. "I'll help clean up." She stepped toward the ruined desserts.

He shook his head. "I'll do it in the morning. I like the thought of coming down here again to find our mess."

"A melted sundae hunt? That's a new one."

"You're right, it's officially Easter now." An arm around her shoulders, he walked her to the door. "What are your plans?"

"Same as yours, I think."

"You're going to Louis Creek?"

"Oh." She laughed. "No. Mom and I are having dinner at Molly's parents'. I assumed you were, too."

"I wish I were, knowing you are. But my mom will skin me alive if I don't show up for her special glazed Easter ham." He fetched her purse from the closet. Dropping a light kiss on her mouth, he handed them to her.

"Will you be back tomorrow night?" she asked.

He missed her already. *This is crazy.* He shook his head. "I want to get in a good visit while I can. I'll return Monday morning. How does lunch sound?" *Ages away.*

"At my place?"

132

"I'll take you out this time." He sat on the chair and tugged on his mud-caked work boots. "I'll walk you to the truck."

"You don't have to."

"I want to." He opened the door, then offered her his arm, feeling gallant and ridiculous in his bathrobe and dirty boots. They strolled across the driveway, gravel crunching beneath their feet. The rain had stopped, and earth-tinged freshness saturated the air. An owl hooted from the fir trees surrounding the yard. Sheba stirred in the carport and barked.

Jess climbed into the truck. Starting the engine, she rolled down the window. Adam settled his mouth over hers for one last, soft, sweet kiss.

"Do you really have to go?" he whispered, and she nodded.

She turned the SUV around in the driveway and sped off into the darkness.

Easter dinner with Molly's family was a boisterous affair. Molly's brothers—Luke, still single, and Brian with his wife and baby—had traveled home to attend. Eleven chairs crowded the huge dining table laden with roast turkey and an assortment of side dishes. Molly's children squabbled about sitting crammed together while the adults argued good-naturedly about politics and hockey.

In the midst of the chaos, Jess's thoughts kept drifting to Adam in Louis Creek. Were the Wrights as noisy and cheerful as the McLeans? Did Adam envision similar holiday bedlam erupting around his dinner table someday?

Visions of blond, blue-eyed children surrounding him—perhaps one or two with curly black hair—zipped through her mind. In each image, she pictured herself sitting beside him, serene and glowing. Like she'd once imagined herself in a future with Danny.

She drew in a breath. *Don't be ridiculous.* Her hormones were working overtime. Hot sex with Adam was one thing, but beyond that? She didn't need the complications.

"I said, 'will you pass the turkey, please, Jess?' " Brian poked her arm. "Can't let that last piece go to waste."

"Huh?" Jess glanced at Molly's brother seated to her left. Had the hockey discussion ended? "Um, sure." She accepted the platter her mom held out to her and transferred it to him.

Brian grinned. "Was it a good one?"

"Good what?"

"Daydream. Or were you trying to block out the noise?" He stabbed the big slice of turkey breast and deposited it on his plate.

Across the table, Molly said, "She was daydreaming. About Adam, I'll bet." She murmured in a selling-national-secrets tone, "They had dinner at his place last night."

Jess gripped her fork. They'd had a lot more than dinner, but Molly wasn't aware of that fact, and Jess had no plans to tell her. She still needed to grow accustomed to the idea.

Luke stared at his sister. "Jess and Adam? Well, what do you know? The guy's finally developing some taste." He passed his brother the gravy boat.

Molly snorted. "What would *you* know about good taste in women?"

"Enough to realize that if I'd had any as a teenager, I would have paid more attention to Jess." Luke nudged his mother. "How about it, Mom? Don't you think Jess and I would make beautiful babies together?"

Sheila McLean flicked a hand. "Don't you dare tease me, Luke. You know darn well I think it's high time you got married." Sheila rose and began collecting empty plates. "Although I wouldn't mind it if a certain nephew of mine found himself someone, too."

"I think she means you, Jess." Molly snickered and got up to help her mom.

"Thanks for pointing that out, Moll." Jess glared at her plate-whisking friend. Her own mother, seated on her right, had quietly absorbed every word.

She didn't want Mom—or anyone else—thinking this "thing" she had for Adam would ever lead anywhere.

Because it wouldn't.

Adam had planned to take Jess to a restaurant for lunch on Monday. However, after a day and night without her, he decided he'd rather go somewhere they could be alone. The waterfall, for instance.

Unfortunately, he failed to inform her in advance, and when he arrived to pick her up, she answered the door in a gauzy, belted, sleeveless dress and delicate-looking high-heeled sandals that would never survive an afternoon in the great outdoors.

But, damn, did she look fine.

"Hi." Tugging the dress's wide belt, he coaxed her into his arms for a kiss. Her spine tensed in the instant before her mouth softened beneath his. One hand on the belt, he skittered the other up her bare shoulder and grazed the vee of the button-front dress. "You wouldn't happen to have something a little more substantial in the line of footwear, would you?"

"I'm a shoe buyer—I brought ten pairs. Why, don't you like these?"

"I love them. Hiking boots or runners would work better for what I have in mind, though."

"I thought we were going out for lunch."

"We are going out. Outside."

"A picnic?"

He nodded. "The convenience store at the gas station sells these incredible take-out ribs and wedgie fries. I thought we could eat out at the waterfall then walk the trails." He fanned his hand like a Hollywood director blocking a scene. "Can't you picture it? Privacy, ambience, the odd black fly buzzing around."

"How romantic."

"If you'd rather eat at the Wander-Inn—"

"After that build-up about the black flies? Not on your life." She stepped out of his arms. "Wait inside. I'll be right back."

Minutes later, she met him in the living room, looking radiant and beautiful in a loose white sweatshirt pulled on over her dress and ankle boots with thick socks instead of fancy sandals.

Part Toronto, part Destiny Falls. She'd fit in perfectly with the granola set.

"What, no jeans?" He kissed her.

"I didn't want to waste more time."

"Honey, I like the way you think."

"You have it."

"No, you have it."

"Nope," Adam insisted. "You."

Her eyebrows arched. "Very well." She plucked the last rib from the take-out box resting between them on the viewing deck stairs. She nibbled the meat. "Mmm, that's *good.*" She dragged out the word on a moan, supercharging his libido. "Betcha wish you hadn't let me have it now."

He laughed. "Betcha?" Had he heard Jess Morgan say betcha?

"Betcha, wanna, gonna—Molly's kids are rubbing off on me."

"Cute. Actually, I don't care about the rib." He pierced the last potato wedge with his plastic fork. "*This* was what I was after." He shoved the spicy wedge into his mouth.

Jess punched his shoulder. "You pig!"

"Me? What about you?"

"A lady is never a pig." She stuck her nose in the air. "A lady merely partakes of the gastronomic pleasures of life with the unschooled appetite of a portly swine." She tore barbecued

136

meat off the rib with her fingers and tossed the morsel to Sheba, curled on the deck at their feet.

Adam thoroughly welcomed her enjoyment of their simple lunch. When she'd left his place in the early hours of Sunday morning, he'd wondered if her mother's morals had really prompted her departure, or had something else? He'd agreed to a spring fling—he wasn't crazy—but sometimes he detected a hint of the old wariness in her eyes or voice. Like in the pickup while they'd driven here. Or when they'd first sat down to eat.

However, now she seemed determined to maintain a carefree mood.

"Finished?" he asked beneath the din of the rumbling falls.

"Yes." She tossed the bone in the box, then licked barbecue sauce from her fingers. The wet, slurping noises conjured erotic fantasies of melting sundaes and amazing lovemaking. His body responded.

"How about that walk?" Sex wasn't the only reason he appreciated her company. Although, at the moment, sex seemed like an excellent idea.

"I'd love it."

"Let's go." He collected their trash and deposited it in the garbage can. They followed a trail that skirted the chain-link fence along the canyon. Then they wound through the woods behind the campsites before emerging to a canyon view again. When the width of the path permitted, they strolled hand in hand, Sheba racing ahead of them, investigating noises, scents, and movements.

"This is nice," Jess murmured. "Mom and I didn't walk the trails when I brought her here. I don't think I've walked them in nine years."

"Since your father died?" And Danny Galloway. Her first love.

She nodded. "When I was little, Dad tried to teach me the

different species of trees. You know, which has two needles, which has three."

Adam looked forward to doing the same with his own kids someday, a woman like Jess at his side. "Do you remember any of it?"

"Not really."

"Then it's time for a refresher lesson." He slapped the bark of the nearest tree. "This one's a Western hemlock. In Latin, *Tsuga heterophylla.* Hetero, like me." He grinned and she rolled her eyes. "Glossy needles, flat and soft, tiny cones, scaly, ridged bark." He pressed her palm to the tree. "Feel that? A Mountain hemlock would have hard, narrow ridges, longer cones, drooping branches."

"How do you remember all that?"

"Four years of university drilled it into my brain." He led her to another tree and pointed out a branch. "When your father talked about two needles or three, he probably meant this tree."

"Pine," she said, and he nodded.

"The needles of the Ponderosa pine grow in clusters of three, the White pine clusters of five, and this baby—the Lodgepole pine—has pairs of short, stiff needles."

Jess slid him an amused glance. "Stiff, huh? And the Latin?"

"For the Lodgepole? *Pinus contorta.*"

"*Pinus?* You're joking."

"Nope." He grinned.

"Hmm. By any chance, is *your* pinus contorta?"

"Not likely. The short, crooked Lodgepoles grow at the Coast. We Interior guys are long and straight."

"Ah." She leaned against the tree, hands clasped behind her back. As if in invitation, her breasts thrust forward. "I remember."

"Do you now?" Desire, hot and heavy, pulled at him. Bending an arm, he planted his hand on the bark above her head.

"Why, Professor Wright. My lesson—"

"Is over."

Swooping down, he kissed her deeply. She laced her hands around his neck and drew him closer. God, he wanted to make love to her.

Beneath the trees. Against the tree. Whatever she wanted. However she wanted.

"I want you, Jess," he whispered. "Don't you know what you do to me? I want you more than I've ever wanted another woman."

"Now?" she whispered, breath warm against his mouth.

"Right here. Right now." He tugged the waistband of her sweatshirt.

Her soft laugh burrowed through him. "Adam, I think we have company. Didn't you hear a car drive in?"

He groaned.

"I think it's stopped now, but—"

"Shh." He craned an ear. The giggling and guffaws of teenagers filtered to them from near the falls. "Damn it, I forgot, no school on Easter Monday. What will we do now?"

A sultry smile tipped her lips. "I know a place."

"My place?"

She nodded.

Heat and pleasure rolled through him. "My kind of woman."

He straightened her sweatshirt and whistled for Sheba to return from exploring. Avoiding the teens, they packed the dog into her airy kennel in the pickup bed, then climbed into the cab. Jess teased him mercilessly while he drove, rubbing his thigh near his crotch.

He raised an eyebrow. "Ever done it in a pickup on the side of the road before?"

"Can't say I have."

"There's always a first time."

139

"Isn't this your driveway?"

"Not a moment too soon, sweetheart."

He parked in the driveway and jumped out of the truck after her, catching her in a breathless hug when she tried to wrestle the house keys from him. Sheba barked in her kennel. Adam freed her, and the dog bounded out of the truck bed, pushing her cold nose into his hand.

"Sorry, Sheeb, this is a private party." Relinquishing the house keys to Jess, he escorted Sheba to the fenced portion of the yard.

He met Jess in the foyer and pulled her into a wild embrace, kissing, touching, caressing while their boots, socks, belts, and his jeans went flying. Shoving his hands under her sweatshirt, he met the resistance of her dress and bra.

"Damn buttons."

"Forget the buttons." Her voice sounded airy.

"You mean get creative?" He hoisted up her dress and slid his fingers into her panties. "Jess, you feel so slick, so good." He peeled off the panties and kissed her deeply. "Upstairs?"

She shook her head. "Too far away. Do you have anything?"

He muttered something about his wallet. The next moments passed in an erotic haze as he readied himself and lay down with her on the carpet. He bunched her dress around her waist and buried himself inside her.

Her gaze softened with desire. She wrapped her legs around his hips, and a moan tore at his throat. Jess, his classy city woman, had become a wildcat in his arms, as bold and uninhibited as the last time they'd made love. Already he felt her going up in flames.

And he loved it. He loved everything about her.

Heart beating like machine-gun fire, he took her hard and fast, plummeting them over the edge together. Laughing out loud with the thrill of their joining, he hugged her close, cherishing her, never wanting to let her go.

His happiness must have been contagious, for she began laughing, too. "I can't believe we did that—again! Although with more clothes on this time." Her body shook beneath his, her dark curls tangling on the carpet.

"We seem to have a thing for floors." He kissed the tip of her nose. "You've worked up quite a sheen, sweetheart. And your hair . . . your mother will think I took you jogging."

"Let's hope." She pushed a hand through her curls. "I'm a mess."

"You're beautiful."

She beamed. "I need a shower. And an iron. Do you have one?"

"Yeah, but I like the idea of a shower first." He eased himself out of her and discarded the protection in a wastebasket by his boot rack that he'd empty later. "Last one undressed washes my back."

She scrambled to her feet. "*Your* back?"

"Well, considering I'm only wearing my shirt and you're practically fully clothed . . ." He yanked open his shirt, popping the buttons. "I win." He chucked down the shirt.

Her mouth gaped. "Cheater!"

"Say that again and I'll toss you in the shower as you are." He hiked her over his shoulder and marched to the stairs.

141

CHAPTER TEN

"You wouldn't dare!" Jess pounded her fists on Adam's naked rump, laughter bouncing out of her chest. Her hair dangled perilously close to the steps. "Adam Wright, I mean it!"

"Did I cheat?" He bounded up the stairs two at a time.

"Yes! Watch out for my hair!"

He lugged her into the bathroom, providing an upside-down view of the sink and toilet. "Did I cheat?"

"Yes! Yes!"

Only one hand gripped her thighs now. The shower knob in the bathtub squeaked, and water pelted porcelain. Adam planted a leg in the tub. Hot drops streamed over her feet. She squealed.

"Did I cheat?"

"No! No!"

"Too late." He swung her beneath the shower spray. She screamed and spat out water. "Now you need a dryer as well as an iron," he said. He yanked shut the shower curtain and stepped toward her with a feral gleam in his eyes.

"You . . . you beast!" She glanced down at her dripping clothes.

"Tut-tut. Watch your mouth. I'll help you with those wet things." He yarded off her sweatshirt over her sodden head, then wrung out the sweatshirt at the far end of the tub and threw it onto the floor tiles. Slowly, meticulously, he repeated the process with her dress and bra. Hot water rushed over her.

Nude and drenched, she crossed her arms beneath her

142

breasts. "Now what?"

"Now we're even." His gaze drifted over her stiff nipples. "Maybe not." He cupped a breast in each hand and gently pinched her nipples. Sensual zings whipped to her core. "You have much nicer equipment than I do," he murmured.

The dizzying sensations rocketed through her, stealing her breath, heating her skin. "That depends on your point of view." She ran her hands over his chest and taut abdomen, then up his muscular forearms. "I'm rather partial to your equipment."

"My equipment is rather partial to you." He hugged her, his big erection grazing her belly. "Let's take it slow this time, sweetheart. Let's make love all afternoon." He kissed her lazily. "When does your mother expect you home?"

"Not until . . . closer to . . . supper," Jess whispered between his wet kisses.

"Good, plenty of time." He slipped the soap off the bathtub shelf and lathered it to suds in his hands. "Because I'm going to need every last second to tide me over the next three days."

"Three days?" she echoed as he soaped and fondled her breasts.

"Uh-huh. The Valemount contract. I need to check it out."

She didn't want him to go. "Can't you do that over the phone?"

His blue eyes glittered. "I prefer a hands-on approach." His hands glided down her thighs, seeking, finding. She moaned. He lathered her thoroughly, then passed her the fragrant soap. "My back, remember?"

They switched positions so he stood beneath the hot spray. She washed his back, then moved to his front, paying attention to every hard, firm inch of his outdoorsman's body. Coaxing him out of the shower, she toweled him dry without speaking, relaying her need for him through kisses, gazes, and caresses.

He returned the favor, hands sliding over her with the thick towel while she shivered with pleasure. Clasping her hand, he led her to his bedroom and cuddled her beneath the billowy quilt. They lay there, wrapped in each other's arms, touching and talking, kissing and embracing, until her heart overflowed with a deep sense of security and belonging she didn't dare examine for fear of breaking its spell.

Gradually, their movements grew urgent. His hands lingered on her breasts. He tugged one nipple into his mouth and slowly sucked.

She moaned, gripping his shoulders. He swept one hand to her other breast, rolling the rigid tip between his roughly padded fingertips. Pulsing currents rippled through her.

His head lifted, and a smile curved his lips. His gaze pierced her, clear and blue and intense in the natural afternoon light.

She shuddered. No holding back. That was Adam. That was how he made her feel.

As if she didn't need to hold back, either.

"Touch me," she said, voice raspy. She guided his hand between her thighs. "Please touch me now."

His fingers slipped into her folds, probing and insistent. She sighed and parted her legs.

"The way you respond to me . . ." He groaned.

"I can't help it." She'd never experienced such elation in a man's arms. She wanted to share everything with him.

She reached down to stroke him, but he stilled her fingers, whispering, "Later, honey. I'm in the mood for dessert."

He slid down her body, dragging the quilt with him, exposing her breasts and tummy to cool air. He kissed the inside of her thighs, cupping her mound with one hand. Then his mouth found her, tasting, exploring, offering the gift of sheer pleasure.

Yes.

The single word seared her mind. This was more than great sex, more than a man and woman sharing their bodies, sharing a bed. This was something she couldn't control, something she didn't want to control, something she wanted desperately to control.

His mouth moved on her again, his hands skipping up to caress her breasts. Coherent thought fled her mind.

Only Adam and ecstasy remained.

Nora smoothed Peter's favorite dress shirt hanging in the bedroom closet. The crisp cotton blend caressed her fingertips as Peter's subtle, masculine scent washed over her, filling her mind and soul with steadfast love and so many happy memories.

Tears pricked her eyes. Her heart ached with missing Peter. Yet, at the same time, a tranquil certainty soothed her. Her spirit would join with his again someday, as surely as it would join the spirits of all her lost loved ones. Her mother, her gruff, authoritative father, and Frank, her first husband.

When she departed this world, wouldn't it be wonderful if Frank and Peter were both waiting for her? Quite possibly, their spirits already battled over who should greet her first. They'd shatter heaven's peace with their ruckus.

A smile touched her lips, and she placed a hand on her chest, over her heart. When she was twenty-two, Frank and Peter had competed for her attention. Although she'd met Peter first, Frank had pursued her with undeniable passion, stealing her away from long hours of caring for her father and giving her a life of her own. He'd been so much larger than life, his magical love overwhelming. Frank, her big, strong lumberjack.

Thirty-seven years ago, Peter's unassuming ways couldn't compete with Frank's verve. If Peter had declared his love sooner, who knew, she might have married him instead of rugged Frank Morgan. However, then she wouldn't have experienced the vibrancy of Frank's love and then her darling Jessie-girl would have never been born.

She smoothed Peter's shirt one last time, then pushed open the wall of clothes. Bending, she withdrew a stepstool from the back of the closet and climbed onto it. She rummaged through the top shelf, finally locating the cardboard box behind old sweaters. She carried the box to her bed, then sat down.

At twenty-two, she'd chosen Frank, hurting Peter with her decision. He'd never married. Instead, he'd lived as a bachelor in a neighboring community. While she was married to Frank, Peter had never once approached her as anything other than an old friend. Yet, when Frank died, Peter's steady hand was there for her, guiding her. Only then had she realized he'd never stopped loving her.

It had been too soon, Frank dead but four weeks. However, grief-stricken and tortured over Jessie's sudden departure, she'd welcomed his support, further alienating her daughter.

Sighing, Nora opened the box and picked up the first of the framed photographs of Frank she'd packed away years ago out of respect for Peter. Frank's broad face smiled at her from the blackened, silver frame. He cradled a drowsy, four-year-old Jessie in his arms.

"Pumpkin's asleep." Even now, his deep voice whispered to her.

Tears welling, she touched the cool glass. Although in some ways Frank had failed as a husband—just like she'd failed as his wife by sublimating her needs to his instead of acting as a true life partner—he'd been the most wonderful father.

She glanced at her and Peter's fifth anniversary portrait on the nightstand, moved there from the wall this morning. Now, this picture of Frank and Jessie would sit beside it, where it should have rested all along.

Tears rolled down her face, hot and salty as they met her lips. She'd loved both her husbands, in such different ways.

In her life, she'd suffered sorrow. Yet, she'd also been blessed.

Now she would try her utmost to impart her life's lessons to her daughter.

Jess waved as Adam's pickup spat dirt down her mother's driveway. Once he'd turned left onto Old Village Road, heading back toward his place, she entered the house through the mudroom. He wouldn't return from his trip north until the evening of the Young Achievers tribute for Pete, allowing her three days to shake the uneasy feeling that their relationship was racing beyond the casual boundaries they'd established.

She removed her boots and hung up her purse. Stepping into the kitchen, she spied a note on the counter: *Went to Thelma and Vince's for supper. Thelma will drive me home later. Sorry I missed you. Mom.* A telephone number followed.

She winced. She'd promised her mother a simple supper for two, but hadn't returned in time to prepare it. *Nice daughter.*

Lifting the wall phone, she tapped out Thelma's number, then hung up before the first ring. If she called now, Mom might feel obligated to change her plans. *Leave it alone, Jess.*

The temptation to return to Adam's pulled at her, but she would not indulge it. Whether it was due to all her excess free time or something else, her feelings for Adam had developed way too fast. She needed to step on the brakes a little or she'd face a ton of heartache when she left.

She fixed herself a sandwich and ate in front of the TV. Two hours later, realizing she could barely recall the shows she'd watched, she carted her laptop upstairs and tried to work sitting on the bed. This morning, Sarah had emailed her the itinerary for her upcoming buying trip. Usually, reviewing her travel plans excited her, but tonight the itinerary blurred on the screen. *Adam. Mom. Adam. Mom.* Could she think of nothing else?

She shook her head. *Concentrate.*

The quiet of the room mocked her. The loud ticking of the

147

old alarm clock marked each passing minute, reminding her with disturbing finality that she was alone. Just like her mom would be when she left again.

Like she would be once she returned to Toronto.

Half the country separating her from the people she loved most.

Stomach churning, she paced the room. The base of her skull thudded. She liked being with Adam—liked it too much, obviously. When she'd fantasized about sleeping with him, she hadn't anticipated how deeply he would affect her. Or that she'd put their needs—her needs—before her mom's. Was she repeating her pattern of the last nine years?

She rubbed her neck. Her gaze drifted to a framed photograph on the dresser she hadn't seen in ages: her mom and dad in dressy clothes beside her and Danny wearing high school graduation caps and gowns. The ceremony had occurred in early June.

Six short weeks later, both Dad and Danny were gone.

She picked up the frame. "Dad, I miss you. Danny . . ." A lump formed in her throat. Biting her lower lip, she struggled to contain the waves of loss for her father and regret for Danny's young life stolen too soon. So much pain and heartache. And now she'd opened herself to more potential hurt by falling hard for Adam.

"Jessie? Are you all right?"

Jess whirled around. Her mom stood behind her. Heart hammering, she set the picture on the dresser. "Sorry about supper." She hugged her mom. "I know I promised—"

"Shh. You were with Adam. I can't hog all your time."

"But that's why I came home—to be with you."

"I know. But I like Adam. I'm happy you've found someone to hang out with while you're here." Her mother drew back, gaze drifting to the photo. "I didn't upset you by bringing that

148

old picture in here, did I?"

Jess shook her head. "You didn't upset me, Mom. I did. I—" How to explain her roller-coasting emotions? "Part of it is feeling I let you down, not returning when I said I would. Another part is just from being here alone. I don't think I've been alone in this house since Dad died." She smiled weakly. "It got to me."

"Oh, Jessie."

"Some comfort I am to you, huh? I can't even find any comfort for myself."

"If I'd known how to talk to you when you were a teenager—"

"No. Don't blame yourself. Dad raised me, too, yet you're always blaming yourself. The other day, you said you chose to pull away from me when I was little. But I think Dad let you pull away from me. Looking back, I realize he was selfish that way."

"But he loved you, Jessie."

"You love me, too. But Dad indulged me. You'd set the rules, and if I broke them he bailed me out. He let you set yourself up as the bad guy. So whenever I had a problem, of course I went to him. I never went to you."

"You can come to me now, dear," her mother murmured.

"Thank you." Jess tried to smile. "Do you agree with what I said about Dad?"

"You idolized him. I didn't want that to change. If I'd been more assertive—"

"I'll always cherish his memory, Mom, but it's not a bad thing to realize my father was human. He had his faults, and that's okay. God knows I have mine. And I don't want to lose the closeness you and I finally share."

"How could we lose it?"

"When I leave . . ." Her voice shook. She sank onto the edge of the bed. Her mother sat beside her, and they clasped hands.

149

Throat scratchy, Jess asked, "I realize this is spur of the moment, but how would you feel about moving to Toronto to live with me?"

"Live?" Her mother's eyes widened.

"I have a second bedroom, so you'd have your own space. I work long hours, so you'd have time for yourself, but we'd still have plenty of time to spend together. We'd go shopping, visit museums—"

Her mom smiled, but tears crept down her cheeks.

Jess pulled in a breath. "I've upset you. Mom, I'm sorry."

"Jessie, I'm not upset. Not really. I didn't expect anything quite like this. It's very sweet of you, dear, to offer your home to me."

"I want to take care of you, Mom. Aren't you tired of taking care of everyone else?"

"Yes, but moving away? Destiny Falls is my home. Sweetie, you have your life and career in Toronto, I have this house and my memories." She patted Jess's hand.

"Exactly. Your mother and father both died while living here. Then Dad, now Pete. How can you live with all the ghosts?"

"Because this is my home. I belong in this house, this town. I couldn't bear to leave." She spoke slowly, each word distinct, yet resounding with love and compassion. "I've failed you, Jessie. You loved Danny Galloway with the same passion I felt for your father—with a woman's passion. Yet, when Danny died, I treated you like a child, hiding my hurt for your father, not acknowledging that you'd lost your whole future. I drove you away," she stated baldly. "Then I started seeing Peter, and my world came alive again. I let him see the parts of me I should have shown to you."

"Mom, we've been through this. I'm okay with what happened now."

"Are you, dear? Or are you still pretending?"

"That's what you think?"

Her mom hesitated. "I know at times it's difficult for you to hear me talk about Peter. To hear me express my grief for him in a way I never did with your father. But I need to do it this way this time, Jessie. I know a lot about pretending, and I'm finished with it. I need to voice my hurt so I can work through it. And I promise that I'll listen to you, too. But I would never ask you to give up your lifestyle for me, and I don't feel you should ask it of me, either."

Jess heaved a sigh. "I know you're right, but—" She leapt off the bed. How much misery should her mom have to rehash three weeks following Pete's death? Their focus should be on *her,* not Jess. "I'm filled with nervous energy tonight, and I can't seem to contain it. I need to take a walk, maybe a drive." She grabbed her purse. "I don't want to leave you alone—"

"But you need to think. I understand." Her mom rose. "Should I wait up?"

Jess shook her head. As she headed to the bedroom door, her gaze lingered on the framed picture of the family she'd lost nine years ago. Her stomach knotted. "I'll be back soon."

Her hands trembled on the steering wheel, anxiety clawing her chest, causing her to forget the turns in the road, the trees and houses zipping past, even the direction she drove. She'd felt so close to Adam today, closer than she'd ever felt with a man. But instead of relishing the excitement of a new relationship, she experienced dread.

Something was missing from her life. Something incredibly important that Mom and Adam and Tim and Molly had all found. Despite her progress with Mom, despite her attempts to fit in while she was here, she was beginning to believe she just didn't belong.

She didn't belong in Destiny Falls, and she had a sinking

151

feeling that she didn't belong in Toronto, either.

Reaching the community baseball park, she parked the SUV and hopped out to walk. A barking tan-and-black blur raced up to her, pawing her sweatshirt and nearly knocking her to the ground.

"Sheba?" She blinked. "Why are you here?" She scanned the fields and dugouts in the gathering dusk. *No Adam.* She grabbed the dog's collar and commanded her to sit. A broken link dangled from Sheba's collar. "Did Adam forget you?"

The young shepherd panted, tongue lolling.

"No, of course not. He wouldn't drive to Valemount without you." She surveyed the fields again. A large yellow Labrador skulked around the bleachers. "Oh, I see. You escaped to meet a buddy. A boyfriend? What will your master think?" Damn it, she couldn't leave Sheba stranded at the ball park. "Come on, girl. I have a plan." Tugging the dog's collar, Jess led her to the truck. "Cooperate with me, and I won't tell Adam about your lover. Do we have a deal?"

"Sheba!" Jess struggled to hold the squirming dog while she wrestled with the yellow cord she'd found in the SUV. "I'll never fix your running line at this rate." The dog's long running leash dangled from a six-meter clothesline set up between two trees in the side yard bordering Adam's carport. As Adam had explained, the line allowed Sheba to explore the unfenced portion of yard while ensuring she didn't chase deer in the woods behind the house.

At least that was the idea.

The dog barked and slipped out of her grasp. "Sheba, no!" Jess grabbed her collar and instructed her to lie down. "Do you hear Adam on the sundeck? Once I'm gone, you can bark at him for all you're worth."

Sheba yapped as if Jess had commanded her to speak.

"Sheba, pipe down!" Adam's deep voice carried around the house. The dog barked again. Seconds later, Adam's footfalls crunched on the driveway.

"Thanks a lot, girl," Jess muttered. "What about our deal?"

Sheba barked and ran toward her master's voice, leaving Jess standing there holding the cord.

"Sheba! Hey, Sheeb, what happened, girl?"

Fingers shaking, Jess stepped out of the shadows. Bare-chested, Adam crouched in the driveway and examined the dog's collar. Jess gazed at him, longing panging in her chest.

"It's me, Adam," she murmured.

He looked up. "Jess? Hi."

"I found her at the ball park. She must have broken her lead."

He stood and dusted his hands on his green-and-white baseball pants. "It's been sticking. I meant to replace it when we returned from Valemount. I had a game tonight. I took her along, but I guess she didn't get enough playtime. Did you, girl?" He scratched the dog's muzzle.

"Guess not." Jess's smile wobbled.

"Why were you at the ball park? Looking for me?" Leaving Sheba, he strolled toward her. "I was about to take a hot tub. Want to join me? Bathing suits not required." Inches away from her, he stopped. His blue gaze searched her face. "What's wrong?"

"Nothing." Jess gripped the cord. He stood too close. She couldn't think. She couldn't breathe. She didn't know what to say.

"Bull." He cradled her chin, his voice tender despite the blunt words. He smelled of salty perspiration and dugout dust. Athletic. Masculine. *Wonderful.* "Tell me."

She shook her head. "I should go."

"No, you should tell me what's wrong."

153

She remained silent. He extracted the roll of cord from her hands.

"What's this for?"

"I wanted to fix Sheba's running line."

"Why didn't you put her in the fenced yard? Or knock so I could help?" He gazed over her head to the SUV. "And why did you park so far back from the house?" He looped an arm around her shoulders. "What's going on?"

Jess sighed. His chest felt so warm, so strong. She was falling in love with him, damn it, and she didn't know how to stop herself. "I need to talk."

Adam tucked Jess beneath his arm as they walked around the house to the sundeck, Sheba at their heels. He didn't breathe a word while she explained her idea for Nora to move to Toronto to live with her—and her mother's reaction. While he admired Jess's desire to take care of her mother, he identified more closely with Nora. Her love for Destiny Falls matched his own.

"This all happened tonight?" He placed the cord on the patio table, then sat with Jess on the cushioned love seat. She rested her head on his shoulder, her warm arm curling around his naked waist. Sheba flopped down at their feet.

As Jess nodded, her curls tickled his chin. The springtime scent of the soap he'd lathered her with this afternoon lifted off her soft skin.

He wanted to absorb her.

"And I don't know what to do about it," she replied, worry lacing her tone. "Mom says she wants to stay here, and I know I need to respect her decision, but I can't help thinking . . ."

"What?" With one hand, he kneaded the tension knotting the back of her neck.

"Oh, that feels wonderful. I know she's only fifty-nine now, but what about in ten years? In twenty? Except for the eight months before she married Pete, she's never really lived on her own. Now he's gone, I'm back east, she's over here." Her hand flip-flopped, her speech gaining speed.

"You'd like her to give a move more thought."

"Yes. I guess so. I mean, I didn't ask her to keep it in mind, but what sort of daughter would I be if I didn't advise her to look out for her own welfare?"

Adam rubbed her arm. "Sounds to me like she's already doing that."

Jess's head lifted. "What do you mean?"

"Well, you have to admit that moving to Toronto would create a drastic change in lifestyle for your mom. Take where you live, for instance." He hugged her. "Hey, I just realized, you've never told me about your place. Do you rent? Own? House or condo?"

"I have a spacious, two-bedroom apartment in a safe urban neighborhood," she replied in a tone that reminded him of a real estate agent listing of amenities.

"So you rent?"

She nodded.

"Any roommates? Pets?"

"No."

"Hmm."

"What?"

"Well, you said once before that you lease your car."

"Yes. So?"

"So, you rent your apartment, you lease your car. Don't take this the wrong way, honey, but is there anything you actually own?"

Her gaze narrowed. "What's that supposed to mean?"

He shrugged. "You're an executive. What's your salary?"

She quoted a substantial amount, and he whistled.

"There's a high cost of living in Toronto." A defensive note

155

entered her voice.

"Yeah, but you still have the resources to buy a car or put a down payment on a condo if you wanted." He massaged her neck again. "The way you live, sweetheart, it's like you're not rooted. You could pack up and move any day. Your mother, on the other hand, is rooted, here in Destiny Falls. Given the difference between your lifestyle and hers, is it any wonder she doesn't want to leave?"

Jess crossed her arms over her sweatshirt and leaned forward. His hand fell away from her neck.

"What you're saying makes sense on an intellectual level. Emotionally, though, I'm having trouble. I love my mom. I want to do what's right for her." She glanced back at him.

"Then quit your job and move back here. She'd love that." *So would I.*

Her gaze flinched. "That's impractical, Adam."

"Why?"

She shook her head so swiftly, her curls bounced. "How would I live? Where would I work? Pete's life insurance and their savings will provide enough for Mom if managed properly, but I want to help her out when and if she needs it, not become a financial burden on her." She sprang off the love seat and paced the deck. He must have hit one hell of a nerve.

"Jess, wait." He jumped up, too, bonking Sheba. The dog yelped and scampered beneath the table. "I know Destiny Falls is small, but you have a wealth of job experience that's bound to fit in somewhere."

"Where?" Her eyes sparked. "Waverly Foods?"

"If necessary. If being with your mom is what you want." He raked a hand through his hair. *Jess, a supermarket checkout clerk or gas station attendant? Get real.* "Look, I know how important your job is to you." Her gaze flew away, and his neck prickled. "Your job is important to you, isn't it?"

Her shoulders squared. "Of course it is."

He wasn't so sure. She made a great show of loving her life and career in Toronto, but she'd told him zip about that life in the weeks he'd known her. In fact, now that he thought about it, she rarely mentioned her work or Toronto friends unless he questioned her point-blank.

And he was tired of being shut out.

"Why haven't you said anything to me about this before?" he asked.

"About what?"

"Moving your mom east. Tonight's the first I've heard of it."

Red splashed her face. "I didn't think of it before."

"Interesting, then, that you'd think of it now." The evening air raised goose bumps on his chest. He grabbed his slo-pitch jersey from a patio chair and jerked it on. "You didn't want to see me tonight, did you? That's why you tried to fix Sheba's running line instead of knocking on the door or risking me seeing you near the fenced yard. That's why you parked so far back from the house. You didn't want me to know you were here." His gut twisted.

She gasped. "That's—"

"Not true?" He threw his hands up. "Come on."

She frowned. "Why are you upset?"

Because I'm falling in love with you, woman, and telling you will only scare you away. He clenched his jaw. "Because. This afternoon was fantastic, Jess. I felt on top of the world with you."

Her eyes grew big as saucers. "I felt that way, too."

She didn't sound very excited about it. "Then why do I get the feeling that this thing with your mother is a way to keep yourself distanced from this town and the people who love you here?"

Her eyebrows snapped together. "I asked my mother to move

157

to Toronto because I want to do what's best for her!"

"I don't think so. You asked Nora to move to Toronto because you want to do what you think is best for you."

"What? What would you know about it? She's not your mother. She's mine."

"I know what it's like to feel rooted to a town, to feel a commitment to a place." He strode to the hot tub and yanked the heavy thermal cover into position. He didn't want to relax anymore. He wanted to get to the bottom of what was happening between him and Jess. "That's something your mother and I have in common, and I don't need to be related to her in order to realize it."

"Low blow, Adam." Her voice quavered.

"Maybe, but it's the truth. I was born here, like you, like your mom. I wasn't as lucky, though—I didn't get to stay. I spent my childhood being dragged from one logging town to another, wondering if Pop would ever pull himself out of the damn bottle. By the grace of God and AA, he finally did. But it wasn't until I moved back here that I felt like I was coming home. Can't you understand what that means to a person?"

"No, I can't! Because I lost any connection I had to this place when Dad and Danny died. Can *you* understand what it means to have the people you love ripped from your life like that?" Her face crumpled.

"Damn it, baby. I shouldn't have said it like that. I'm sorry." He crushed her to his chest.

"No." Pushing away, she wiped her eyes on her sweatshirt sleeve. "You're not sorry you said it, only for how you said it. Am I right?"

His hands stiffened. If he spoke his mind, he could lose her. But he had to risk it, for both their sakes. He softened his tone. "I believe there's some truth in what I said. I could deny it, but that wouldn't be fair to either of us."

A bitter laugh popped out of her. "Then I guess that's that."

"Oh, no, you don't." With one step, he closed the space between them. "We can talk this through, Jess. We can work it out."

"Great. Now I'm an emotional screw-up, and you have all the answers. It must feel wonderful to be so on top of things."

"I don't think you're a screw-up. But I do think you're looking for an excuse to run as far away from me as you can." He touched her arm. "Does the thought of having a relationship with me frighten you that much? Is caring for me too much for you to handle?"

She brought up a hand. "Stop right there. We never said we were looking for anything heavy between us."

"But feelings aren't easily controlled, are they, Jess?" Clasping her hands, he drew her to him and kissed her. A squeak escaped her, but she didn't resist. She opened to him like she was drawing her last breath.

"I care for you, Jess Morgan," he whispered against her mouth. "I care for you a hell of a lot. And I think you feel the same."

"Adam, I—" Her voice broke. "My feelings for you are complicated."

"Damn it, baby, they don't have to be." She glanced away. He fanned his fingers along her jaw, urging her gaze to connect with his again. Those velvet doe eyes he loved. "I know you have a lot of bad memories associated with this town. I'd like to give you some good ones. Not so complicated."

Her shoulders lifted. "I don't belong here. Why force it?"

"Because forcing it might prove you wrong."

She shook her head. "I think we should cool things off for awhile."

A knife gouged his gut. "Oh, really?"

Gaze lowering, she whispered, "Yes."

He swore. She hadn't said she never wanted to see him again. Although, if he pushed, that might come next.

"Whatever you want." It went against every instinct he possessed, but he backed down. "You need the space, and I have to finish the Jamison bid when I return from Valemount. I'll still expect you at the Young Achievers meeting Thursday night, though. Not just your mom."

Expression numb, she nodded. Turned and bolted to the SUV.

Adam scraped his hands over his face, chest cramping. He had no choice—he had to let her go.

But if she thought he would give up on her, she'd quickly discover it wasn't so.

CHAPTER ELEVEN

"What a gorgeous day for a slo-pitch tournament! There's not a cloud in the sky." Molly paid for their coffees at the concession stand and passed a cup to Jess. "I'm glad you came."

"Me, too." Jess trailed her friend to the bleachers from where they would watch Tim's game. Aside from the Young Achievers tribute for Pete two days ago, during which she'd avoided Adam enough not to pique her mom's curiosity, she'd spent the week cooped in the house. Coordinating the buying trip had absorbed most of her time, including several conference calls with the junior colleague accompanying her. Although she risked bumping into Adam again at the two-diamond ball park, she couldn't bear wasting this sunny Saturday indoors.

"We haven't seen much of each other lately," Molly said as they climbed the steps, "and I'm sorry. What with the deal for the boutique and all—"

"You haven't neglected me, Molly. It's the other way around. Besides, now that your boss has decided to sell, this is an opportunity you can't pass up."

"Thanks for understanding."

"I wouldn't make much of a best friend if I didn't." Jess sat on the wooden bleachers beside the team scorebook Molly had placed there to save their places.

Her friend smiled. "Back in a minute." Moving to an upper row, Molly checked on her three-year-old daughter perched with two little girls and the team babysitter.

161

When she returned, Jess asked, "What happened with the bank yesterday? How does it look for a loan?"

Sitting, Molly opened the team scorebook on her lap. "Considering the monthly payments, it's not something I can handle on my own, but"—she crossed her fingers—"I might have found a business partner. Anne's a substitute teacher at the high school, and she's looking for something steady to get into. She thinks this might be it."

A strange sensation moved through Jess. "You'll set a great example for the Young Achievers group."

"Especially if we hire a couple of members for retail experience. I told Adam that if the sale goes through, I'll show the group my business plan and explain the purchasing process. Anne has taught business ed. dozens of times, so she'll be a lot of help."

"How long have you known her?" Sipping her bitter coffee, Jess wrinkled her nose.

"Since Christmas. Her husband plays with the Eddies, so we started talking at the team party last night. One thing led to another, and here I am—another step closer to achieving my goal."

Jess fidgeted with the hem of her shorts. How could Molly consider going into business with someone she'd only known a few months? What if this Anne found a permanent teaching job in the future? What would Molly do then?

Quit overthinking the negatives. Molly knows what she's doing.

Pushing a hand beneath her hair, she scratched her neck. "Do you feel you can work well with her?"

"Sure. Not as well as I could you, of course, but since that isn't an option . . ." Eyes twinkling, Molly elbowed her. "I need a partner, Jess. Buying The Clothes Horse is my dream, but I don't want to sacrifice my family life to do it. This is the perfect solution."

Nodding, Jess looked at the softball diamond, where the Educators and the opposing team assumed positions. Not a green-and-white Mountaineers' uniform in sight.

Her gaze drifted to the second diamond. Red-and-gray in the first dugout and . . . *yes!* . . . green-and-white in the next.

She picked out Adam right away. His broad shoulders strained his team jersey as he warmed up near the dugout. Images of their passionate lovemaking swamped her mind and her breasts tingled.

Her face heated. What was she now, a sex fiend?

She returned her attention to Molly, busily entering the batting lineups in the scorebook. Five-year-old Sean scampered up from the Eddies' dugout, excitement brightening his freckled face.

"Mommy! I get to be water boy!"

"Way to go, champ!" Molly hugged her son over the scorebook. With a grin to Jess, she murmured, "It's a coveted position."

"Hey, guy, high five!" Jess slapped Sean's little raised hand.

"I can't sit with you now, Auntie Jess."

"I hope not! Whoever heard of somebody as important as a water boy sitting in the bleachers with two cranky old ladies?"

Sean giggled and Molly said, "Auntie Jess is right, champ. Go hang out with your dad and the other big, strong men. Have fun! We'll see you at lunch."

"Yay!" Sean clambered down the bleachers and hopped onto the earth, raising dust.

Jess laughed. "He keeps you running."

"I love it. Kids are a blessing, Jess."

"A blessing I'm not planning on dealing with anytime soon."

"You say that now, but you're great with my two. All it takes is the right guy."

The elusive Mr. Right.

163

Or Wright.

Jess wiped her hands on her shorts, thankful Molly had resumed her scorebook duties. The bleachers slowly filled with spectators as the Eddies went up to bat. She glanced at the second diamond, where Adam now played shortstop for the Mountaineers. Just as many fans occupied his stands.

Her spine stiffened. *Enough.*

She swung her gaze to Tim's game. He stood at the plate, bat raised.

Thwack! The ball whizzed to right field, earning Tim a two-base hit.

Molly jumped up, hollering, "Yay, hubby!"

Jess cheered, too. However, as the game progressed, she couldn't stop peeking at Adam's diamond. He wore his ball cap shoved up on his forehead. Although she couldn't distinguish his features, she easily imagined him zeroing in on every swing of the opposing player's bat.

"You're supposed to be watching this game, Jess," Molly chided.

"I am." She clapped, shouting, "Go, Eddies, go!"

"We struck out." Molly smirked.

"Oh. Yeah, I knew that. Sorry." She watched Molly scribble in the scorebook, filling in the miniature boxes that tabulated each run and play. "How do you know what to do?"

"It's easy. I'll teach you, if you can tear yourself away from Adam's game."

"I'm not watching Adam." Jess sipped the bad coffee.

"I didn't say you were. I said you were watching his game." Molly put down her pencil. "What's up with you two, anyway? I called Adam this morning, but when I mentioned your name he changed the subject. Have you two made a pact not to talk to me about each other?"

"No." Jess shifted on the uncomfortable wooden seat. "Things are at a stalemate between us, that's all."

"Aw. I thought you'd hit it off."

"That's the problem." She pressed her lips together. "We hit it off too well."

Molly's eyes popped. "You slept with him?" she whispered.

Jess nodded.

"You call that a stalemate?"

Thumping her coffee cup onto the bleachers beside her, Jess waved a hand. "Calm down," she whispered. "It was a mistake. There's no point in Adam and me becoming more deeply involved with each other, and we both know it."

"Wow. Sounds serious."

"I wish it weren't. Then maybe I could handle it."

Molly studied her. "What are you saying?" she whispered. "Are you in love with my cousin?"

Jess's mouth dried. *Oh, God, am I?*

A ruckus erupted in the neighboring bleachers. Molly pointed, shouting, "Someone's hit a home run! Look, it's Adam! His team just went up to bat and already he's hit a homer. Way to go, Adam!"

Jess's pulse quickened as Adam raced for home plate while the opposing team's center fielder scrambled over the fence for the ball.

"The Wright stuff! The Wright stuff!" the Mountaineers chanted, each team member thumping Adam on the back as he trotted into the dugout.

Pride swelled in her chest.

Go away!

"They sure make a big deal out of a home run," she muttered, tearing her gaze from him.

"The Mountaineers have won the first tournament of the season every year for the past five years. It *is* a big deal. And it drives the Eddies crazy."

"Let's give them a run for the money, then." Standing, Jess cheered on the Eddies. Who cared if she looked like an idiot—or if Adam saw her? She'd come to the ball park to have a good time with Molly, and that's what she planned to do.

Three o'clock came and went without Adam and his kick-butt Mountaineers getting a chance to slaughter Tim's slacker Eddies. The roster in the outdoor beer gardens indicated the two rival teams might not compete for the duration of the tournament, a result of games won versus games lost and a bye allotted to the Eddies Sunday morning. Lucky stiffs.

After his team won their last game of the day, Adam paraded into the packed beer gardens with the excited guys. As he reached their table, a glimpse of long, curly dark hair and beautiful toffee eyes slapped him in the face.

Jess? He narrowed his gaze at the Eddies' table, several meters away. There she sat, wearing a T-shirt and shorts, laughing along with the rest of the wives and guys at Tim's corny jokes.

What the hell?

"Adam, want a beer?" A teammate held out an overflowing plastic cup.

"Thanks, Bruce. In a minute." He plopped his glove onto a chair. "Save me a seat."

"Yup."

Dodging partiers, Adam bee-lined toward Tim's table. At the halfway point, Jess glanced up. Their gazes met. Eyes widening, she spoke to Molly, then hightailed it to the makeshift bar.

You can run, honey!

Adam caught up to her as she grabbed a beer cup from the bartender and gulped a mouthful of foam.

"Well, well," he said. "I'm surprised to see you here."

She faced him, color high on her cheeks. "Molly invited me."

"Uh-huh. How many games have you watched?"

166

"Um, all of Tim's."

The first of which had begun at ten fricking A.M. He squinted. "Having fun?"

She nodded. "You?"

"Peachy." He poured on the sarcasm. Hell, he'd counseled himself to be patient, and look where that had got him—Jess ignoring him at the Young Achievers meeting whenever Nora wasn't within listening distance, and now she'd spent all day at the ball park and hadn't even attempted a polite hello.

Did he have fungus growing out of his ears?

"I thought you'd feel out of place at a community function like this," he bit out.

Her mouth turned downward. "What?"

"You heard me. On Monday you said you don't belong in our little backwoods town." He jerked a thumb toward the Eddies' table. "But it looks to me like you fit right in."

She shifted her feet, sipping her beer. A foam moustache decorated her upper lip. What he'd give to haul her into his arms and kiss the foam and her stubbornness away.

"You can't give it up, can you?" he muttered. "You've decided you're an outsider in your hometown, and nothing anyone says will change that."

Her gaze flicked to a group of ball players loitering near the paper-covered, plywood-and-sawhorse bar. "Don't do this here," she whispered, setting down her cup.

He lowered his voice. "Then where would you suggest I do it? If I asked you to go somewhere and talk, I'm betting you'd turn me down."

She stared at the ground.

"I thought so." He lifted his ball cap and pushed a hand through his sweaty hair. Why suffer this aggravation? He should turn around and walk away. Instead, like a sucker for punishment, he asked, "Then how about going to the dinner-dance with me tonight? You'd meet the team, the people I work with. Good times, good food, good conversation."

She looked up. "I would if we—"

"Didn't feel something for each other? Then you'd go? Damn it, Jess," he whispered. "Caring for me isn't a crime. Why do you treat it like one?"

"Because I don't want to get hurt."

The hot afternoon sun beat down on his head. "Who's going to hurt you, honey? I wouldn't, I swear. The only person who might hurt you is you, because you're too stubborn to admit that this is where you belong. With your mother, with Molly." *With me.*

He touched her wrist. She shrank away.

"You won't even listen, so why do I bother?"

Because you love her, Wright. The truth slammed into him. He loved stubborn, fixated-on-a-dead-guy Jess Morgan.

Damn it, couldn't he have fallen for a local girl who wanted nothing more than to build a life here? After Crysta, you'd think he could have bought himself some brains, but apparently his were a rental.

"Hey, Adam! Buddy!" A drunk pitcher from another team staggered toward them. "Lemme buy you a beer!" The guy plunked two tickets onto the bar.

"No, thanks." *Look at me, Jess. Just look at me.*

"Aw, c'mon!" The pitcher whacked his back. "Be a sport, Mr. Homer-Run Simpson!" The fellow eyed Jess. "Hey, Wrightsi, you gonna introduce me to yer little hottie?"

Adam's jaw clenched. "Not a chance. And if you talk about her that way again, I'll deck you. The lady's mine."

Mission accomplished: Jess looked straight at him. Unfortunately, just when he sounded like a cave man.

She mumbled, "I told Molly I'd check on her kids." She arrowed for the swing sets as if he'd set fire to her shorts.

168

The pitcher guffawed. "There she goes! Hey, dude, I don't wanna rain on your parade, but it looks like she ain't too thrilled about being yer woman, know what I mean?"

"Yeah, I know." Scowling, Adam stepped up to the bar. "You can buy me that beer now, if you still want. I need it."

Jess stood beside the SUV in the community hall parking lot. If she entered the hall, she risked seeing Adam, unless he'd left the tournament dinner-dance early. If she didn't drop in, she might upset Molly, who'd insisted on holding her a chair at the Eddies' table.

Neither option appealed—especially following her encounter with Adam in the beer gardens this afternoon. If he'd wanted to get a rise out of her with that outdated comment about her being his lady, he'd succeeded big time. Jess Morgan didn't want to be anybody's "lady."

Yes, I do.

No, she didn't.

The night breeze ruffled her hair, carrying the scents and noises from the hall. A layer of cigarette smoke hung above the crowd milling at the open double doors, and loud dance music spilled into the parking lot.

Make a choice, Jess.

Stomach tight, she stepped forward. If she saw Adam, would he think she'd come to the dance to make up with him? She couldn't lead him on. She'd done too much of that already.

The crowd at the doors parted, and she stepped back again, heart pounding. *Please don't let it be Adam.* But it was only the guy from this afternoon. Sobered up, it appeared.

The fellow must have recognized her, because he gave a cheery wave before lighting a cigarette for the woman with him. The woman kissed his cheek, and they strolled off across the parking lot. Arms wrapped around each other. Obviously in love.

Jess squeezed shut her eyes, rooted to the earth. She wanted what that couple shared. She wanted it with Adam.

But fear had a stranglehold on her.

And love couldn't keep her safe.

Following his last game on Sunday, Adam picked wildflowers from a field behind the park, then drove to the Olson farmhouse and rapped on the door. Jess hadn't returned to watch the tournament finals today, not that he'd expected her to. The woman gave new meaning to the definition of stubborn.

Stubborn, hell. Try intractable. Stuck in an emotional rut so deep, she'd need an extension ladder to climb out. None of which had prevented him from falling in love with her, idiot that he was.

He raised his hand to knock again, but the door swung inward before his knuckles met the wood.

Jess stepped into the doorway. He thrust the bouquet at her. "We won!"

"What?" She blinked, not taking the flowers, evidently not making the connection between his sweat-soaked slo-pitch uniform and his presence on her front porch.

"We won! The Mountaineers won the first league tournament of the season for the sixth year running! Tim's team came on strong in the semi-finals but didn't stand a chance against tradition." He tipped his ball cap. "And, thanks to you, honey, I snagged MVP."

"Most Valuable Player? Thanks to me?" Her hand skimmed along her jean-clad hip.

"Yep." He leaned against the doorframe. Her elegant perfume drifted off her, teasing his nostrils. "I put all my frustration about what has and hasn't been happening between us lately into smacking that little white ball. Hit four home runs in the final game."

"Is that good?"

He laughed. "It's fantastic!" Behind Jess, he glimpsed Nora exiting the kitchen. Moving back, he greeted her. "Good afternoon, Mrs. Olson."

"Adam!" She joined her daughter. "What a nice surprise. We didn't expect to see you today."

Didn't he know it? "Then my intention to surprise the two of you has succeeded." He offered Nora the wildflowers. "I was telling Jess that I won Most Valuable Player, thanks to her inspiration. Could you take these for her, please? She's in shock."

"Flowers! How sweet!" Nora accepted the bouquet. "Aren't these lovely, Jessie?"

Adam dipped his head to kiss Jess before she could answer yea or nay. Her lips softened, then tensed beneath his.

"Oh, my," her mother murmured in an amused tone.

Adam broke the kiss, and Jess glared at him. Turning to Nora, he said, "To celebrate, I'd like to take you both to dinner at the Wander-Inn. A few other people are coming, including Tim and Molly. The restaurant closes early on Sundays, so we'd better hurry."

Jess's gaze shot daggers at him. "We—"

"Why, thank you, Adam." Her mother beamed. "I haven't been to the Wander-Inn—oh, I can't remember how long." She smoothed her cords with one hand. "Should I change?"

Adam laughed. "Look at me. If you can tolerate my *eau de sweat sock* aftershave, that's half the battle. Tonight is strictly casual. No fancy clothes permitted."

Nora's eyes crinkled. "Then I'd love to go out to dinner with you and Jessie. Please come in while I put these in water."

She strolled to the kitchen with the flowers, leaving Adam

and Jess alone, which didn't seem to ingratiate Jess with him any.

Crossing her arms, she whispered, "Why did you do that?"

"Ask your mom to dinner?" He kept his tone light. "Number one, because I like her. Number two, because she deserves a night out. Besides"—he touched the top button of her blouse—"I figured it was the only way I could get anywhere near you tonight, considering your rather hardheaded behavior in the beer gardens yesterday."

"Hardheaded?" Her eyes flashed. That was okay. Her anger promised more than her indifference ever could. "You're using my mother to get to me, Adam."

"You're using her to keep me at a distance, Jess. You tell me, what's the difference?"

"There's no comparison!"

"Know what? I agree."

"But you said—"

"I changed my mind. Or is that only a woman's prerogative?"

Aggravation floated off her in waves. She stepped back, and he murmured, "I enjoy your mother's company, Jess. I don't care what you believe. I'll gladly take her to dinner tonight, whether you decide to come or not."

Her gaze threw indignant sparks at him. He glanced toward the kitchen, where Nora was selecting a vase from the buffet.

He looked at Jess again. "Now, are you going to make a scene about it when she returns or will you be a good girl and play nicely?"

She huffed out a breath. "Why do you insist on baiting me?"

"Why did you come to the community hall last night?" Her eyebrows hoisted, and he grinned. "Yep, I heard all about it. The woman from Toronto, lurking in the parking lot. When you drove off like the hounds of hell were chasing you, someone thought you'd stolen my SUV. It was quite funny when they told me. Not to mention illuminating."

He grazed her collar with two fingers, and she bumped his hand away.

"It's okay, Jess, you showing up, even if you couldn't bring yourself to stay. At least I know now that you still want me. I also know you don't want to want me. In fact, it's probably safe to assume you don't know what the hell you want anymore."

"Adam, I swear—"

"Want to know how I know?" He maintained his quiet tone. "Because I feel the same way. After Crysta, I vowed never to date another woman who didn't feel the same connection to this town as I do. But then you came along—"

"Don't give me that," she half-whispered. "You knew from the start that my stay here was temporary. A visit. Nothing more."

"You think that mattered to me a few weeks ago? Then I got to know you, and I began fooling myself. I thought we could date casually for a few weeks. Hell, I thought I could take you into my bed and be done with it. What a joke. Hooking up? For you and me, honey, it's impossible."

Her mouth thinned. "I don't want to hear this, Adam. We have no future. This is too fast. It isn't real. And you know it."

He shook his head. "What I know is that you've built a cage for yourself in Toronto, and you're terrified to break free. You have your reasons, but you're soaking them with all you've got. You're feeding your own damn fear." He glanced toward the kitchen. They had maybe a minute before her mother returned. Sixty short, precious seconds. "The flowers are in a vase on the table now, sweet cheeks. What will it be?"

She glanced over her shoulder then looked at him again. "I'll come with you and Mom tonight on one condition," she whispered. "Mom doesn't know that we've slept together or that we've broken up. That's how I want it to stay. Tomorrow's a month since Pete died, and I don't want her worrying about me when she has her stuff to deal with. As far she's concerned, you and I are dating casually while I'm here." She had the grace to blush. He guessed it was because she'd used the same ridiculous wording as he had a moment ago. "And never, I repeat, *never,* pull a stunt like this on me again."

He smiled. "That's two conditions, Jess. I'm afraid I can only agree to one."

CHAPTER TWELVE

Nora assembled the popcorn maker on the kitchen counter while Jessie and Adam quarreled in the living room over which of two rented DVDs to watch. When she'd asked Adam to dinner tonight to repay him for Sunday at the Wander-Inn, she hadn't imagined he'd bring along his old DVD player and then give it to her. Evidently, he'd upgraded.

She and Peter had never purchased a VCR, much less a DVD player. They'd preferred to drive to Kamloops once or twice a month and enjoy carefully selected movies in a darkened theater, a nostalgic reminder of their long drives in the classic car in the months before Frank had moved to town. However, with Peter gone, she appreciated Adam's gift.

Tears burned her eyes, still a frequent occurrence whenever she thought of her husband. The first-month anniversary of his death yesterday had been hard, but Jessie had been there for her. They'd hiked in the hills behind the pasture, Nora wearing Peter's sheepskin coat, his fading scent comforting her while she'd walked.

She'd felt so close to his spirit, and to her daughter. If only she could help Jessie in return. Yet, despite her efforts to encourage her daughter to open up these last few days, Jessie kept insisting nothing was wrong.

Sighing, Nora poured the kernels into the hot-air popper and turned it on. Behind her, Jessie and Adam's voices grew quiet.

Seconds later, Adam strolled into the kitchen, shadows sobering his gaze.

"I came to help," he announced too cheerily. He glanced at the popper. "What, no microwave?"

"It broke a month before Peter died. I love cooking from scratch, so I didn't get around to replacing it. I suppose I should." The kernels began their merry dance, pinging against the plastic cover.

She sliced a pat of butter. Adam passed her the small saucepan she'd set on the counter. She tumbled the pat into it and placed the pot on the stove.

"Glad to see we're having butter," he said. "Salt, too?"

She nodded. Why was he talking to her instead of remaining in the living room with Jessie? She didn't need help melting butter! Did they think her so burdened with grief that she didn't realize they felt something for each other and that those feelings were the source of their arguing?

"Which movie are we watching first?" she asked.

"*Titanic,* if it's okay with you. It's a chick flick and an action movie."

It was also a long film. Good. She'd feign tiredness partway through, allowing Jessie and Adam time alone.

"Oh, I love *Titanic.* It's a classic."

Adam tapped the counter. "Will the ending bother you? Jess wanted to ask, but I said I would, seeing as how I rented it."

"You mean because the hero dies? No." If she remembered correctly, the heroine in the film derived so much joy from loving the hero that she lived a long, adventurous life despite losing him. In a way, the situation mirrored Jessie's experience with Danny Galloway, except Jessie hadn't truly moved on. She pretended she had, but Nora knew better.

"Love is a precious gift, Adam," she murmured. "I treasure every reminder of Peter."

"You have the right attitude." A pensive light entered his gaze, and Nora knew he was thinking about her daughter.

"He's driving me crazy!" Jess complained to Molly Wednesday morning. They sat at a table for two in the back of crowded Clara's Café, catching up during Molly's coffee break.

"How do you expect him to react?" Glancing around, Molly lowered her voice. "From what you've told me, you slept with him—not once, but a few times—and then you cut him off. Don't get me wrong. I'm not saying Adam only wants you for sex. It might be easier for you if he did." A wry smile curved her mouth. "He's a guy, Jess. If he wants you, he'll pursue you. That's what guys do."

"Can't he take a hint? I've given him enough, but he's relentless." Last night, when he'd nestled beside her on the couch, his large hand resting possessively on her thigh as she'd tried to concentrate on *Titanic,* her ire had been roused to no end. She'd been roused *and* aroused, while her mother had sat in the swivel rocker, hopefully oblivious.

Molly pulled off a chunk of her banana-nut muffin. "This 'dating casually' routine you're faking for your mom works in his favor, you know."

"He's using her." Jess bit into her massive cinnamon bun— her first taste of the Clara's staple in nine years. She'd looked forward to the treat for days. However, the warm, raisin-studded roll didn't inspire the sigh of contentment she recalled.

Molly gazed at her. "He's not using her any more than you are. The poor guy wants some time with you. He's getting it any way he can."

"Well, last night he got it in spades." Jess licked sticky cinnamon syrup off her finger. "Mom went to bed halfway through the movie, but did he leave? No, he insisted on staying until it ended."

"Maybe he thought leaving too quickly would alert her that you're fighting."

"That's what he said." It was her idea that they perpetuate the charade, so she shouldn't grumble. However, she hadn't anticipated her mom inviting him to dinner last night—or that he'd accept.

How was she supposed to fight her feelings for him when he kept invading her life?

"Aw, sweetie, you didn't see this coming, did you? If it helps you feel better, I don't think Adam did, either."

"See what coming?" She frowned.

Molly nibbled another chunk of muffin. "I think he's in love."

Her heart soared. *No, no, no!*

"Has he told you that?"

"He doesn't have to. He's my best friend, next to you. I know him inside out. If he's not in love with you, I'm a monkey's aunt."

Jess's throat tightened. She swallowed. "Maybe it's not love. Maybe it's infatuation or . . . or lust."

Molly flicked a hand. "I don't think so. Look at this." She retrieved an envelope of pictures from her purse and riffled through them. "Remember that shot I took of you and Adam the night of my anniversary? I printed them up. I think Adam was halfway in love with you then."

Jess snorted.

Molly slid the picture across the table. "See how he's looking at you? How about the way you're looking at him? The beginnings of love, my friend, not lust. I'm an old married woman, remember? I know of what I speak."

Jess picked up the picture and glanced at it. Adam sat with his arm wrapped around her shoulders. A nervous yet excited expression brightened her features.

Later, for a brief time at the drive-in, she'd relaxed easily enough.

Her gaze misted. The picture blurred. "I don't believe in love at first sight." She held the picture out to Molly.

"Yeah, right. What about Danny?"

"He lived here a year before I even noticed him." Granted, she'd only been fifteen.

"Interesting. So you're saying you love Adam in a way you never loved Danny?"

"Don't be ridiculous." Sometimes Molly's tenacity was as irritating as Adam's.

"Sounds to me like that's what you're saying, Jess."

Jess flapped the picture. "My arm's getting sore, Moll. Are you taking this back or not?"

"Keep it. I saved them to my computer."

"I don't want it."

"Don't be silly."

"I mean it. I don't want it." Jess tossed the picture onto the table.

Molly blew out a breath. She tucked the photo into the envelope and shoved the packet into her purse. She drained her coffee, then stood. "Thanks for the break, but I need to get back." She tossed five dollars onto the table.

"Already?"

"Sorry, hon, twenty minutes is my max. Tomorrow again?"

"I'd like that."

Molly left and Jess gazed at her unfinished cinnamon bun. Mom wanted some items from the drugstore. She should go.

She fetched her purse from the floor. As she sat up again, her pulse clattered. Adam stood at the counter, chatting to the waitress pouring him a cup of take-out coffee. He paid for the cup, turned, and then he saw her.

Her heart raced. *Please leave. Just turn around again and go.*

179

But Adam Wright didn't follow telepathic orders any better than he did spoken ones. He said something to the waitress, then headed to Jess's table, looking sexier than he had a right to in the same faded jeans and ivory shirt she remembered from the night he'd picked her up at the airport.

Her knees weakened as she gazed at him, memorizing each line of his body, every curve and angle of his handsome face.

He planted a hand on a chair back. "Mind if I sit down?"

"Could I stop you?"

"Not unless you want to leave without finishing your coffee. Not to mention that monster cinnamon bun." His scarred eyebrow quirked. "Reminds me of your sundaes."

Her grip tightened on her purse. She wouldn't let him chase her out of here.

Placing her bag by her feet again, she replied, "Go ahead, sit."

He draped himself in the chair Molly had vacated. "Thanks. I ordered a sandwich."

Him and his appetite. "What brings you downtown?"

He lifted his coffee cup. "Meeting at the Forest Service. They make lousy coffee. Tastes like sawdust." He paused. "How are you doing?"

As exasperated as she'd felt last night, considering his DVD shenanigans. She ran a finger up and down her coffee cup. *He's not funny. He's not charming. He's not.*

"I'm sure you can tell me, Adam. We've spent enough time together lately."

"Well, then, I say you're a bit testy." He sipped his coffee. "Mmm. Much better than at the Forest Circus."

She narrowed her gaze. "Did Molly put you up to this?"

"I just said I have a meeting." He glanced at her. "Do you wish she had?"

"No." *Maybe. Stop it!* "Why would I?"

"Because then you could get all ticked off about the set-up instead of admitting you're thrilled to see me." His eyebrows rose. "We're good for each other, Jess. You just refuse to believe it."

Her spine stiffened. "That's because I decide what I think, Adam. Not you."

"Then tell me what you think, Jess."

"Persistence is outdated."

"So is the fear of intimacy."

"I don't have a fear of intimacy."

"Denial. A bad sign."

"I don't have a fear of intimacy," she repeated through clenched teeth. Her stomach felt like a rock.

"Actually, you have a point." Voice low, he murmured, "You're quite good at physical intimacy. It's the emotional kind I'm thinking of."

Her face stung as if she'd been slapped. She leaned over the tiny table. "Look, Adam, I thought I told you no more stunts. It's not enough that you tricked Mom and me into going to the Wander-Inn Sunday. No, you had to weasel an invitation to dinner last night, and now you insist on sharing my table. Did you ever consider that maybe you're not welcome?"

A muscle flexed in his jaw. He plunked down his cup. "In the first place, I didn't weasel an invitation to supper, Jess. Your mother asked, and I accepted. That's it."

"You didn't have to accept," she whispered.

"Yes, I did." The waitress delivered his sandwich. He chomped into it, chewed, and swallowed. "You won't be around much longer, and Molly's busy with her job and family. Someone's got to keep tabs on your mother when you leave. I'm available."

"Why you?"

"Because I like her, as I've said before. Because I was friends

181

with Pete. Because her nearest family is in Kamloops—the sister I met at his funeral. Because she needs someone she can rely on here. Those reasons enough for you?"

She pushed aside her plate. "She has a lot of friends."

"Now she'll have me, too." He bit into his sandwich. "Relax, Jess. Eat your cinnamon bun. Hell, I thought I was doing you a favor, volunteering to keep an eye on your mom."

She pulled in a breath, head throbbing.

"What now?" He drank from his cup.

She fixed her gaze at a point beneath his chin. "I need to make sure your motives for paying all this attention to my mother are honorable, and not a ploy to get me back."

He sputtered on his coffee. "Get you back? I haven't had you, Jess. At least not in the way I'd like. Could we please try to have a civil conversation? All this tension is giving me indigestion."

She sighed. "I know what you mean."

"Good. Then eat." Tone softening, he slid her plate toward her. "And tell me how the car's running."

Last night, while her mom was making popcorn, she'd told him the car had come out of the shop. She'd asked about returning his SUV, but he hadn't wanted to discuss the issue while her mother was within earshot.

She replied, "The car's running great. Thank you. Getting the new transmission was the right thing to do." She picked at a raisin on her cinnamon bun. "Adam, I wish you'd let me give you back your truck. Now that Mom has the car again—"

"Jess, how many times do we have to go through this? You're keeping the SUV until you leave. It's what works best for you and Nora, and I don't mind at all."

"But now that you and I aren't—"

"Your mother thinks we are. Or have you told her that we're not 'dating casually' anymore?"

"No." She stared at the tabletop.

"Then it makes sense for you to keep the truck. If I take it back now, she'll know something's up." He devoured the remainder of his sandwich. "Besides, what about her idea to visit your aunt?"

Jess held in a breath. "She's leaving Friday."

"You going along?"

"No. Molly's hosting an end-of-season dinner for the high school boys' basketball team. I already promised to help."

His gaze narrowed. "How did you intend to get around this weekend, with your mom taking the car to Kamloops and the SUV sitting idle at my place? Molly?"

She shrugged. "The taxi."

"Right." He slapped sandwich crumbs off his hands. "I can see right through you, Jess Morgan, and I'm not sure I like what I see. You're not indebted to me for the loan of the truck, so I'd appreciate it if you'd stop thinking I have ulterior motives in mind. It's not like I plan on dragging you to bed in exchange for using a damned SUV."

Her face baked. The idea didn't sound half bad.

He shoved back his chair. "I may be persistent to the point of being obnoxious now and then, but I'm not a begging man. Remember that when you're holed up in your ritzy apartment with nothing but an electric blanket to keep you warm."

He stormed out.

"Jess, I'm sorry. That doesn't sound like fun." Molly stirred the sizzling sloppy joe mixture on her stove. "My cousin can be a pain sometimes." She offered a commiserating smile.

"I need space. He has a tough time accepting that." Jess rinsed the lettuce head beneath the tap, the water cool on her hands. Tim's voice filtered through the closed pocket door leading to the living room. Muffled teenaged laughter arose at

183

something he said, then another male teen voice bounced back a reply. Ah, to feel that vibrant and free. "I haven't heard from him since."

"Does that bother you?"

Yes. "Why should it? I told him to stop pulling stunts, and he has." She turned off the tap and glanced at her friend. "Wait. He's not coming here, is he?"

"No. I planned to ask him before I knew how bad things were between you. But he was too busy, so I didn't bother. I think he had a long day planned in the bush."

Or he was avoiding her, Jess thought. Some definite irony happening there. She'd wanted it like this—Adam at a safe distance, as if they'd never made love. However, she hadn't counted on feeling so lost, so alienated and ignored.

Molly's three-year-old daughter toddled into the kitchen from the rear hallway. "Mommy. Wanna help."

Molly smiled at Kaitlin. "Can you carry a big bag of taco chips, sweetie?" She secured the medium-sized bag in Kaitlin's hands and walked her to the pocket door. "Give the bag to Daddy, and he'll let you have some chips. But you have to share with the players, okay?"

" 'Kay!"

As Molly slid open the door, a jumble of teenage voices poured from the living room. Molly saw her daughter through, then closed the door again and walked back to Jess.

"Sorry. Kaitlin's in a 'big girl' stage."

"That's okay. She's darling." Jess's heart squeezed. "I'm sorry I didn't fly out to see her when she was born."

"If I remember, you weren't even in the country."

Story of her life. "I know. I can't believe she's three, and I've just met her."

"Time flies."

"Yes, it does." And she'd missed out on so much. Dreams

184

that had once felt as vital to her as breathing. Had she stayed in Destiny Falls, she'd probably have two or three of her own sweet babies by now.

With whom?

Biting her lip, she blotted the lettuce with a paper towel. "Does Tim know Adam and I aren't getting along?" She tore bite-sized pieces into a wooden salad bowl.

"Well, he's not blind. But I didn't tell him." Molly stirred the sloppy joe mixture. The hearty scent filled the kitchen.

"I'm more concerned with what Mom might think."

"Didn't she go to Kamloops?"

"Yes. At noon. You know, I thought I wanted her in the dark about my problems with Adam. But now . . ."

"It doesn't feel right?"

She nodded. "We're starting to relate to each other like women, not just mother and daughter."

"Like you always wanted."

"It's still new to me, but once she returns I want to try talking to her about him. Not sure how successful I'll be."

"She might surprise you, Jess. She'll probably have great insight."

"Maybe." Her lungs pinched. How had her situation with Adam grown so complicated? Why did he have to be such a . . . such a man?

"It's just that he wants a whole lot more than I'm prepared to give." Jess shredded the lettuce head.

"I assume we're talking about Adam again." Molly stepped to the counter, opened a bag of buns, and began buttering.

"It feels like we're in some sort of competition. It's like, who'll be the first to break? Him or me?"

"You both are stubborn as hell."

"I'm not trying to be stubborn. I want—no, I *wish* we could have some laughs and then be realistic about it and go our separate ways. But he keeps pushing me—"

"Because you pulled away from him, Jess."

"I pulled away because I had to."

Molly set down the knife. "You do love him."

Her heart thudded. "I didn't say that."

"And it scares you, doesn't it?"

"Only out of my mind! What if I stayed here to be with him? He may not be a logger, but he works in the bush nearly every day. A forester, like Danny wanted to be. What if—"

"Uh-uh, don't play what-if, Jess. I can see where you're going with this, and, I have to tell you, it's not fair to you or Adam." Molly pried the tattered lettuce head out of her hands and calmly tore up the remaining leaves. "Losing Danny was horrible, but supervising contracts isn't in the same danger league as logging. It's more likely you'll get hit by a bus while crossing the street in Toronto than it is that Adam will die in the bush."

"Tell that to my heart, Moll."

"Listen to your heart, honey. I know you're scared. Who wouldn't be? Your whole life is changing." The telephone rang. Molly grabbed a tea towel and dried her hands, glancing over her shoulder as she picked up the cordless. "But if you don't take this chance with Adam now, you'll regret it."

Crossing her arms, Jess stared up at the ceiling. Molly made love sound easy. And maybe it was—for her. To Jess, love felt like she teetered on a cliff while unknown dangers lurked below. And Adam stood behind her, poised to push, too impatient to wait for her to tip-toe to the edge with him.

"Oh, my God!"

Jess whirled around. Molly clutched the cordless, eyes like saucers. Her freckles stood out in stark relief against her pale skin.

"Molly?" Jess raced to her.

"I'll be right there." Hand shaking, Molly disconnected.

"Molly, what is it?"

"Adam! He's in the hospital. Oh, Jess, the nurse said he's been attacked by a bear!"

CHAPTER THIRTEEN

Stupid. Stupid, stupid. Adam sat on a gurney in the emergency room, supporting his sore left wrist with his right hand. *What kind of moron stays alone in the bush at the height of bear season?*

"You won't hear any arguments from me," the nurse cleansing his abrasions murmured.

"Huh?" He gritted his teeth as she dabbed his tender shoulder with a gauze pad. The strong scent of antiseptic seared his nostrils. "Did I say something?"

She nodded, still dabbing. "And I have to agree. Going in the woods alone at any time of year isn't smart." Her friendly smile tempered the criticism.

"I didn't go in alone. I just stayed later than the other guy."

"Same difference."

"Yeah, well . . ." Great role model he made for the Young Achievers group. Start your own business then ignore safety rules while conducting it. He'd have to use today as an example of what not to do.

The nurse's eyebrows rose as if she wanted to hear more, but he wasn't about to elaborate that his reasons for staying after his employee had left revolved around an aggravating woman named Jess. He'd hoped an extra hour deep in the serenity of the forest would help him sort through the barrage of emotions he'd experienced since stalking out of the café two days ago. Fool that he was, he hadn't considered the possibility of encountering a mean-tempered, black bear sow.

188

"You're right," he admitted. "It was dumb. But falling the last three meters out of that damn spruce was even dumber."

"Better a fractured wrist and a few abrasions from falling out of a tree instead of what might have happened if that bear had reached you." The nurse applied a dressing to his shoulder, and he tensed against the pain. "Speaking of what-might-have-been, I think your cousin got the wrong impression when I phoned her while you were in X-ray."

"What did she say?"

"Not much. She seemed distracted when she answered, and she hung up before I could explain everything. I'm afraid she might think you're hurt worse than you are."

Shit! "Did you call her back?"

"Yes, but she'd left by then. Her husband answered. It was noisy. Something about a team dinner, he said."

"Right." He'd forgotten about the basketball dinner. His rotten luck, Jess would have been at Molly's already when the nurse called.

And what would he do if she had been? If she showed up here with Molly? An upset cousin he could deal with. Jess, however, would probably treat this whole episode as an excuse to race back to Toronto.

The friction of footsteps on the linoleum floor sounded beyond his curtained cubicle. The nurse's head popped up. "That might be your cousin now. I'll head her off, let her know you're okay."

Adam returned her smile with a pathetic version of his own. Once the curtains fell closed, he swore. The nurse's voice lifted to him, then Jess's, then Molly's.

Fantastic. The worst case scenario: Jess was here.

His chest hollowed out as he imagined her panicking when Molly received the call.

The curtains tore open, and she burst in, eyes huge, face

chalky. Her gaze locked with his, and a wave of hope rolled through him. However, instead of speaking or coming to him, she averted her gaze.

"Jess, I swear, this was nothing like Danny," he said quickly.

Molly barged in. Jess moved aside, her long curls veiling her face. Adam's gut clenched. She couldn't even look at him. Wouldn't say one heartening word.

Molly raced to his side. "Adam! Are you okay? We thought you were mauled—or worse!" She studied the mild swelling on his arm above his wrist.

"Hairline fracture, most likely." He glanced at Jess. She picked up his torn work shirt from the visitor's chair, then sat and draped it across her lap. The whiteness in her face persisted. "The nurse said a sprain would actually hurt more."

"Did she give you painkillers?"

"I don't need painkillers." He spared another glance toward Jess. Wearing dark blue jeans and a scooped-neck T-shirt the color of jade, she could do more for him than a triple dose of painkillers, if only she'd look at or talk to him. "The doctor will slap a cast on me, and in six weeks I'll be good as new. I won't be playing any more slo-pitch this season, though."

"As if that should be your primary concern." Molly slapped his leg. "You scared us silly, you doofus."

"Me? You overreacted." But he clasped his cousin's hand, wishing he could do the same with Jess. "Sorry for putting you through the wringer like that when all I really needed was a ride home."

Molly's gaze flicked to Jess. "That was my fault. Sorry. We were discussing something related when the call came—"

"Related to being treed by a huge black bear?"

"Oh, stuff it, Adam. I remember the nurse saying 'bear attack' and 'X-rays.' My brain stopped functioning at that point." She crossed her arms. "So, tell us, Tarzan, what really happened?"

"The usual. A mother bear protecting her cub." Should he relate the tale in front of Jess? Damn it, she needed to understand that not every bush accident resulted in tragedy. "Only I didn't realize there was a cub in the area until after I'd been treed by the sow. When I saw her, I did what I always do—climbed the nearest tree. Unfortunately, she charged up after me."

Jess gasped, and he steeled himself. *She has to hear it.*

Molly squealed like a kid caught up in a ghost story. "Omigod, what did you do?"

"Climbed! By the time all was said and done, I must have climbed seventy feet. Good thing I didn't pick a shorter tree." He extended his right hand for Molly's inspection. His unsupported left arm throbbed. "I got most of these scratches from climbing. I kept looking for the cub, thinking it must be in my tree. Otherwise, why would the sow keep charging me?" He repropped his arm.

"Keep charging you?" Jess blurted. "How many times did she charge you?"

Adam looked at her. She might not stick around once she heard his reply, but he intended to work in the bush his entire life. She deserved the truth. "Four. The first and second times, I kept climbing. She'd run up so high, then scoot back down. By the third charge, I'd snagged my jeans. I couldn't get away from her fast enough, so I kicked at her with my caulk boots." He lifted one foot to display the metal studs. "A handy weapon in a tight spot, eh?"

Jess stared at him, mouth hanging open.

"Did you hit her?" Molly asked.

"Grazed her ear. Must have surprised her, because she scampered back down. That's when I finally saw the cub—in the next tree, up seventy feet, the same as me."

"In the next tree?" Jess and Molly chorused.

191

He nodded, adrenaline surging anew. "I couldn't climb much higher. The branches were thinning out, and the top of the tree was starting to sway. So I did the only thing I could do." He lifted his boot again to demonstrate. "I lined up my weapon and I waited for her."

Molly squeaked. "You kicked her in the head?"

"I had to. She was protecting her cub, so she wouldn't stop. If I'd had any other choice, I would have made it. But short of sprouting wings and flying away, I didn't. So I kicked her hard, and she took off." He touched his injured arm. "This didn't happen until I tried to climb down, after the cub left his tree and ran off to find Mama. I'd weakened a few branches on my way up, and one gave out on me. I fell three meters, tried to break the fall with my hand, and that's how I fractured my wrist."

"Wow!" Molly hooted. "What a story!"

Jess leapt from her chair, anger replacing the shock on her face. "I don't believe this! How can you both treat this so casually? He was charged by a bear!" She clutched his ripped shirt.

"He's fine, Jess," Molly said. "That's why we can treat it so—"

"He's not fine. He's hurt." Her head whipped to Adam. "Why didn't you use your cell?"

"Left it in the truck. Not that it matters. Service doesn't reach there."

Her lips curled. "What about Sheba? Is she hurt, too?"

"No, thank God. She used the back of my pickup as a toilet yesterday, so I left her at home as punishment. Lucky thing, because I doubt she would have come out of this alive."

"You were lucky to have come out of this alive! You could have been killed!"

"But I wasn't."

"You know what I mean—the risk was there."

He met her fiery gaze head-on. "The risk is always there, Jess. Risk is a part of life."

Molly fake-coughed. Parting the privacy curtains, she mumbled, "I think I'll call Tim." The curtain closed behind her and her footfalls echoed down the hall.

Jess glared at Adam. He returned her stare.

"It'll be another hour before I can go," he said as evenly as if he were making dinner plans. "There's no sense in both you and Molly waiting."

Her cheeks assumed a rosy hue. He'd provided her with an out—all she had to do was take it. Instead, she flipped a hand, sputtering, "The basketball dinner is tonight."

"I know."

"Molly has a houseful of teenagers to entertain."

"Excuse me for getting treed by a bear."

She flashed him a dirty look. "Molly can leave. I'll take you home."

"I wouldn't want to put you out. I can always call that one-car taxi service you're so fond of."

Her shoulders firmed. "I said I'd stay, Adam. I said I would, and I will. So let's just drop it, okay?"

The next two hours crept by so slowly that Jess could have sworn the time ran backwards. A growing irritation with Adam's lax attitude replaced her feelings of helplessness upon hearing the news. As he joked with the nurse and the on-call doctor, all the while teasing and tormenting her, he seemed intent on provoking her, almost as if he wanted her to remain angry. As if he thought that keeping her annoyed would help get her past what had happened.

If that was his plan, it wasn't working.

Visions of him scaling the tree assaulted her each time she so much as blinked. Along with those images flashed memories of

Dad and Danny: the hot summer day Dad died, Jess and Mom canning peaches in the kitchen, the dusty brown pickup careening down the driveway, the grizzled landing foreman knocking on the door to deliver the awful news.

After that, the memories blurred: watching the blood drain from her mother's face, the air contracting painfully in her own lungs, the rigid set of Mom's spine as she'd struggled valiantly to regain control.

And she'd managed it, but Jess hadn't. Hadn't been able to deal with or handle it. Not the horrible knowledge of her father's death or the crushing realization that Danny was being ambulanced to the Kamloops hospital with an injury Destiny Falls Memorial lacked the resources to treat.

Now fate had tossed her another turn in the shape and form of Adam. Sweet Adam. Infuriating Adam. Persistent, bullheaded, demanding Adam.

Why had she stayed at the hospital with him? The question looped through her mind as he trailed her in the darkened parking lot. Why had she insisted that Molly go home?

As they approached his pickup, she turned, nearly knocking the cast covering his arm from hand to elbow. The doctor had torn the sleeve of his work shirt, and a strip of red plaid rippled like a flag in the warm evening air.

She stuck out a hand. "Your keys."

"Use yours. You have a set."

"Not for the SUV. For the pickup. I came with Molly in her car." Jess hadn't been in any shape to drive. The truth be told, she still wasn't. Not only because of the danger Adam had faced today. Her insides fluttered each time he came near her. The mere thought of driving his pickup stirred memories of their crazy dash from the waterfall when he'd threatened to pull over and make love to her on the side of the road. "If I can manage the truck, I can manage your pickup. The keys, Adam."

"Manage away."

His hand brushed hers as he passed her the keys, and a current zapped her. She turned and climbed into the truck.

"We'll have to decide about tomorrow," he said, sliding in on the passenger side and ushering in his wonderful, woodsy scent.

She fumbled with the seat's adjustment latch. "Huh?"

"Tomorrow. In the morning. When the doctor said I could drive."

"Oh. Right." She pulled the seat forward and released the latch. She hadn't considered tomorrow. It was all she could do to survive tonight.

"The way I see it, you can drop me off now, go home, then tomorrow you can pick me up again, we'll drive to Molly's, and you can get the SUV."

"Sounds like a plan."

"Or . . ."

"Or?"

"You could sleep over."

"I could sleep—" Face heating, she stopped parroting him. He'd probably said that last part half to irritate her. However, it also had the disturbing effect of making her feel guilty. She turned the key in the ignition and the engine's roar filled the pickup. "I don't think that's a good idea."

"No, I'm sure you don't."

She gripped the steering wheel. Couldn't he let up for a minute? They'd agreed to a spring fling. If she thought he could live with that, her answer might be different. However, she knew as surely as she knew her own name that he needed more.

During the drive, she fought to remain distant, but an invisible line seemed to cast off him, hook her in the soul, and reel her in. By the time she turned onto Red Rock Road, tension hummed between them—part promise, part threat.

"Want coffee?" he asked as she pulled up to his house. "Or

would you rather head back to Molly's?"

She avoided his gaze. "That's okay, I'll come in." She wouldn't stay long—she couldn't risk the temptation—but she couldn't dump him on his doorstep with a fresh cast. He'd need help getting settled, and she'd volunteered, after all.

His eyebrows lifted, but he said nothing. She climbed out of the truck and fetched Sheba from the back yard. The dog hung her head and slunk toward him.

"It's okay, girl. You're forgiven." He crouched, and the dog sniffed his cast. "Don't make a mess in the back of my truck again, all right?" He scratched Sheba's muzzle, his voice gentling. "Although it worked out for the best in this case. You should have seen that bear."

Jess steeled herself against a lightning-quick image of Adam, boot in position as he waited for the bear to charge. Only this time she visualized a horrific outcome—the bear lashing out and striking him, gashing him, dragging him to the ground.

Stomach pitching, she concentrated on the house keys. After a moment, she succeeded in jamming the correct key into the lock.

She inhaled. She'd just see him settled. Thirty minutes at most.

As Sheba raced toward the kitchen, Adam sat on the chair in the foyer and bent to unlace his work boots. He groped with his left hand and swore. "Damn cast will take some getting used to."

"I'll help." Jess knelt and carefully slipped off his right boot. His skin warmed as she touched him, and he glanced at her sideways.

"I'm not an invalid," he muttered.

"I know. But the doctor said to take it easy. I'm here. I might as well help you out a bit."

He grunted. She could help him out a whole lot if he knew what was going on in her beautiful head. He could ask, but he didn't want to push his luck—for once—or she might leave.

With a need bordering on desperation, he wanted her to stay. So he stuck out his left foot and let her tug off the other boot like a kid needing help from his mommy.

"There." She brushed dried mud off her hands. "I'll put on the coffee and build a fire."

"A fire isn't necessary."

"You want to be comfortable, don't you? But first the coffee." She cut a trail ahead of him into the kitchen. Sheba at her feet, she fetched the coffee can from the fridge freezer and scooped grounds into a filter. "Do you have cocoa? I can make mocha instead of coffee."

Adam withdrew the can of sweetened chocolate powder from a cupboard and handed it to her. If she wanted to play nursemaid, who was he to argue? Besides, he recognized all her hustle and bustle as a ploy to keep her distance from him.

But if she wanted to keep her distance, why the hell was she here?

He filled Sheba's food and water bowls, then set them in the laundry by her indoor sleeping mat. The dog wolfed down the kibbles with vigor. Stepping into the carport, Adam retrieved three puny chunks of firewood for the fire Jess insisted on building. His sore wrist ached beneath his cast. He might have to break down and take a painkiller.

Entering the house, he nearly collided with Jess. "Sorry." Her nearness spiraled around him, an intense, compelling vibration.

As if sensing the connection and not wanting any part of it, she stepped back. "You shouldn't be carrying that."

"Like hell." Her exasperated sigh reached his ears. Ignoring it, he strode past her. Sheba, nose buried in her bowl, peered at him, but didn't follow. In the great room, Adam dumped his tiny load onto the hearth.

Moments later, Jess appeared, carrying a larger load.

"Where's the dog?" Adam asked.

"On her mat." Jess stacked the wood, then knelt and scrunched newspaper from the basket flanking the fireplace set. "Sit down. I've built fires before." She placed a crumpled ball of newsprint on the grate.

She spoke to him like he was too brainless to add one plus one. Kneeling beside her, he wadded up a second sheet and tossed it in. "Where? In the remote-controlled natural gas contraption you probably have in your swanky apartment?"

Her gaze narrowed. "What's your problem?"

"You." And he meant it.

"Me?" Dropping her newspaper, she stood.

"Yes, you." He got up, arm throbbing. "The coffee, the fire. What are you up to, Jess?"

She flinched. "Why do I have to be up to anything?"

"Oh, I don't know. A few days ago you wanted as little to do with me as possible. Now you're acting like an overzealous Girl Guide out to earn a new merit badge."

She rammed her arms across her chest. "Would you rather I leave?"

"No, damn it, I'd rather you be honest with me."

A crimson stain suffused her face. "I wanted to just do something for you, that's all."

"Why? To appease your conscience for dumping me?"

"I did not dump you. I—oh, what the hell?" Her hands scissored the air, voice rising. "Why can't you accept what I have to offer, Adam? Why do you have to keep pressuring me?"

"I wasn't aware you were offering, Jess. Sounds intriguing, though. What did you have in mind for the patient? A sponge bath?"

Her gaze snapped. "You know, sometimes you can be a real

boor. That's b-o-o-r, in case you didn't know."

Down and dirty. They'd finally lost their minds. But he wasn't about to stop this train until they ran out of track. "One of my more endearing traits. And better than being a bore, in my opinion. That's b-o-r-e."

She glared at him. "This is ridiculous. I'm leaving." Whirling around, she plowed into a chunk of wood that had fallen onto the carpet. "Damn it!"

"My thoughts exactly." He balled his good hand into a fist at his side to prevent himself from reaching out to her. "I love you, Jess, but you're so inflexible in your thinking it's a wonder we ever got together in the first place. The more I talk to Molly or your mom, the more I think about this great life you supposedly have in Toronto, the more I realize it's all a sham. You're not happy living back east. You're not happy with your globetrotting job. We have a chance to be happy, Jess, but you won't risk taking it."

She whipped around, hair flying in her face, breath heaving. "You love me?"

"Damn straight!"

"Well, you have a strange way of showing it! You never stop pushing until you get what you want. Is that it, Mr. Perseverance-is-my-middle-name? I'm a challenge to you, aren't I? To your damned determination and willpower. But this time it's not working for you. You can't fix me, Adam!"

"You're right, I can't. You have to do it yourself. Are you up to the challenge?"

"Oh, sure, turn it all back on me." She jabbed his chest. "I could have lost you to the bush today. You could have been killed by that bear." Her gaze glittered. "Do you think I'm happy about that?"

"That's not the point."

"Grief is a terrible thing, Adam. It eats away at you, bit by

199

bit, until nothing's left but a husk." Her voice shook. "Why am I telling you this? You can't understand."

"Oh, no? What makes you think so?"

"Because! I lost two people I loved more than anything—to those damn woods. And it ripped me up in here." She pounded her chest. "People say they understand, but they can't, unless they've experienced it."

"Then here's a surprise for you, honey. I know grief—I've lived it. Crysta was pregnant when she left me. With a baby she didn't want. But I did."

Her eyes popped. "Crysta died?"

"No. Won't you listen? She left town, and I couldn't find her for weeks. Finally, her mother took pity on me and told me where she was." Initially, Priscilla Jenkins had vowed secrecy to her headstrong daughter. However, once she'd learned about Crysta's wild partying, she'd called Adam in tears. "I'll never forget that grimy Vancouver apartment block, the steep stairs leading to Crysta's hovel. Only, when I finally caught up to her, she wasn't pregnant anymore."

"She had an abortion?"

Throat squeezing, he shook his head. "It was too late for that, but nature took care of things for her. She was seventeen weeks pregnant and hung over as hell when she fell down those damn stairs. Seventeen weeks, Jess." Ten fingers, ten toes, the little heart pumping blood. If the miscarriage had occurred just three weeks later, his baby would have been considered stillborn, he'd discovered later.

"She'd been drinking and snorting coke. Partying every night, doing whatever she wanted, with whoever she wanted. Letting loose in every way she claimed that I and this town had prevented her from doing. She saw our baby as a burden. When she told me she was pregnant, she didn't want me to want the baby, Jess. She didn't want me to want her."

"But you did." Jess's hand flew to her mouth.

He nodded. "I was raised by a father who couldn't see beyond his own pain for years. Who dragged his family from one logging town to another before realizing he was tearing us apart. When Crysta became pregnant, yes, it was a surprise, but that didn't stop me from wanting her and our baby, the stable lifestyle I'd never had." He fisted both hands, the fingers extending from his cast clenching and unclenching. "I grabbed my chance with her, Jess. I grabbed it so hard I couldn't hear her trying to tell me that she didn't want what I did. Showing her the blueprints for this house was her wake-up call, seeing how Tim and Molly lived the last straw. She didn't want a cozy little family life like Molly's, so she took off."

"And if she'd told you she didn't want the baby? If you'd heard her?"

"If she'd agreed to carry the pregnancy, I would have raised our child on my own. But we never had that discussion. Not only because of her selfishness, but mine, too." He stepped toward her. He yearned to gather her into his arms, absorb her hurt and make it his own, so she wouldn't have to struggle anymore. He gentled his voice. "So, you see, honey, I do understand where you're coming from. I won't pretend our circumstances are the same, because they're not. But I can identify, and I have moved on. Can you?"

"I don't know." Her shoulders slumped. "Oh, Adam, maybe you're right about me, after all. Maybe there is something wrong with me."

He closed his eyes for space of a heartbeat. Damn it, he'd done it now. "Jess—"

"Maybe I have built a sanctuary for myself in Toronto, where no one can touch me, where I can be safe." Her stricken gaze lifted. "Don't you get it? Being alone keeps me safe."

His heart constricted. She painted such a lonely picture. This time, he couldn't stop himself from reaching out to her. The need to touch her was too strong.

He brushed her arm. "Come on, honey, you're full of contradictions. Being alone keeps you safe? If you honestly believe that, why did you ask your mother to move to Toronto to live with you?"

"That's different. She's family. She's my mom."

"All right. So marry me. Then I'll be your husband, and we'll be family, too."

CHAPTER FOURTEEN

"Marry you? You're asking me to marry you?" Disbelief shone on her face, in her eyes.

"Yes, honey, I am." Clasping her hand, he lifted it to his mouth and placed a soft kiss on her fingertips. "I love you, Jess, and I think you love me, too. Marriage is what I want with you."

"But where would we live? You belong here, Adam, in this house, in this town, and I don't know if I'm capable of—" Slipping her hand free, she sank onto a brass trunk near the fireplace and looked down.

He knelt before her. "I won't lie to you, Jess." He rested his good hand on her leg, above her knee. Her thigh muscle jumped beneath her jeans. "I'd love for you to move back here and live with me in this house." She glanced up, and he smiled. "However, I can be flexible, believe it or not." *Please believe it.* "I could move east, look for a job with a Toronto consulting firm. Or we could try Vancouver, Victoria, a small town on Vancouver Island." He caressed her leg with slow, soothing strokes. "Honey, you mean so much more to me than where we are. Any major center, and I'd have to travel for work on a regular basis, but we'd figure it out."

Her gaze swirled, revealing her tumbling emotions. "But Adam, you would hate the city. It isn't fair to ask you—"

"*Life* isn't fair, Jess." He pulled in a breath. "Sweetheart, I know this is sudden. You don't have to answer me tonight, or

203

tomorrow, if that helps. Right now I think I could wait ten years for you to decide if it meant spending my life with you."

Relief washed over her features. And something else. Hope? Love? He couldn't tell, and suddenly it didn't matter. She hadn't shut him down or pulled away. For once, he'd said the right thing.

He rose up on one leg and kissed her mouth. "Stay," he murmured. "Please stay with me tonight. In my bed. All night."

Her lips trembled. "Adam."

The raw need in her voice unleashed a corresponding burn within him. "No strings, no pressure, no decisions. Just stay."

He pressed his mouth to hers again, and she leaned into him as if she were melting. Her lips parted and her tongue slipped out to tangle with his.

Silken honey. His lower body ached.

Tearing his mouth away, he tipped up her chin. Desire glimmered in her eyes. He wanted so much more.

He whispered, "Are you sure?"

She nodded.

"Then say it."

"I'm sure."

"Louder."

She licked her lips. "I'm sure!"

It was enough. It had to be. His need for her would drown him if he didn't find release.

Ignoring the twinge of pain beneath his cast, he urged her to stand, then led her upstairs to his moonlit bedroom. Cherishing her smooth skin beneath his hands, he helped her undress as best he could and endured the sensual torment of allowing her to undress him. She slipped his torn shirtsleeve off his cast, her movements slow and tender. Her honey scent wove around him.

Favoring his broken wrist, he lay with her on the bed. Wanting to touch. Wanting to move. Nearer. Closer. Instead, mindful of his cast, he surrendered the lead in their lovemaking. Murmuring seductive words, he allowed her to set the mood and pace.

She complied. Shyly at first. Then bolder, freer. Avoiding contact with his cast, she feathered kisses onto his chest. His nipples tightened beneath her warm mouth.

Ah, Jess.

As she positioned herself above him, her long curls trailed sensation along his skin. Her eyes glazed with pleasure, anticipation, and the same heat that flared in him.

She shifted again, breasts bobbing above his mouth. He tugged one pointed tip with his lips, then circled his tongue around her nipple. She moaned, straddling him. Her sleek hips rocked against his erection.

Grinding his teeth, he reached for the condom box on the nightstand. However, Jess, without a word, stilled his hand and assumed that task for him, too.

Her fingers pressed the length of his heated flesh, infusing him with the need to possess her. She raised her hips and slowly sank onto him. His breath hissed from his lungs.

She pulled up then sank back down. Hot, wet, slick. Once. Twice. Torturing him.

He groaned and surged into her, fondling her breasts with his mouth and hands. She angled against him, pressing down. Deeper. Closer. So close. Her breath came in short gasps.

Suddenly, she arched with a cry, her inner muscles clenching as she climaxed. Thrusting into her, he released the full force of his love and passion.

Slowly, clinging to one another, they relaxed. He held her in the hushed quiet of the room until she fell asleep. Nuzzling her neck, he glided his hands over her, remembering every detail of their lovemaking.

Remembering it all.

Jess shot up in bed. Heart pounding, she glanced at the blue glow of Adam's radio alarm clock.

Nearly dawn. She'd spent the night. Her mother would be frantic.

Her feet met the cool wood floor before reality descended. At four-fifty A.M., her mother would be fast asleep. In Kamloops—at Jess's Aunt Marion's. In fact, probably the only person in the world having a conniption at this particular moment was herself. A grown woman of twenty-seven.

Loosen up, Jess.

Sweeping a hand through her tangled hair, she snuggled beneath the sheets again. Adam slept soundly in the pre-dawn shadows. His cast rose and fell with the rhythm of his breathing as it rested on his flat stomach. The quilt rode low on his hips, creating a picture that reminded her of an exquisitely carved marble statue.

Except Adam was real and very much alive.

Her heart fluttered. He'd asked her to marry him last night. Was his proposal sincere, or had he just been caught up in the moment?

She didn't have a clue. Did she want to find out?

One thing she knew. If he was serious about marrying her, he'd probably ask her each and every day of the two weeks remaining in her visit. Sooner or later, she'd have to reply. She'd have to reach a decision about their future.

Our future. Our life together.

A peaceful calm settled over her. Last night, when he'd offered her time, she'd felt a rush of love more powerful than anything she'd ever felt for Danny. She loved Adam with an intensity she hadn't thought possible at eighteen. And that was okay. The memories of her first love weren't any less precious because she loved Adam more. Had she at long last learned what it meant to feel grounded again?

I could wait ten years for you to decide. Last night, those words had sent her, both eager and cautious, into his arms. How she hoped he'd meant them. Oh, how she prayed that he wouldn't wake up and shatter her warm bubble of contentment by pressing for an answer right here and now.

She caressed his whisker-stubbled jaw. His head turned to meet her touch. Her heart stumbled, and warmth and need spread through her. Cuddling him, she grazed his lower lip with a finger, then sprinkled kisses from the corner of his mouth to the hollow below his ear.

He shifted again, moaning. Eyes closed, he smiled. "Please don't wake me, whoever you are. I'm having the most wonderful dream."

She wriggled her fingers through his chest hair, tracing a small abrasion on his shoulder. "I'm checking out your injuries."

"My what?" His eyes opened and he gazed in fake wonder at his cast. "Oh, yeah, my wrist is broken." He propped himself on his good arm. The quilt fell off his hips, exposing his morning arousal. His gaze dipped. "Nothing broken down there."

Curling her hand around his erection, she stroked him. Desire bloomed within her. "You're right, Percy has never felt better."

He drew in a breath, expression blissful. "Percy?"

She stroked again, nodding.

"Let me get this straight, sweetheart. You're naming my guy Percy?"

"Mm-hm." Lying on her side, she hooked her right leg over his hips and nudged him closer. "It's short for Perseverance," she said as he slid into her. "I think it suits him perfectly, don't you?"

★ ★ ★ ★ ★

Over the weekend, Adam avoided any further talk of love or marriage. He thought about the subjects often enough, however, each time he considered broaching either of them, he'd sense Jess's wary anticipation and remind himself to back off.

When she felt ready to discuss their future, she'd let him know.

The waiting wasn't so bad. On Saturday, they stayed in bed until noon, making love over and over again between revitalizing naps. "Percy" received the workout of his life, despite Adam's awkward cast. A couple of painkillers eased his discomfort, as did the ministrations of "Dr. Jess" wearing nothing but her birthday suit.

Eventually, other appetites intruded. When Adam's stomach growled through a particularly energetic bout of lovemaking, they submitted to the inevitable and went downstairs. After sleeping in the laundry room all night, Sheba craved the outdoors. Adam played with the dog in the fenced portion of his big yard while Jess fixed pancakes. He left Sheba to sniff her territory, and he and Jess ate standing at the kitchen counter, she wearing his good navy bathrobe and he slumming in the ragged one he kept for hot tub sojourns. After breakfast, he cleaned the kitchen while Jess phoned Molly to explain that they wouldn't fetch the SUV until Sunday.

"Let me guess," he said after Jess had completed the laughter-infested call. "Molly thinks I engineered the bear-treeing incident to get us together again."

Her eyes twinkled. "Did you?"

"I may act deranged at times, but even I wouldn't stoop to such desperate measures."

"As long as we've got that straight." She flipped through the Kamloops section of the telephone book. "I'd better call Mom at Aunt Marion's, too. She'll worry if she calls and I'm never home."

"Won't she try your cell?"

"She's never had one, so she forgets I do." Jess picked up the kitchen phone and punched in a string of calling-card numbers. Adam grabbed the phone while she still held it. "Don't even think about charging the call to your card, lover. It's on me."

She beamed at him, and a fist of emotion clenched in his chest. God, he loved her. What would he do if she returned to Toronto without responding to his proposal, if she went away?

Patience, Wright.

He wandered into the great room, granting her privacy. Sank onto the couch and thumbed through a logging magazine, then flicked on the TV. He stared at the screen without interest until Jess joined him on the couch. A smile curved her lips.

He hugged her. "How did it go with your mom?"

"Better than I expected, really. To be honest, I thought she'd be a little more old-fashioned about me spending the weekend with you."

"You flat-out told her we're sleeping together?"

"I didn't have to. She figured it out when I said she could reach me here until tomorrow afternoon."

"That would be a major hint." He squeezed her arm through the terry cloth robe. "Don't sweat it, sweetheart. Your mother's been married twice—she knows the score."

Jess rested her head on his shoulder, her little, burrowing movements reminding him of their last lovemaking session, when she'd nestled her face into his shoulder as she'd climaxed.

His body stirred. *Concentrate. She needs to talk.*

"It came as a surprise, though." Her hand drifted onto his thigh. "I've never been very good at sharing my personal life with her, not even when I was with Danny. When I decided to go on the Pill, I didn't ask her to take me to the doctor. I took

209

care of it on my own."

Adam tilted his head. In her roundabout way, she'd told him that she and the Galloway boy had gotten it on. *Not a problem.* Danny Galloway was her past. *He* was her future.

"Then I'd say you and your mom are growing closer." She and Nora still had a lot to learn, though. If Jess married him and moved back to Destiny Falls, she'd have all the time in the world to nurture her relationship with her mom.

He'd have to find a way to convince her of that over the next two weeks, all the while appearing the epitome of patience, of course.

"So am I a rascal in your mom's eyes now?"

"Actually, she gave us her blessing. She even cautioned me about safe sex."

"That was admirable of her." His mind fixated on the word sex. As did his body.

But then his feelings weren't only about sex, were they?

Rising from the couch, he killed the TV.

Jess's eyebrows lifted. "Don't you want to watch the bowling?"

"Hardly." He grabbed her hand.

"Where are we going?" she asked, all tousle-haired, wide-eyed innocence.

"To Percy's lair, for a safety drill."

She squealed with pleasure as he hauled her upstairs.

Jess floated around her mother's kitchen with a bowl and whisk, whipping the dressing for the pasta salad she and Adam would share at the waterfall in an hour. Mom nursed a mid-morning cup of tea at the table, her wide smile reflecting the joy bubbling inside Jess.

The last five days had been amazing, both because of her happiness with Adam and because she and Mom had shared several candid conversations. After Jess had vanquished her awkwardness over speaking frankly, they'd discussed everything from the painful period of time following the logging accident to how falling in love again didn't have to mean erasing fond memories of the good times.

Finally, they were talking like two women, not just mother and daughter. Yet the friendship that had blossomed between them strengthened their mother-daughter bond, enriching it more than Jess had ever hoped.

Her visit home had certainly initiated its share of pleasant surprises. Discovering this new give-and-take relationship with her mother and falling in love with Adam topped the list.

Especially falling in love with Adam.

Continuing to whisk, she smiled. Without looking, without even wanting to, she'd found a man who respected her and was willing to give her all the time she needed to reach a decision about their future.

One short week ago, she never would have believed Adam Wright could be that man.

The bear attack had changed everything: her illogical fear of losing him to the bush, his pushing for a commitment. He'd survived, and, while a vague uncertainty lingered in the back of her mind, reason dictated that she couldn't live out her days waiting for disaster to strike, rejecting love for fear of what might happen down the road.

"Jessie?"

"Hm? Oh, sorry, Mom."

"Daydreaming again? I asked about your dinner with Molly and Tim at Adam's last night. How did it go?"

"Great. He's been working so hard on the Jamison bid that he really needed the break."

"Peter mentioned that contract once. Adam's doing a marvelous thing for our young people."

"I know." If Adam won the bid, several local university kids would enjoy well-paying summer jobs. For two recent forestry graduates, the work would extend into winter. Potential annual contract renewals were another bonus. "Wouldn't it be nice if he didn't have to keep working out of town?"

"Nice for him, and for you too, when you visit again this summer. Did Molly bring her famous pecan pie for dessert?"

"Yes, and it was delicious. After dinner, we had drinks on the sundeck and talked about her plans for buying The Clothes Horse. She's partnering with a substitute teacher from the high school. They finalize the sale details next week."

Mom sipped her tea. "Good for Molly."

"Isn't it?" Moving to the counter, Jess poured the dressing over the cooked pasta spirals. Last night, she'd almost blurted that she wanted to partner with Molly, which was ridiculous. Molly needed someone now. Not a silent partner, either, but someone willing to share the heavy load that building a successful business required.

With Jess living halfway across the country, she wasn't that person.

"Tim and Molly left around ten, so Adam and I walked Sheba in the woods behind the house. Then we talked out on the deck." And made love on a thick Mexican blanket with the stars twinkling overhead and the night air cooling their heated bodies. "It must have been two before I finally got in."

"No wonder you slept so late."

Jess tossed the pasta salad. "I'm sleeping in a lot these days." A result of her long nights with Adam. She'd seen him at least twice a day all week, usually at noon and then in the evening after her mom went to bed. "I'll try to get in earlier tonight. Then I can wake up in time to make us a big breakfast."

"That sounds nice." Her mother's gaze lowered, then rose again. "You know, dear, I hope you aren't coming home every night, to sleep here, I mean, on my account. I understand you'd like to spend as much time with Adam before you leave, and I don't want you thinking I disapprove."

"After everything we've talked about lately, how could I think you disapprove?" Jess ran a hand along the hip of her jeans. "I know you don't mind if I stay overnight at Adam's, Mom, but if I spent all my time with him I'd never see you and he'd never get any work done."

"As long as those are your reasons."

"They are." She sealed the pasta salad in a plastic container, then dug in the fridge for cold fried chicken.

The phone rang. Her mom got up and answered it. "It's your office, dear. Mr. Lind." She held out the receiver.

"Gareth? I didn't expect to hear from him today." *What is it this time?* Sighing, Jess placed the platter of chicken on the counter. "Thanks, Mom." Accepting the receiver, she injected false sincerity into her voice. "Hi, Gareth. What's up?"

His terse greeting soured her stomach. He spoke hastily and urgently—for good reason. A stone dropped in her chest. She listened while her mom moved to the sink and filled it with bubbly water. As Gareth finished, Jess murmured her acquiescence and hung up.

She sagged onto a chair. "Oh, Mom."

"Bad news?" Her mother hung the dishrag on the faucet.

"I'll say." Jess pinched the bridge of her nose. "I have to leave sooner than we thought."

"When?"

"The first available flight. Tomorrow, I guess." Melancholy pressed on her like a heavy, hot, wool blanket. She hated the thought of disappointing her mother—and Adam. How could she leave him now that she'd just found him? "Gareth needs me in the office first thing Monday morning, and he wants to brief me over dinner Sunday night. He had to bump up the buying

213

trip by ten days to accommodate a factory owner in Asia. Mr. Wong is a new contact and my responsibility." Supposedly her responsibility. Gareth and Sarah had been covering for her.

"I thought you were traveling with a colleague?"

"I am, but it doesn't matter. I have my contacts, and she has hers. Besides, I'm her senior. If one of us has to go early, it should be me." Her stomach clenched. Despite the emails and conference calls, she'd lost the pulse of the current buying season. She barely recalled the styles she'd studied at the European trade shows in March. Yet, in two weeks she'd be overseas, working with the factories to knock off those same styles. "I need to make this trip work, Mom. Gareth is bucking for a promotion. If I look good, he does. If he looks good, he moves up, and then I'll have a chance at his job. That means less overseas travel, more money and vacation time. I can use that time and money to visit you."

"Oh, Jessie." Her mother's voice saddened.

"What a mess, huh? I was counting on another week, too. But this factory could save Arlington a bundle on the new women's line, and Gareth needs me in the office to prepare. I have to go back."

"I know." Her mom's chin trembled.

Jess swallowed the lump in her throat. "Even if I don't get the promotion, I'll take time off in the summer for my birthday, like we talked about. And two weeks at Christmas, I promise."

"But you've taken so much time already. Can you manage Christmas?"

"Even if I have to hijack Santa to bring me in on his sleigh. There's no way I'm missing another Christmas with you." *Or Adam.*

Her mom smiled. "We'll work it out."

"You know what? I believe that, too." Getting up, she hugged her mom. "I'm proud of you, Mom. I know these past few weeks haven't been easy. I know how much you miss Pete. But you seem so much stronger now. Do you feel stronger?"

Her mom nodded against her shoulder. "Thanks to you. Thank you, Jessie."

Jess blinked back tears. "Will you be okay? Will you call me if you need me? Even at the office or on my cell. Any time of day or night. You know that, don't you?"

"I do." Her mom pulled away and gazed at her, eyes shining with love and affection. "Jessie, my sweet girl. We've come a long way, haven't we?"

Jess paced the back porch. The summons to return to Toronto had tipped her entire morning off-balance. An investigation of airline websites had brought even more bad news. Where was Adam? They needed to talk.

The horses in the pasture nickered. Needing the distraction, she approached the fence and stroked the chestnut mare's muzzle. "You understand, don't you?"

The mare whinnied. Translation: *I really don't care. Get me a carrot.*

Jess's nerves receded. She retrieved a carrot from the kitchen and fed it to the appreciative horse.

Within moments, the rumble of Adam's pickup in the driveway tripped her heart into overdrive again. She turned. He'd spotted her, and his long legs quickly swallowed the meters between them.

Oh, he looked good—in boots, a blue T-shirt, and faded jeans. His scarred eyebrow quirked a hello as the warm breeze ruffled his dark blond hair.

Her heart soared. Throwing herself into his arms, she kissed him with all the love and urgency coursing through her.

He chuckled against her mouth, and the gravely sound vibrated through her. His cast tickled her arm.

"Hey, I missed you, too. Ready for our picnic?"

"I can't go! Gareth called." She blurted the schedule changes. "I checked, and the only available flight leaves tonight."

A dozen emotions flew over his face. "Tonight?"

"I know! At nine-forty, out of Kamloops. It was the best I could do, because of the short notice. For the connecting flight, I mean. I had to book the red-eye out of Vancouver. I still need to pack and spend time with Mom." *And you.* "The bus for Kamloops leaves at six."

"The bus?" Backing away, he scrubbed his good hand over his face. The mare nudged him over the rail, but he didn't acknowledge her. "No. Don't take the bus." His tone flattened. "I'll drive you to Kamloops."

His gaze lifted, sorrow reflecting in his eyes. A whipcord wrapped around her heart, squeezing until she could barely breathe. They'd both known this day would come, but that didn't make the reality of their parting any easier.

"You shouldn't drive," she said. "Your wrist is broken."

"Honey, I have a cast."

She touched his injured arm. "But it's a three-hour round trip. I don't want you driving that far when you don't have to."

"You'd rather say good-bye to me now?" He pushed his undamaged hand into a front pocket. The mare startled. Snorting, she trotted away to rejoin the other horses.

"Of course not. I'm sorry. I'm not making sense." How could she, when the thought of leaving him tore her in two? "But I can't go to the waterfall. There's not enough time, considering everything I have to do. That doesn't mean we can't have our picnic here, though. On the porch, or the lawn, or in my room." She caressed his upper arm. "Mom left to buy groceries for an early supper. I asked her to give us an hour."

"To indulge in a little afternoon delight?" He brushed a stray curl off her cheek. "As tempting as that sounds, sweetheart, it

216

doesn't solve the problem. You see, I thought you had another week remaining in your leave of absence. In fact, I was counting on it. I'd hoped that, somehow, during that time . . ." He glanced away, jaw firming. Then, looking at her again, he gave a hollow laugh. "The truth is, I don't want you to go at all. Call Garth and—"

"Gareth."

"Whatever. You're entitled to your full six weeks leave, so call him back and tell him you can't make it."

A tremor raced up her spine. "Excuse me?"

He waved a hand. "Look at it this way. You don't own Arlington Shoes. You're a valuable employee, but they've survived the last five weeks without you. Is it imperative that you take this trip? Can't someone else go instead?"

The back of her neck prickled. She'd expected him to understand, as a businessman if not as a lover.

"Two of us are going, but that's not the point. Gareth Lind is my boss, and these trips are a major facet of my job."

"A convenient facet. I don't know, Jess, maybe this phone call from Garth—"

"Gareth!"

"His name's not important. What's important is the way you hop-to when he snaps his fingers." Adam's features hardened. "Okay, maybe I'm wrong. Maybe you are doing the right thing. But it seems to me—no, it's pretty damn clear—that this phone call is an excuse for you to run out on me. On us."

Hurt carved deep lines on his face. *Oh, Adam.* If she were in his position, she might not immediately understand, either.

"But I'm coming back in July for a few days, then two weeks at Christmas. You can fly east to see me—I have a million airline travel miles that need using. We'll fly back and forth for a while, take long weekends whenever we can. Can't we start from there and see how it goes?"

CHAPTER FIFTEEN

"See how it goes?" Why hadn't he pushed the marriage talk when he'd had the chance? This waiting-for-the-right-moment business sounded noble in concept, but proved useless in practice. "I asked you to marry me a week ago, honey. My feelings haven't changed."

"But you said—"

"That you didn't have to answer me right away. I know. But that was when I thought I had two weeks to encourage you otherwise."

Her gaze softened. Spirits lifting, he cupped her chin. "How about it, Jessie Noreen? Will you marry me?" Her lips parted, and he placed a light kiss upon her mouth. "I love you, Jess. Please don't say no to me . . . to us."

Tears sparkled in her toffee-brown eyes. "I love you, too. But the thought of marriage is too much for me right now. It's too fast, too soon. I thought you understood that."

She loves me. "And a long-distance romance isn't too much?"

She shook her head. "It's a beginning, something we can build on. And far more than I could have offered two or three weeks ago." Her gaze pleaded with him. "Don't you see?"

A rope of tension knotted inside him. "I wish I could, honey, but I can't." There it was—his failing, his shortcoming. He couldn't stop from feeling that this was his last chance with her.

He let his hand fall away from her face. *Out of sight, out of mind.* If he didn't fight for her now, he might lose her forever.

"Don't get me wrong, Jess. I've tried seeing your point of view. But every time I think I do, something else happens and we have another setback." He paused. He sounded like a jackass. "The thing is, I want a life with you, honey, not a now-and-then relationship where we see each other maybe twelve times a year. I want to hold you in my arms each night, not talk dirty to you over the phone."

"It's too soon for me, Adam. Please understand."

He dragged in a breath. "I understand. In fact, I think I'm beginning to understand too well."

Her mouth thinned. "What do you mean?"

Out with it. She has to know. "I mean that you're still playing the same old tune. You want to be with me, but only for the present. You love me, but there's no future, no hope. Face it, Jess, you can't take a chance."

She stepped back. "I'm willing to take a chance," she said, her voice trembling. The breeze fluttered her long, dark hair. "For me, a long-distance relationship *is* taking a chance."

Adam's heart twisted—for her, for himself, for the dreams disintegrating right before his eyes. "And, for me, it's not enough. If you'd be honest with yourself for one damn minute, you'd realize it's not enough for you, either."

Her gaze snapped. Voice low and controlled, she said, "There you go again, telling me what I should think or feel. I had to learn to trust that my mother knows what's best for her. Can't you at least try to do the same for me?"

He ground his teeth. "It's not—"

"But, no, you've already made up your mind. You know what *you* want. Now all you have to do is convince poor, deluded Jess that *she* wants the same thing." She glared at him. "Did I say I would never move back here and marry you? Did I? If you'd let me deal with our relationship at my own pace and in my own time, you might be pleasantly surprised. I might actually

219

decide—without being bullied—that I want to return to Destiny Falls and spend the rest of my life with you!"

He grunted. "That sounds jim-dandy, Jess, but what guarantee do I have that you won't get sucked back into your mile-a-minute life in Toronto? That you won't leave me hanging on the line for the next two, ten, or, given your style, twenty years while you decide what you want?"

"And here I thought you've been trying to show me that life comes with no guarantees. That I have to reach out and grab one of those fabulous risks you're always raving about. Remember what you said about Crysta? You pressured her. Even if you didn't mean to, you did. And she wasn't ready." Jess poked her chest. "Well, neither am I. You're pressuring me, Adam, and I can't take it. I *won't.*"

Fury lanced him. He didn't need his mistakes with Crysta thrown in his face. Not now. Not ever.

"Let's leave ancient history out of this," he said.

"To quote you, I don't think I can. Because it's not just me with the problem here. You asked me to marry you. I asked for a compromise. But you won't take any less than exactly what you want." Tears welled in her eyes. "Well, guess what, Adam? I'm leaving town tonight because my job demands it. I'm leaving because I need time, I need space, and I won't allow you to 'encourage,' pressure, or otherwise bully me into rushing into marriage!"

Ceasing her tirade, she began trembling head to toe. Sobbing, she ran into the house. The door slammed behind her, windows rattling.

"Jess!" He pounded the fence, pain stabbing his injured arm. He spun around, swearing, fighting the urge to storm in after her and press his case until she stopped playing hardball with his emotions.

But what would that accomplish? He'd given her a choice—

she'd made it. More pressure wasn't the answer.

He threw back his head and searched the clouds scudding across the pale blue sky.

A shroud of utter hopelessness fell over him.

"I'll miss you, Jess."

"I'll miss you, too, Molly." Jess hugged her best friend tightly, blinking back the tears that sprang up all too often since her fight with Adam this afternoon. They stood in the convenience store parking lot, the bus idling nearby. The acrid odor of diesel permeated the early evening air. "But I'll be back in July for our double birthday party, remember?"

"If your boss lets you."

"He will. I've already promised Mom."

Molly released her. With an unhappy expression, she smoothed the collar of the jacket Jess wore with her jeans.

"And Adam?" Molly asked.

Jess stared at the pavement. She'd told Molly about her argument with Adam when she'd called for a ride to the bus stop. After spending the afternoon unloading her hurt onto her mother, she couldn't bear reliving the pain and heartache. "Moll, I'm sorry, but if I talk about Adam again, I'll cry."

"Aw. I shouldn't have mentioned him. I'm sorry."

"No, it's okay. It's just been a harrowing day." Jess rubbed the tension between her eyebrows. "Part of me expects him to pop up again, determined to 'talk some sense' into me. Even Mom thought it might be him when we heard your car in the driveway."

"Do you wish it had been?"

Yes. But only because she hated leaving with so much bitterness between them. If he had tried contacting her, would they have fought all over again? Probably. The pain from this afternoon was too fresh, the time afforded them too sparse, the

221

stress and pressure of her hasty departure all too real—for them both.

"I need to put some space between us," she mumbled.

"Well, you're doing that." Molly glanced around the deserted parking lot. "I don't think he's coming here, if that's what you're afraid of. He knows when the bus leaves, right? If he were coming, he'd have shown up by now."

Insides freezing, Jess nodded.

"Aw, Jess, don't discount my cousin completely. He's stubborn, but he's not stupid. He'll realize what he has with you, what you can have together. It'll work out. You'll see."

"I don't know." In the meantime, she wouldn't cross her fingers. She needed to concentrate on the buying trip instead of dwelling on Adam and his thinly veiled ultimatum.

At the moment, however, she found it impossible to think of anything *but* Adam.

The stocky bus driver approached them. "Excuse me, Miss? This yours?" He pointed at her luggage on the pavement.

"Yes." The word felt charged with finality.

He stowed her suitcase and carry-on, then returned for the spare suitcase she'd borrowed from her mother to carry her purchases from The Clothes Horse.

"A couple more minutes, but that's it." The driver tapped his thick-strapped watch. "I got a schedule to keep."

Jess thanked him and turned to Molly. "I have to go." She pasted on a smile. "Return Adam's truck soon, okay? I don't want Mom worrying about it."

Molly patted her jeans pocket. "Key's here, instructions duly noted. Now, climb onto that bus and get out of here before I try to stop you myself."

The sheer curtains drifted away from Nora's fingertips. Although the bus route to Kamloops didn't follow Old Village

Road, she hadn't been able to resist stealing one more glance out the living room window. Five minutes ago, she'd thought she heard the bus rumbling down the highway, which was silly. The highway was miles away.

The Greyhound was taking her daughter away, yet contentment flowed through her. *I'm proud of you, Jessie.* Her daughter had found love again, yet hadn't allowed that love to rule her the way Nora had let Frank Morgan's love swallow her up so many years ago, the way Jessie had allowed Danny Galloway's love to consume her following his untimely death.

It wasn't that she didn't want Jessie to experience the richness of a deep, mature love like she'd experienced with Peter. *Oh, how I do.* But a rich love couldn't be forced. When the time was right for Jessie and Adam, Jessie would know.

Nora wandered to the kitchen and put the kettle on the stove. The silence of the house descended, but she didn't mind. She was home, in her heart and soul. And one day soon her daughter would find her way home, too.

Whether Jessie remained in Toronto or returned to Destiny Falls, Nora remained confident that Jessie would find home. Because home was a certain sense of peace, a welcoming, a gathering warmth, belonging. Home had very little to do with geography and everything to do with finding that peace and contentment within oneself.

While waiting for the kettle to boil, she returned to the living room. Yesterday she'd arranged several framed pictures on the fireplace mantle. Photos of her and Peter, and the Waverly Foods photo Marie Shaverton had delivered. Then pictures of her with Jessie, Jessie and Frank, her and Frank, and several smaller photos of family outings.

One by one, she touched each photograph.

"I love you all," she whispered.

★ ★ ★ ★ ★

She's gone.

He could tell without looking at his watch. He felt it in his bones.

Adam leaned his good hand on the railing of the viewing deck, staring out at the waterfall. The rushing cascade thundered in his ears. The wind blew moist and cool against his skin. But his heart ached for Jess with every beat. The waterfall held no solace for him tonight.

Coming here hadn't been his first choice. When he'd stalked out of Nora Olson's back yard this afternoon, he couldn't think straight. He'd holed up in his office and drowned himself in computer work. Later, trying to run off his frustration on the trails behind his house, the need to go to Jess, to say, do, offer anything to make her understand his behavior and open her life and heart to him again, had devoured him. He'd jumped in the pickup and sped halfway to her house before realizing she might think he was trying to bully her. So he'd pulled a U-turn in the middle of the damn road and sought refuge at the waterfall instead.

"What do you think, girl?" he muttered to Sheba. "Dumb move, huh?"

The dog gazed up at him with her big brown eyes and panted.

"Yeah. I haven't a clue, either." Hell, he was exhausted. As he scraped his casted hand over his face, he focused on the trees in the distance. They lined the canyon walls like proud, wooden guards.

It's not just me with the problem here. Jess's words reverberated in his mind. Harsh words, however, in this case, so very true.

Wright, you really are king of the idiots, aren't you?

He knew he could be pushy at times—all right, damn often. Knew he didn't like to lose out on anything he perceived as a challenge. And, although it cut him to the quick to admit it, he

224

knew Crysta had walked away from him two years ago for about the same reasons as Jess had today.

Because he was too damn pushy.

Pressuring Crysta had stolen the life from their unborn child. Had she not felt so cornered by *his* desires, *his* wants, she might not have gotten drunk or high night after night. Might never have fallen down those damn stairs.

And today, instead of being alone, Adam would have an active toddler in his life. *My son or daughter.*

He tightened his grip on the railing, and a splinter bit into his palm. Hell, he'd thought he'd learned his lesson with Crysta. He'd thought he'd mellowed over time. During these last couple of weeks with Jess, hadn't he exerted effort after conscious effort to pull back, to be patient? He'd almost succeeded, too . . . until today, when he'd finally pushed her too far.

She'd said she was returning for a few days in July. Two long months away.

Could he handle two months without calling or emailing or buying a one-way ticket to Toronto? Could he give her the time and space she needed? And if she decided against him—that was, if she hadn't already—could he deal with that, too?

The breeze rustled his hair, cooled his skin, however, neither it nor the canyon offered any answers.

He felt like he'd hit the wall of pain in a marathon.

He just didn't know if he could survive the race, let alone win.

Purse tucked beneath one arm and laptop case bumping her hip, Jess tossed her mail onto the dinette table. Then she trudged to the spare bedroom she used as a home office.

The same room she'd asked her mother to move into.

Whatever had possessed her to do such a thing? Considering her long hours and unpredictable travel schedule, the idea now seemed doomed to failure. Even if she replaced Gareth when he obtained his promotion and her travel decreased as a result, her take-home work would escalate. Her mother deserved so much more than to get treated as a tag-on to a harrowing day. Besides, her mother belonged in Destiny Falls . . . as surely as Adam did.

Chest heavy, she plopped her purse and computer case on the desktop, then sagged onto the swivel chair with a groan.

Work had never felt so much like work as it had since her return to Toronto twelve hectic days ago. From discovering that Gareth had hired a senior buyer out from under their fiercest rival to facing the collapse of a favorite line, every time she turned around another crisis erupted or a meeting required her presence. She'd spent most of last week in dazed shock. Then she'd poured herself into readjusting to office routines. On Sunday she'd finally come up for air, but tonight was Tuesday and she was flying to Asia with the new senior buyer on Thursday, ready or not.

Tramping into the kitchen, she fixed herself a cup of tea in the microwave and sat at her desk again with the steaming mug. After firing up her laptop, she began inputting the number-crunching she rarely had time for at the office. The mundane task allowed her mind to roam as she paused now and then to sip her tea.

She'd hurried back to Toronto at Gareth's bidding, believing he'd meant her to travel to Asia alone. Her colleague was to have caught up with her after she'd met with Mr. Wong. However, as Gareth had explained over their briefing dinner, their new senior buyer, an energetic woman named Louisa, already possessed connections with the factory responsible for Jess's schedule change. As a result, Louisa was too valuable an asset to leave behind. So now two of them were going, three once their colleague arrived. A waste of manpower, if Gareth had bothered to ask her.

How about tossing the trip in the bag and flying home to see Adam instead?

As if that was an option. She set down her mug and continued data entry. Adam had taught her so much during her five weeks home. Because of him, she'd finally learned to let go of her haunting memories of Danny. Through Adam, she'd discovered what it meant to feel whole again.

She snorted. *Feel whole?* What a joke. If she felt whole, then why did the old, hollow sensations keep swelling up inside her?

Shaking her head, she forced herself to concentrate on the flickering computer screen. Hours later, hungry and exhausted, she pushed back her chair and stretched.

"I need a break," she muttered to the empty room. Her time in Destiny Falls had spoiled her. No matter how hard she tried, she couldn't seem to muster the same enthusiasm for buying that she'd possessed before Pete had died. As she lay in bed night after sleepless night, the thought often occurred to her that she hadn't felt truly enthusiastic in ages. At some point during the last four years, the constant pressure and deadlines inherent in merchandising had buried her love for the business—and she hadn't even realized it was happening.

Until Adam.

No, not even falling in love with Adam had helped her break through the safe but sterile wall she'd erected. Yes, he always pushed, but she, every bit as often, refused to listen. Digging in her heels, acting more than stubborn. She'd wasted nine years of her life looking backward, thinking she was moving forward when all this time she'd been running away.

She swore. "I don't have time for this." Getting up, she kicked off her pumps and shut down the laptop. "Business. I need to focus on business." She'd have plenty of time to dwell on the rubble of her relationship with Adam while she was in Asia.

227

Sighing, she tromped to the dinette table and sorted through her bills. Two envelopes into the pile, a light floral scent drifted to her. She glanced at the address on a pale yellow packet. Molly! Why hadn't she emailed?

Jess opened the letter and withdrew a sheet of daisy-dotted stationery. A photograph slipped out and fluttered to the carpet. As she picked it up, goose bumps dotted her arms.

Adam and me at the Wander-Inn! The picture Molly had tried to give her at Clara's Café.

Tears blurred her vision, and her throat pinched. *Damn it!* She hadn't heard one word from him since her outburst in her mother's backyard. Which was what she'd demanded, but which had left her feeling hurt and alone. Adam Wright was the most persistent man she'd ever met. When he wanted something, he went after it. He'd said he wanted *her.* Obviously, he'd changed his mind. He'd only wanted her if he didn't have to wait.

A hot tear rolled down her cheek. Slumping onto a chair, she scanned Molly's note:

Thought I'd send you a memory of home. Don't be mad, please. It's only been a week, but we all miss you. Adam misses you. Says someone named Percy is having a rough time of it, too. Don't know who he's talking about. Do you?

A laugh bubbled in her throat. Wiping her face, she reached for her cell and punched the speed dial for Molly's, then paced the living room as the rings sounded in her ear.

"Hello?" Molly answered, voice deflated.

"Molly, it's Jess. What's wrong?"

"Jess! Tim and I were just talking about you! Did you get my letter?"

"Yes." Jess smiled. "You rat."

"You're not upset I sent the picture?"

I treasure it. "No. Hearing from you made my day."

228

"Phew!" Molly paused. "He's miserable without you, you know."

Jess stared at a framed museum print on the wall. "He hasn't called."

"I know. He told me. Isn't that what you wanted?"

"I guess. Well, I did. I mean, I thought I did."

"He's trying hard to restrain himself. Hey, have you asked your boss about taking that time off in July yet?"

"Yes, but it depends."

"On what?"

"Oh, you know . . . if I apply for Gareth's job, it wouldn't look right if I booked off holidays right away."

"Jess, you have to come back! I'm already planning our twenty-eighth birthday party."

Jess squeezed shut her eyes. She was letting down everyone. Molly, her mother, Adam. *Herself.*

"I'll try, Moll. Give me some credit." Not wanting to end the call on a sour note, she asked, "How's it going with the sale of the store? Have you signed the legal documents?"

"No." Molly's voice sagged. "I didn't get the chance to sign anything. My so-called business partner bailed."

"What? When did you find out?" Jess paced back to the dinette.

"A few days ago. She kept postponing, so I confronted her. Turns out she and her husband might move again this summer. They miss the conveniences of the city. Jess, I'm so frustrated! To have my dreams snatched out from under me like that!"

"But—I don't understand. If Anne didn't plan on staying in Destiny Falls, why did she agree to partner with you in the first place?"

"Because it was the only opportunity other than substitute teaching available to her at the time, she said. She wanted to leave her options open, in case she and her husband do stay.

229

But Adam thinks she's afraid to take the risk. And, I have to admit, even with the boutique's good reputation, any business in a place the size of Destiny Falls is a definite risk."

Jess's heart thumped. Hadn't Adam said something similar about her lack of adventure?

Molly's voice broke. "My boss is listing with a real estate agent tomorrow. She waited on this deal, and I didn't come through for her. I think that hurts as much as losing the deal."

"Can't you find another partner?" *Me.* The thought floated up from a secret place inside her. A place that beckoned her to take a chance, to break free.

"I dunno," Molly said. Kaitlin's cheerful voice piped up in the background. Molly murmured a few words to her daughter, then said to Jess, "I gotta go. Tim has a meeting, and Kaitlin wants her bath. I'll email you in a few days."

"Molly, wait! I'm leaving Thursday."

"Oh, right, your buying trip. I'll phone tomorrow instead. Same time, okay? I'll be in a better mood, I promise."

Frowning, Jess disconnected and plunked the cell on the table. Rarely had her best friend sounded so depressed. The Molly she knew would already have a contingency plan in place for buying The Clothes Horse. In fact, her Molly would badger her best friend to come in as a partner.

Unless Molly had given up on her. Like Adam had.

Heart aching, Jess stared at the tabletop. The dinette light glinted off the shiny surface of a postcard amid the remaining mail.

Absently noting the waterfall scene, she flipped over the card. A single word graced the back: "Okay."

Adrenaline shot through her veins like a drug. The unsigned card was from Adam, of that she had no doubt. But what the heck did "okay" mean? That he was okay? Was she okay? Damn

230

it, did he have to pick now to be cryptic? She couldn't handle this!

Then it hit her—what he might be saying. Crashed over her like a tidal wave.

Knees wobbling, she flopped onto the chair. Was he saying he would wait for her? That he'd finally learned to let go? Or was he simply baiting a line, trying to reel her back in?

The apartment walls swam. She dropped her head into her hands.

It doesn't matter, Jess. Whatever he meant, whatever he might mean—it didn't matter. Hadn't she learned from her phone call to Molly that life held no guarantees? How many times did she have to re-take that lesson?

She raised a shaking hand to her mouth. She had to make some decisions. She had to take a chance. It was the only way she'd ever learn if she had a future with the man she loved.

CHAPTER SIXTEEN

"All right, all right, quiet in back!" Tim's hearty voice boomed into the microphone. "We're trying to conduct a respectable charity event here!"

Adam squinted against the glaring stage lights Tim had borrowed from the high school drama department. Did the two guys standing on either side of him feel as ridiculous as he did?

In response to Tim's opening monologue, cheers, jeers, and guffaws continued to erupt from the rowdy slo-pitch crowd cramming the community hall for the bachelor and bachelorette contest the Eddies had organized for this year's Lumberjack Festival. Thanks to the blinding lights, Adam couldn't see past the second row of dinner tables. If the proceeds from this stupid contest didn't benefit Destiny Falls Young Achievers, he would have refused to participate. Jess's sudden departure three weeks ago had left him reeling. However, yesterday Molly had called with the news that one bachelor had been forced to drop out due to illness. Considering Adam's connection to DFYA, she'd begged him to take the guy's place. She'd even promised the festivities would lift his spirits.

Yeah, right.

His postcard brainwave had been a bust. Either Jess had received his one-word message and hadn't given two rips about it, or the postcard had arrived after she'd left for Asia and she hadn't received his message at all. Whatever, he felt caught between gears. He couldn't contact her again for fear he might

232

be pushing her. Yet, if he did nothing, he could lose her anyway. He probably already had.

Tim spoke into the mic. "This mob is noisier than a gym full of sweaty teenagers! I appreciate the enthusiasm, folks, but let's get the show on the road!"

The audience quieted enough for Tim to continue. "Thanks. Now, on behalf of the Destiny Falls Young Achievers and in memory of the group's hard-working co-leader, Peter Olson, let me extend a great big thank you to everyone who plunked down ten bucks per vote for the top three bachelors and bachelorettes brave enough to be standing here beside me. Next weekend a limo will chauffeur the lucky winning couple to an all-expenses-paid evening in Kamloops!"

Loud clapping sounded from the back of the hall. Again, Tim shushed the crowd. "The money raised tonight will help fund DFYA fieldtrips and workshops throughout the year. Votes were tallied over dinner. Minutes ago, I learned that between the guys' contest and the girls' contest, we'll raise nearly three thousand dollars tonight—thanks to your generosity!"

The applause and whistles hammered in Adam's ears. He glued on a smile. Jess was due back from her buying trip soon. Due back to Toronto, that was. Had she thought about him at all while she was overseas? He'd never restrained himself more in his life, but he would keep at it even if it sent him up another tree with a disgruntled black bear nipping at his heels.

". . . with twenty votes, raising two hundred dollars!"

The guy to his right stepped forward and waved to the cheering crowd.

"And our second bachelor, Wade Jones, playing third base for the Buzzards, captured forty-three votes tonight, raising four hundred and thirty dollars!"

As Wade stepped forward, Adam cringed. His arm itched beneath his cast. Two weeks until it came off. He couldn't wait.

"And last but not least, according to these numbers," Tim declared with a chuckle Adam thought unnecessary, "Adam Wright, currently water boy for the Mountaineers but expected to make a comeback next season, grabs a walloping seventy-seven votes, bringing in seven hundred and seventy bucks!"

Adam stepped forward amid a cacophony of hoots and catcalls. "Aw, shaddup!" he ribbed his hecklers.

Tim held up a hand until the audience calmed, then announced in a voice resounding with melodrama, "Not to worry, ye Adam-trouncers. I'm sure Wright's large number of votes has *nothing* to do with the new jobs he recently provided to several of our local young people."

"Ain't that nepotism?" somebody yelled.

Tim waggled a finger. "I think you'd better check a dictionary, Bill. Like maybe under G, for Gratitude. And for all the Gracious ladies and Gents who voted for Adam. Because Wright's votes carry an added bonus!"

Adam sucked in a groan, glancing at Tim. *What are you up to?*

Tim said, "An anonymous donor contacted me yesterday offering to buy back Adam's votes—should he win—at twenty dollars per vote. For those of you who failed high school math, that raises another fifteen-hundred-and-forty dollars! DFYA isn't greedy, so we're splitting all of tonight's proceeds with the elementary school's playground equipment fund! Adam and the donor will enjoy a complimentary dinner at the Wander-Inn. Wade Jones and the winning bachelorette will claim the Kamloops prize."

Adam rolled his eyes. Who in their right mind would spend over fifteen-hundred dollars for an evening in his dour company?

A male member of the audience sounded every bit as perplexed. "Who the hell would do that?" his deep voice hollered.

"Maybe it's your wife, pal!" a second guy shouted.

234

"Maybe it's yours!" the first guy retorted.

"Maybe it's neither!" a female voice sang out.

Adam blinked. *Jess?*

Squinting against the stage lights, he peered into the crowd. *It can't be.*

Then he spotted her. Threading her way through the dinner tables from the kitchen at the rear of the hall. Wearing jeans and a vibrant red T-shirt, her dark curls bouncing around her shoulders, she waved a slip of paper in the air.

His brain froze. His legs refused to budge. His mouth gaped stupidly.

Was he seeing things? He blinked.

In the next instant, she was standing beside him in the glare of the hot stage lights and passing a check to Tim. "It's good at the local bank. I opened an account there yesterday."

Turning, she winked at Adam. "Surprised you, didn't I?"

The crowd roared. Adam stared at her. Her toffee eyes sparkled, and her cheeks held a rosy glow. Her T-shirt sported the white outline of a heart, the words HE'S MINE emblazoned in white script across her breasts.

"What are you doing here?" He sounded stunned. Not a big stretch. He *was.*

"Buying up your votes." She looked smug.

"No. What are you doing *here,* in Destiny Falls?"

"Giving you the shock of your life, I gather. About time, too. God knows you've thrown me for a loop often enough."

She took a step closer. Then another. A riotous cheer swept from the crowd.

Adam squelched the urge to reach out and swallow her into his arms. He couldn't figure this—her—any of it—out. Jess Morgan didn't act on impulse. Every move she made originated from a need to protect herself.

"What about your buying trip? I thought you were in Asia."

"Don't argue with me, Wright." Grabbing the front of his shirt, she drew down his head. "Fifteen hundred and forty bucks. You'd better be worth every red cent." She planted a kiss on his lips that spun his brain into the next galaxy.

Pulling back, she shouted to the hooting and hollering crowd, "We're leaving! Find yourselves another bachelor, ladies! This one's mine!" She hauled him toward the exit.

"You heard her, folks!" Tim swung back into his ringmaster routine. "Wade Jones of the Buzzards is on his way to Kamloops! Now let's move on to the women's division!"

The double doors banged shut behind them, muffling the noise inside the hall. Excitement flooded Jess as she tugged Adam into the privacy of the shadows between the rows of parked cars.

"I'm here!" She threw herself at him. The night sky wrapped them in a twinkling blanket of stars. "Can you believe it? I'm really here!"

"No, I can't believe it, but I don't give a damn." His gaze flicked over her face, warming her to the core. "I've missed you, Jess. I'm sorry for pressuring you. I'm sorry—aw, hell."

His mouth covered hers, tender and insistent. She parted her lips, inviting the thrust of his tongue. Placing her hands over his, she guided his touch from her face to her hips. Urging him closer, nearer, more intimate, until his hands roamed over her body and their mouths fused in a kiss so full of memories and promises that she knew she would rather die than ever leave him again.

Finally, his head lifted. "How much time do we have?" he murmured.

"How much time do you want?"

"All night, then all day, then all the next night, until you have to leave again."

She smiled. "Did you win the Jamison contract?"

He nodded. "I don't want to talk about that now, though. I want to talk about you." Still embracing her, he leaned back. "Aside from the fact that you spent over fifteen hundred dollars to impress me in front of my friends, why did you open a bank account here?"

Her pulse jumped. "It made sense, considering I gave up my apartment, broke the lease on my car, and, let's see . . . oh, yeah, quit my job one day before the buying trip so I could move home and buy The Clothes Horse with Molly."

His eyebrows shot up. "What?"

"You heard me. I bought The Clothes Horse with Molly. We're changing the name to MJ's. M for Molly and J for me, like we dreamed about when we were teenagers."

His hands rested on the small of her back. "So, you've been in town since when?"

"Yesterday. I met Molly at the bank to sign the loan as soon as I got in."

"She picked you up in Kamloops?"

"No. I drove."

"From Kamloops?"

"Toronto."

"You drove from *Toronto?*"

"Yep. I arranged to sell some of my stuff, packed up my new little SUV, and drove the Trans-Canada. It was great." And nerve-wracking, thinking of Adam, hoping he'd still want her. "After driving your standard for a month, I couldn't get used to an automatic again."

"Let me get this straight." His forehead furrowed. "I try everything short of kidnapping to get you to stay, but no go. Then Molly cries the blues over losing a business partner, and you change your life to run to her rescue?"

Jess's heart sank. She'd risked everything—her job, the

promotion, her industry reputation. Gareth had gone ballistic when she'd quit, but she'd needed to make a clean break, regardless if doing so meant destroying her chances of ever working for Arlington Shoes again.

She'd needed to prove to herself—and to Adam—that she finally knew where she belonged. She belonged in Destiny Falls, whether Adam wanted her or not.

"I didn't run to Molly's rescue," she murmured. "I ran to mine. I couldn't have done it without your support, either. You gave me the time I needed, finally." Beaming at his confused frown, she pressed on, "And I love you dearly for it. Without that time, I couldn't have reached the decisions I reached."

"I didn't give you time, Jess. I—"

"Shh." She touched a finger to his lips. "I know about the postcard, and I don't care. In fact, I'm thrilled you tried to contact me. It made all the difference in the world."

"It did? Why?"

"Because, one word? From you? I've never known you to act so restrained. It helped me realize how stubborn I've been." She clasped his good hand. As her thumb grazed his palm, warmth spread through her. "And then I missed you like crazy, too. I dreamt about you every night. It got so I never wanted to wake up."

His forehead smoothed. "Every night, huh?"

She moved back into his arms. His breath fanned her neck, hot and sensual. She raised her head to meet his gaze. What she saw in the clear, blue depths of his eyes gave her the courage to continue.

"I know what I want. I realize it's been a long time coming. When Dad and Danny died, I couldn't cope—with my memories, with the betrayal I felt when Mom married Pete."

"You were scared." Adam brushed her cheek. "You felt alone."

She nodded against the comforting heat of his palm. "But

238

now I'm through running. You were right. See? I can say it." She felt weightless, devoid of gravity, as if she could drift like a kite on a spring breeze, taking Adam with her. "You pressured me, and I didn't react well. Yet you were right about so many things. Especially that I've been running scared since I was eighteen, refusing to face what I really want out of life for fear I might lose it."

"And what do you want?" he asked, voice husky. His gaze searched hers, alight with hope and love and trust.

"To live with you. After the wedding. Mom says she doesn't mind if I spend the night at your place now and then, but she frowns on out-and-out living together without benefit of marriage."

He tugged her snug against him. " 'Mom says,' huh?"

"Okay. I say, too. I want to marry you, Adam. I want to have your babies, to build a life here with you in Destiny Falls. I'm not talking a halfway commitment. I want it all."

"Ah." His eyes glittered as he gazed at her. "You took a big risk there, Jess, thinking I'd still want you. If tonight is anything to go by, I'm the most eligible bachelors in these parts. I could have my pick of all twelve unmarried women in town."

She laughed. "In case you've forgotten, Mr. Swelled Head, I just bought back every one of your votes."

"You were that eager to win me over?" He swept her hair off her neck and gently nibbled her flesh.

She closed her eyes, swaying to the pull of his mouth. "I was that eager to prove to you that I finally know where I belong. That's why I didn't contact you earlier. Why . . . , that feels so good. Um, why I wanted to sign the loan with Molly first. Why we cooked up the vote buy-back scheme, why I left my job so quickly, so there'd be no turning back."

His mouth shifted from her neck to her ear, but she stilled his questing lips with her hand. Every moment in her life from

239

this point forward depended on his answer to her question. She wanted to look at him while she asked it.

She gazed up at him. "So, how about it, Adam Thomas Perseverance Wright? Will you marry me?"

He grinned. "Just try to stop me."

Then his lips dipped to hers again, claiming her mouth, her soul, and her heart.

ABOUT THE AUTHOR

Cindy Procter-King earned a B.A. in English Lit. before unleashing herself on the unsuspecting workforce. She quickly realized her aversion to fluorescent lights and the numbers 9-2-5 wouldn't earn her kudos from her various bosses. So she moved to a tiny town where she couldn't find a job—unless you count a stint as a prison secretary. There, she began writing novels, and she hasn't looked back.

Cindy is an RWA Golden Heart® finalist and author of poignant contemporary romances and rollicking romantic comedies. Her mission in life is to see her surname spelled properly—with an E. That's P-r-o-c-t-E-r. So take heed. Cindy lives in beautiful British Columbia with her family, a cat obsessed with dripping tap water, and Allie McBeagle. Visit her website at www.cindyprocter-king.com.